forbidden CRAVINGS

forbidden CRAVINGS

WICKED CRAVINGS

BOOK TWO

JL JACKOLA

livshe

Paperback ISBN 978-1-960784-50-6
Hardback ISBN 978-1-960784-51-3
Electronic ISBN 978-1-960784-52-0

Distributed by Tivshe Publishing
Printed in the United States of America

Cover design by Tivshe Publishing

Visit www.jljackola.com

Also by J. L. Jackola

UNBOUND PROPHECY SERIES

Ascension

Descent

Surfacing

Submerged

Riven

Adrift

UNBOUND PROPHECY NOVELS

Unbound Kingdom (the trilogy omnibus)

Orlaina (an Unbound Prophecy prequel)

UNBOUND KINGDOM TRILOGY

Severed Kingdom

Cursed Kingdom

Prophesied Kingdom

WICKED HUES SERIES

The Forgotten Hues of Skye

The Coveted Hues of Skye

The Shattered Shades of Crimson

The Impossible Shades of Crimson

The Endless Shadows of Pete

Author's Note

Welcome back to the world of wicked cravings where morally gray is the norm and cravings are hard to resist. Forbidden Cravings is a mafia romance with dark aspects, so be prepared to expect:

Explicit sexual content
Language
Threats of s. a. (not by the mmc)
References to trafficking (not by the mmc or anyone in his circle)
Violence and death

For those who crave the commanding bad boy.

Chapter One

There were those who were hunters, and those who were prey. I was a hunter. I'd always been a hunter. But something had gone wrong. I'd miscalculated, and it had cost me dearly.

Soft breaths came from where Riley slept, curled in the nook of her window seat. Clutched in her hand was a small black box. I knew what was in that box and what it would mean to our family, the potential for unforeseen change that it held. A ring. A fucking engagement ring. I had the urge to tell Tyson to throw it out when he had called to tell me about it. He would have done it, no questions asked. But I'd ignored my desire, thinking of Riley and how she hadn't healed yet.

I walked over and draped a blanket across her frail frame, hating that she was still suffering, and I didn't have the cure for it. Christmas had come and gone, as had New Year's, yet she was still a shell of herself. Riley had run from me and the lies I'd woven to protect her from my world, but my way of protecting her had failed drastically.

After one last glance, I closed the door to her room, careful not to wake her. Returning to the main room of my home, I poured myself a glass of scotch and sat, thinking about the mistakes I'd made and the situation that now faced me. Snow was falling in thick flakes that broke up the moonlight, and I stared at them as they slowly covered the back deck. No matter how I thought about it, I couldn't find a way out of the predicament my lies and Riley's impulsiveness had left me in.

Greyson Tides. The last man I ever would have considered for my sister. A lethal boss who nobody fucked with, yet I'd attempted to do just that in my ambitious, arrogant plan to increase my territory and take a chunk of his. It had been rash, and I'd failed, expecting him to come after me, to retaliate. But Tides wasn't rash. He was a patient, calculating man who played games only the best bosses could survive. Years had passed, and I'd thought it was over. I had matured, changed to the point that I now considered myself his equal, yet he still didn't strike. Until his patience paid off and Riley landed right in his city, in his hands. And that was a complication I couldn't unravel because Riley's heart was entwined within it.

Resting my head in my hands, I tried to simmer my frustration. I'd been gone three days, dealing with meetings between the territory bosses that sat north of me and mediating a dispute between them. And in those three days, nothing had changed. Tyson had stayed with Riley, watching over her. Not that she ever moved. She stayed in that damned room, barely eating, not moving from her spot at the window. The only time she'd left the room was the day I allowed Tides to see her.

I'd known Tides since I first climbed my way to power, and never had I seen him so vulnerable. I could have taken him out then and there. He was alone, his men not with him, and he'd come unarmed. I'd contemplated it. Stepping foot in my territory and daring to come to my home was grounds for war. Hiding the fact that he'd known my sister was in his city the entire time, that he'd touched her, and broken her heart, gave me every reason to fill him with holes and be done with him. But the man who'd stood at my gates that day asking to see my sister wasn't the notorious mob boss I knew. This man was disheveled, desperate, broken even. And I knew then that whatever had happened in his twisted game, it had changed. He was in love with Riley as much as she was with him, and the knowledge of it killed me.

My phone rang, jerking me from my thoughts, the sound loud in the house's silence.

"You there?" I asked Tyson when I picked up.

"On my way."

"Then why are you calling?" I asked, knowing he was on his way to the airport to pick up his sister.

"Checking on you, buddy."

I took another drink, staring at the floor, my silence my only reply.

"What are you gonna do?" he asked. He'd been my best friend since grade school and knew me well enough to read the silence.

"I don't know," I answered honestly.

With the Clint Randall debacle, Riley had been weepy for the days following her hospital stay, but she'd bounced back quickly. Even if she wasn't talking to me, I had my men watching her. She returned to work, returned to life.

But this? This was different. Something in her had broken that I couldn't fix, and I could fix anything. Not this time. This time, I had a feeling only Tides could fix her. So, I'd instructed Tyson to leave the ring for her and when I returned earlier in the evening, she had it clutched in her hands while she slept.

"Although," I continued, "I don't know that it's up to me. Riley needs to make the decision."

"And if she chooses Tides?"

I cringed, hating the idea. My sister doing anything with my enemy was difficult enough to deal with, but to think of her marrying him was like a stab in the gut. Shit, all of this had been a stab in the gut. But she hadn't known. I'd left her in the dark and she had no way of knowing who he was until it was too late.

Leaning back in the chair, I considered my options. I could kill him...well, I could try to kill him. He was a difficult man to kill, and he was the most powerful of all the bosses. But killing him would crush Riley and leave her more devastated than she already was.

"As much as I hate it, I'd learn to deal with it," I answered. "I just want her to be happy again."

Tyson let out a heavy sigh. He was as close to Riley as he was to his sister, maybe closer, and I knew he considered her to be another little sister. "I could kill him," he finally said.

My chuckle felt out of place. "But you wouldn't for the same reason I wouldn't."

"Damn, we're fucked, aren't we?"

"That's the perfect word for it."

"I just got to the airport. Maybe Casey can talk some sense into her when I get her home, or at least convince her to leave her room."

"Let's hope," I answered absently before hanging up.

Setting the phone down, I looked out at the snowy night sky. There was nothing more important to me than Riley, and there was nothing I wouldn't do for her. Maybe this wasn't what I wanted, but maybe it was the right thing for Riley. If I had to deal with Greyson Tides in my life, I'd bear it as long as Riley came back to me. As long as she was happy again.

I pulled my jacket tighter, missing the warmth of home as I made my way through the airport terminal. Even inside, it was cold. Snow had started falling as the plane landed, and I'd peered out, watching how the flakes gathered on the ground below. My mother had moved us from the province so long ago I'd forgotten what snow looked like. Armina was situated on the far west coast where the air stayed warm and pleasant year-round. I hadn't returned since she packed us up when I was thirteen. That day had been emotional, having to leave my older brother Tyson behind. It had been his choice to stay. He was eight years older than me, and he and his best friend, Mason, were already building their empire.

Unlike Riley, Tyson had kept me informed. I knew what they were doing, as did our mother. Which was why she'd moved us, and why Tyson had suggested it after our father passed away. He didn't want us anywhere near the business; it was too dangerous. But that didn't mean he'd left me in the dark. Instead, we talked regularly and when he came out to visit, he would teach me. At first, it was the basics of the business and as I matured, it was the more dangerous aspects. I could defend myself, use every gun

Tyson had bought for me, and read people and tell the threatening ones from the ordinary ones...something Riley had never learned.

I shifted my oversized purse and rested it on my carry-on, then returned to my hike through the airport. My brother had wanted me to take the private jet, but I'd argued about how wasteful that was. He'd still sent the two men currently tailing me and bought all three of us first-class tickets after making me promise to take the private jet back. My arguments had fallen on deaf ears, and I'd consented, happy that I'd at least gotten him to compromise.

Even though the airport was small, it was busy, and I couldn't stop myself from looking around. It seemed odd to see people bundled up in heavy coats, and I plowed into a woman in front of me with my sight on everything but the path I was walking. She gave me a dirty look, especially when the man with her let his eyes linger on me a little longer than he should have.

I could have flirted with him just to annoy her, but I had other things on my mind and two intimidating men at my back. Throwing her a quick apology, I looked away from her companion and caught the eye of a cute pilot making his way down the terminal. I flashed him a sexy smile, which he returned with a grin that made me want to stop and give him my number. If Tyson hadn't been waiting for me and Riley's mental health hadn't been in jeopardy, I would have. Giving him a wink, I kept my eyes locked ahead of me. I could go back to flirting and playing when I returned to Armina.

I already missed the sound of the waves on the coast and the smell of saltwater that wafted in through my open balcony at home. Maybe that was what Riley needed—a trip to the beach with me. Away from the cold winter air and depressing lack of green. I couldn't remember the last time she'd come out to visit me.

Riley and I had been close as kids, and we still were, but I rarely saw her. We spoke infrequently, especially over the past year when her life had unraveled because of the secrets Mason had kept from her. She would come out with Tyson sometimes and visit me, but the last visit was years ago. And I never returned home, even after our mother grew sick. I was old enough to fend for myself when she passed away, mature enough to handle her death and the arrangements that went with it. Tyson had flown out, and we'd discussed my options as we'd packed up her house. Mason had remained behind to run the business, giving Tyson time to settle things, time to grieve. Even if my brother wasn't the grieving type, he'd still needed the time, and Mason knew him well enough to make him take it.

As we'd packed the last of her belongings up, we'd agreed that I would stay in Armina. Tyson wanted me as far from their business as possible, and so I'd remained on the other side of the country, thousands of miles from him. As much as he'd wanted to keep me away, I'd still ended up in the business. Acting as a liaison to the family that ran the southern side of my province. It had taken some convincing, but I'd talked Tyson into it. They were allies, and having me work with the Donelli family ensured the relationship stayed secure.

"Do you ever work, Case? You look like all you do is sit on the beach." Tyson's voice broke through my thoughts.

"Better than looking like your pasty white ass," I teased before dropping my bags and running into his arms.

He gave me a massive bear hug, his muscular arms squeezing me tight as he planted a kiss on my head. We may have lived on opposite sides of the country, but we were still close and being in his arms felt like coming home. He pushed me back and looked me over.

"You look good, Casey." His brow creased as he pulled my jacket aside. It lifted when he spied the skin my crop top left exposed. "Really?"

I smacked his hand and pulled the jacket closed. "Shut up. It's the style at home."

"You are home. And that's not a style I want my little sister in. Too much skin, Casey. Damn, I'll have to kill everyone who looks at you now. Did you wear that skimpy thing on the plane?"

"Of course. It's only cold enough to freeze my tits in this province."

He pursed his lips. "Language, Case."

"If you don't stop with the overprotective bullshit, I'll turn around and get back on that plane," I replied, reaching up and mussing his thick, brown hair.

"No, you're not because you're here for Riley."

He picked up my bags and started walking. His men followed close behind, joining the two who had been my shadows since leaving Armina.

"How is she?" I asked, trying to keep up with his long strides. Tyson took after our father. He was tall and built, towering over the petite frame I'd inherited from our mother. The only similarities between us were our curly brown hair and hazel eyes. Where he was a solid wall of muscle, I was soft and curvy. I'd struggled when I was younger, especially when I'd moved to a province where bikinis were regular attire and looks were everything. I was petite in height, but that was all. Everything else about me was full. It had taken me a long time to appreciate the larger curves, the bigger breasts, and handful of waist, hips, and ass that my body was. Now I worked it, knowing what parts to flaunt, and which ones left men weakened.

"She's...not Riley," Tyson replied, the sadness coating his voice.

"Well, I can guarantee her mopey ass will not remain that way with me there."

"Always the obnoxious ray of sunshine," he muttered.

"Always," I said with a wink before climbing into the car.

THE SNOW WAS COMING DOWN HARDER by the time we pulled up to the house. It was massive, a mansion that sat brightly against the night sky. Once we made it through the large iron gates, I sat forward in my seat, taking in the sight. The Donelli's lived in a home of similar size, so the size didn't intimidate me. It was what the house represented that astounded me. A sign of the power that Mason with Tyson alongside him had accumulated. A confirmation that Mason was a boss to be feared, one who was just as dangerous and powerful as the others. I'd known it from what Tyson had told me through the years and how Donelli talked about him. But seeing it was different and cemented the fact. And with Mason's power came my brother's. The two were a pair, which meant my older brother, who had once comforted me when the boys had bullied me for my changing body, who had let me snuggle with him during thunderstorms, who was my rock anytime I needed him, and would kill anyone who wronged me, was just as lethal.

"Stop gawking. You look like an idiot," Tyson teased.

"Shut up, Ty."

I followed him into the house, my eyes taking in Mason's world and wondering how the cute older brother of my friend had amassed so much power. As we walked further into the home, I spotted Mason. His green eyes met mine, and I tried to breathe. Everything I remembered about Mason Brinks was a distorted memory to the man who sat before me. He was gorgeous, and the way those eyes devoured me left me completely drenched. His black hair was messy, as if he'd combed his hands through it, and I wondered what it would feel like to have my fingers running through it. He put his glass aside and stood, the rolled sleeves of his black button-down revealing sexy tattooed arms that looked strong enough to hold my body in place as he pounded me.

"I'd ask if you lost your sister along the way and picked up a treat, Ty, if that hair wasn't the same mop of curls as yours."

"Fuck you, Mason. That's disgusting," Tyson grumbled.

Mason laughed, his eyes sparkling with humor, and I struggled to find my voice. I was wondering how inappropriate it would be if I took my clothes off and straddled him.

"You look good, Casey," he said, waking me up.

"The Armina sun helps," I muttered, trying to get a grip. "You don't look so bad yourself, Mason. I see you added some ink since the last time I saw you."

"Damn, has it been that long?" he asked.

"Fifteen years and enough time for me to get my own ink. It's good to see you, Mason," I said, giving him a hug and questioning why the feel of his arms around me had my thighs quivering.

"You what?" Tyson asked.

"Let her be. She's not a kid anymore, Ty." His voice sent butterflies soaring through me.

"And what if Riley got a tattoo?" Tyson asked as I shook my head at his overprotective behavior. I was twenty-eight, not eighteen.

Mason shrugged, a move that made him even sexier. "I'd say that would be the least of my troubles with her."

His face dropped, and I could see the toll this had taken on him.

"Well, I'm here to help and if I have my way, she'll be back to her normal perky self before you know it."

"Just a ray of sunshine, aren't you?" Mason joked, his smirk returning.

"Too much of that west coast sun." I elbowed my brother playfully for the comment. All the while, Mason's sage eyes burned into me, turning my legs to jelly. "She still in her room?"

"Yeah, she's sleeping. I tried talking to her earlier, but she made me leave." He ran a hand through his thick hair, making it messier. The look only enhanced his sex appeal. "When I checked back in on her, she was asleep."

"Did she take the ring?" Tyson asked.

"Ring?" I asked. Tyson had filled me in on the situation and we'd chatted about it on the way, but there had been no talk of a ring.

"He sent her a ring," Mason said, his teeth slightly gritted. I noticed the pulse of the large vein in his neck. He was angry about the situation still, and I couldn't blame him. Greyson Tides was a legend among the bosses, a feared, deadly, aggressive boss who no one crossed. Tyson had told me how they'd tried to cross him years ago, on edge since then that he'd strike back. I'd cussed him out, calling them both fucking idiots for doing such a stupid thing. They were both cocky, thinking they could outplay someone like Tides, who was older and wiser than both of them. He'd been in the business a lot longer and there was a reason no one crossed him.

It made me more in awe of Riley. Greyson wasn't one to slip up, and he had with her. Something had happened between the two of them that had morphed whatever plan he'd had and left them both broken. I was curious to hear her side of the story, but I knew better than to ask Riley right away. She'd be in no condition to tell me. And I certainly couldn't ask Mason or Tyson. The situation had them both pissed. Clint Randall was dead by Greyson's doing, and he'd done it to protect Riley. That was the only reason he was still alive. He'd been vulnerable the night they found her, and they could easily have killed him, but they hadn't. And that was saying a lot. Although I didn't live near them, Tyson kept me informed and I knew from everything he'd told me that Mason didn't play. He was a younger version of Greyson Tides. Just as deadly.

"An engagement ring," Tyson said.

My mouth gaped, and I closed it quickly, not wanting Mason to see me dumbfounded. "He wants to marry her?"

"Wanted," Tyson said. "I opened the box. It's clear from the note he left that he bought the ring before things went south."

"Shit," I muttered. "That's serious."

Mason clenched his hands, and I tilted my head, studying him. "And if she says yes?" I asked him.

His eyes darkened, his sculpted jaw, which was covered by a few days' growth, tensed. "We'll make it work." But I could tell he wasn't happy about it. I didn't blame him. Having your younger sister marry your enemy would be an awkward position to be in. "Why don't you show Casey to her room, Ty."

"She staying near Riley?"

He nodded and Tyson grabbed my bags. I lingered for a moment, lost in Mason's eyes, until I forced myself to follow Tyson. I could feel his eyes on me, watching each step I took, and I wondered why my body was suddenly craving my brother's best friend and what I was going to do about it.

Chapter Three

MASON

Casey was nothing like I remembered her. Stunning was the word that came to mind, and that didn't seem strong enough for the reaction she evoked in me. Those hazel eyes were mesmerizing, and I found myself lost the moment I gazed into them. The sexy woman standing next to Tyson couldn't have been the same awkward Casey I remembered from years ago. That middle-school version of her had been unsure of her changing body, unconfident, and awkward. Tyson and I had threatened each of the bullies who had tormented her before she'd moved away with her mother.

But the woman in front of me was confident and stunning. From the auburn curls that framed her round face to the thick lashes that layered her hazel eyes to the curves that lay below her jacket. I could barely breathe before I reminded myself that she was my best friend's sister and he would kill anyone who so much as touched her, even me. My overprotectiveness for Riley was nothing compared to Tyson's with Casey. But that hadn't helped my body's response to her appearance.

My eyes followed her as she walked away, her curvy ass swishing with each step. All kinds of dirty visions filled my mind, and I wiped my eyes, grabbing my glass and pouring myself another shot of scotch before downing it. Those thoughts would get me in trouble. Tyson came first and no matter how hard hugging his sister had made me, there was no way I was finding satisfaction there. She was only here a few days and then she'd be back in Armina. Tyson had talked her into coming to help Riley, hoping she could bring my sister out of the shell she had closed herself off in.

After a few minutes, Tyson returned.

"Casey's washing up." He yawned, and I raised my brow. Tyson was like me, a night owl, and it was rare to see him tired. "I didn't sleep much last night."

"No? Why not? I was doing all the work. You were babysitting Riley."

"I may have had some company."

"Fuck, Ty. You were supposed to be watching Riley, not wetting your dick. Who did you bring to the house this time?"

Tyson was a playboy. I wasn't innocent and enjoyed the occasional night of debauchery, but he had a bad habit of it.

"China."

"The brunette with the big tits?"

"Damn nice tits, and yes."

"I thought she was too kinky for you?" I joked because I knew Tyson well enough to know he was into things even I wouldn't touch.

"Eh, I was in a mood." He rolled his neck. "She was worth the distraction and Riley was fine. It's not like she even leaves her room."

"Did you leave the house?" I crossed my arms, feeling the anger build. I'd left him with her to keep an eye on her, not to spend the night at the club.

"No, I texted China and had Leo pick her up."

"You're messed up. Don't pull that shit when I put you on duty. If the guys can't do that shit, neither can you."

"Do what?" Casey asked, coming into view.

The air stuck in my chest again. The jeans she wore were snug, highlighting her hips and the shapely legs below them. She wore a short-sleeved shirt that came halfway down her stomach, her tan skin soft and begging to be licked. She'd grown into the breasts that had made her so uncomfortable when she was younger. They were perfect now, full and pert, amply overflowing the black lace bra I could see under her shirt.

"What the fuck, Case?" Tyson yelled. "Is that what you go out in at home? You can see right through that shirt. I'm gonna need to return with you so I can kick every guy's ass that comes within view of you, aren't I?"

"Shut up, Ty."

I wanted to tell him to shut up because she looked hot, but I kept my mouth closed. He was even more protective of Casey than I was of Riley, even if he argued he wasn't because he'd let her into our world early on and I'd kept Riley sheltered. I swallowed, trying to calm the reaction my body was having to her.

"Don't tell me to shut up, Casey!" He stood over her, threatening and overbearing. I had the urge to push him away, to defend her, but I kept out of it. To her credit, she didn't blink. Instead, she stood taller, which still wasn't very high. She was tiny compared to Tyson's six four and my six three. Either of us towered over her. Exactly the way I liked my women, small but full of fire, and I could see from the look in her eyes she had fire.

"Fuck off, Ty. I'm twenty-eight years old. I'm not some little kid you can boss around. We go through this every time you see me."

"And every time I see you, I make you cover your ass up. What happened to the clothes I bought you last time?"

She laughed, a sound that reverberated against my skin. "You mean those matronly things I gave to charity?"

The vein on his forehead popped.

"Calm down, Ty. She's right. She's old enough to dress

herself. And if I remember correctly, what China wore the last time she was going down on you makes Casey look like she's in a nunnery."

Tyson threw me a look.

"China?" Casey asked, her brow arching. Her smile was devious, making her even more attractive.

"Thanks, Mace."

"Who's China and why was your dick in her mouth?" Casey walked around the bar and my eyes followed her, spying the tattoo on her back that peeked above her jeans as she reached for a shot glass. My hands wanted to push her pants down and follow the design's path with my tongue. I looked away quickly, hoping Tyson hadn't noticed.

"None of your business." He punched me in the arm, and I glared at him.

She dropped the glass next to mine and motioned for me to pour. She was so close to me, the smell of her perfume tickled my nose, making it difficult to concentrate. I didn't understand why I was so enamored with this woman or why she was having this effect on me. The feeling left me out of control and I hated it.

I poured her a shot, saying, "She's a stripper at the club, one your brother enjoys playing with when he's bored."

"Seriously? Don't you guys own that club? That's completely inappropriate."

I couldn't help laughing. "So the fact that she works there bothers you and not that she was giving him a blow job?"

She shrugged, her eyes sparkling with an amber hue. "If that's what she's into, but it's still completely inappropriate."

"It's only once in a while," he groused.

"It's my club, anyway," I said. "Besides, she's kinky, and your brother likes kinky."

Casey didn't bat an eye. "And what do you like?"

I almost spit out the sip I'd taken, choking on it instead.

"Yeah, Mace. Tell her what you like," Tyson urged, completely missing the seduction in her voice and how it reached in and gripped my balls.

"Just a good hard fuck," I answered, gaining my composure.

"Hard?" she asked with the lift of her eye. "You strike me as the controlling type."

Good god, she was sending my desire into a frenzy. I took another sip and calmly put my drink down. I wanted to thread my fingers through her hair and jerk her against me before I wrapped my hand around her neck.

"Controlling is a good word for it," Tyson teased.

"I'm not a dom, fucker," I growled. Although I had some tendencies that leaned that way.

"Keep telling yourself that, buddy."

Casey's mouth had parted, and she seemed flushed. The conversation had gotten both of us hot and all the while Tyson remained oblivious. She took another sip of her scotch, gulping the rest down before wiping her mouth with the back of her hand.

"That's enough talk for me. I'm beat," Tyson said. "I'd text China to come back tonight, but she was getting clingy and that's definitely not something I'm into."

"No, you just want to tie her up and use her," I said, flicking my eyes to his.

He gave me a wicked smile. "Damn right I do. I'm turning in. Don't let my sister drink too much. She might end up with another of those tramp stamps on her ass. You show up with another of those and I'll burn it off you."

"I'd like to see you try. I guess I shouldn't mention the one on my tit?"

Oh, she had a mouth on her, and I was loving it. I wanted to answer that I wouldn't mind seeing that tattoo, but again, I kept my thought to myself. Tyson would tear me up if he had any inkling of how turned on she was getting me. It would be a bloody fight because we were both strong, but in this case, I didn't doubt he'd have me black and blue.

"I'm gonna move you home. And you wait until my next meeting with Donelli. What the fuck is he thinking, letting you do that shit? He's supposed to be watching you."

"Eh, I went with his daughter for the last one. She got one right here." She rubbed her finger along her pelvis just before it would have dipped between her legs and my eyes followed, longing to see that finger travel further.

"Bad influence. I'll be having a talk with him and with her. She's a piece of work, spoiled brat," he mumbled as he walked away, leaving me alone with Casey.

There were a few moments of silence where our eyes locked, and the sound of Tyson's footfalls faded as he made his way to his end of the house.

"You've changed, Mason," Casey said, her smooth voice breaking the silence.

"That happens after so many years. I could say the same about you, Casey. Without the braces and pre-teen awkwardness, you're..." I wanted to tell her how sexy she was, but I knew it wouldn't be appropriate. No matter how attracted I was to her, she was Tyson's sister and that crossed a line.

"What?" she asked, tipping her chin up and waiting for me to finish.

"Different."

Her brow lifted with a beautiful arch. "Huh."

"Huh? What does that mean?" I scratched my neck, forcing my eyes from her and looking back at my glass.

"I thought you'd say something more definitive."

"It's no different from what you said," I countered, daring to look back at her.

Humor lit her eyes, and she rested her back on the bar as she perused my body slowly, her tongue coming out to lick her lower lip. Her confidence was a turn on that I didn't need, especially now that we were alone.

"Well then, you're...larger than I remember, definitely sexier." Shit, this was not a conversation I wanted. I needed to take control before she rattled me more and worked her way into my bed. Crossing my arms, I hardened my look, but she only inhaled in a way that sank into my body. "And that right there, along with those tattoos, is enough to break any girl."

I cleared my throat, desperate to get away. There had never been a woman who worked me the way Casey did in just the short time she'd been here. "That's probably not the best response," I said, hating that I sounded like a scolding parent, or worse, like her brother.

"Why not? Afraid Tyson will hear you tell me how you can't keep your eyes from lingering on my body?" She stepped closer, but I stood my ground, not moving back like I wanted to. "That I'm not the little girl who left all those years ago?"

"No, you're not." I looked down at her as she pressed her breasts against my arms. It was taking all my strength not to grab a fistful of her hair and smash my lips into hers. Although another part of me wanted to yank her head back and admonish her for her brazenness. "But you are Tyson's little sister," I said, releasing my arms, intent on taking her by the shoulders and pushing her back. My move caused her to lean further and left her chest resting against mine. Those hazel eyes shimmered with desire as they looked up at me. "And you're entirely too easy, Casey. You don't do this in Armina, do you?"

The thought caused a strange streak of jealousy to run through me. One I didn't like.

Her lips pursed, and she stepped back. "I'm not easy, Mason. I just know what I like, and I don't hesitate to stake my claim on it when I find it."

That was it. I needed my control back and to remember who I was. She'd left me rattled, and that was a weakness. I grabbed a handful of her hair and yanked her head back, hearing her sexy exhale. "I'm not one to be claimed, little girl. And you're not one I can take, even if I want to." Her eyes were sparkling with excitement, which wasn't making this any easier.

"And what would you do to me if you could take me?"

Fuck, she was killing me. I jerked her forward, her body slamming into mine. "Things that would make even you blush. And things I know your brother wouldn't want anyone doing to you."

"What if I want you to do those things?"

I clenched my jaw, lowering my face to hers. Her lips parted, a sigh escaping. I could feel a slight tremble run through her and it left me wondering how she liked it.

"That's a shame because I won't. Now, I'm going to pretend you didn't throw yourself at your brother's best friend and expect me to stab him in the back like that. And I'm going to assume this is some sort of test of my strength. But if it isn't, you're playing with fire, Casey, and I guarantee the heat will be too hot, even for your sun-kissed skin."

I shoved her away and turned away from her. "Go to bed, Casey."

"Good night, Mason. Will you be thinking of me when you're jerking off?"

I halted my steps. Damn, she'd gotten the last play, and I hated that she'd beaten me. I glanced over my shoulder at her and slowly surveyed her body once more. There were so many things I wanted to say back, dirty things I'd regret in the morning. Keeping my mouth shut, I returned to walking away, leaving her there and wishing I could get her out of my head just as easily.

Chapter Four

CASEY

I poured myself another shot of scotch before I returned to my room, drink in hand and alone. Not that I'd thought I would have company. But damn, I wished I did. I'd had a crush on Mason when I was a kid. He was older, cute, and tall, with eyes that could see into your soul. But now...now he was every type of man I loved in one package. And that package was enough to drive me mad.

I changed into the soft nightie I'd brought, wondering what Mason's large hands would feel like pushing it up my body. He was right. I'd been easy, throwing myself at him, but my attraction to him caught me off guard and I told him the truth—I was never shy about telling a man I wanted him. I'd been shy in my younger years and learned quickly that it was the confident, sexy women who got what they wanted. And I always got what I wanted.

But Mason Brinks was someone I couldn't have. He was Tyson's best friend, and I didn't want to come between that. Being out of the same room as Mason cleared my head, and I could see how naughty I'd been. I couldn't do that to Tyson, no matter how desperately I wanted to. Nor could I put Mason in that position. They were like brothers, and Tyson wouldn't forgive him if he touched me. He was too overprotective, and he would expect Mason to be the same with me. It was bad enough I had to keep my party life in Armina from him. If he knew half the things I did with men, he would have brought me back to Treemont years ago and locked me down. And then there was Riley. I was here for her, not for sex with her brother. I wasn't so sure she would mind, but I needed to stop.

Crawling into bed, I promised myself I would keep my cravings under control, something I didn't know if I could easily do. The way Mason's hand had tugged my hair told me exactly what kind of lover he would be. I was self-assured, a demanding presence, but the type of men who ran in my circle were the powerful types, built to kill, not afraid to play dirty or hard. And I could tell from how Mason slammed me to his chest, his grip in my hair tightening that Mason was as controlling and aggressive in the bedroom as he was in life.

The thought sent my heart pounding, and I flopped down on the soft pillows, cursing myself for letting my mind wander back to him. I needed to keep Riley in my forethought. I was only here a few days. There was no way to avoid Mason during that time, but I could tone it down and stop my flirting. The question was, did I want to?

I SMACKED my phone as my alarm buzzed, chastising myself for not changing it. This province was two hours ahead of mine, and I should not have been up this early. The morning sun filtered through the light curtains, and I knew I wouldn't be able to go back to sleep. Especially when Mason popped back into my mind.

"Dammit," I groused, rising.

Throwing the curtains open, I took in the snow that covered the ground. I'd forgotten how beautiful snow was. It made me want to run out and play in it like I had when I was a child. I hopped in the shower, taking time to fix my hair and check my appearance before I left my room. This time, I made sure to cover my skin, choosing a long-sleeved shirt of a soft pink that fell just to the rim of my jeans. My figure was still prominent, my breasts pushing above the neckline to provide the perfect cleavage, but it was more conservative than most things I owned.

Ty had shown me where Riley's room was, so I stopped by and checked on her first. Peeking my head in, I couldn't believe the shape she was in. This was not my friend; this was the ghost of that person. She was unkempt, her hair matted and dirty, her clothes hanging on her because she'd lost weight. My heart broke, and I knew when her eyes turned to me, there was no recovering from this. Those green eyes that had once held the same life as her brother's did, a beautiful emerald that was hard to turn from, were dull and lifeless. There was a twinkle of life when she realized it was me and not Mason, but that faded quickly.

I talked with her, eyeing the rock that Greyson had sent her. My friend had broken the most ruthless boss in the provinces and from the looks of it, he had broken her. I vaguely wondered what Mason would do if she accepted Greyson's proposal. If she returned to him. When I asked her if she still loved him, I knew she would go back to him. I'd known Riley since we were children. Knew her well enough to see that this kind of love wasn't the kind you gave up on. And like I told her before I left, Greyson had risked everything to come see her and Tides didn't take risks. It was something that made him the most feared boss, the one all the others wanted to be. He held the power in this entire province, no matter what Mason or any other family in the province thought.

I closed the door, hearing her grossed out response to my mention of Mason's sex-appeal, and hoping my chat with her would wake her up. Maybe having Riley around would distract me from Mason. I doubted it and as I padded through the house, finding my way to the kitchen, I discovered that wouldn't be an easy feat. Mason was leaning against an island that took up the entire kitchen, the black marble shining in the sunlight from the large windows that lined the room.

"You know for someone who lives on the edge of constant threat, you'd think you would have fewer windows in your house," I teased, ignoring how hot he looked with his damp black hair, his white button down partly unbuttoned, the sleeves rolled up again.

He took a sip of his coffee, peering over the ridge at me. "It's the living on the edge part that encouraged me to add them."

His gaze was intense, warming my entire body, and I was finding it difficult to breathe.

"I see you found something more covering," Tyson said, walking into the room.

He headed straight to the coffeemaker, fixing himself a cup while Mason and I continued to stare at each other. I couldn't tear my eyes from Mason, feeling the heat in them as if he was touching every part of me. He gave me a sexy smirk before his eyes dropped to my cleavage, his jaw clenching. Grabbing the paper, he turned from me just as Tyson brought his cup to the table and sat.

"Tell me what happened with Rinala and Thompson," he said to Mason. They were family names, but ones I didn't know well. Their territories sat north of Mason's, on the outer edge of the province.

Mason took another sip of his coffee, and I forced my legs to move. Turning my back to them, the air returned to my lungs. I found some bread and toasted it as they talked.

"They're worried," Mason said.

"They should be."

There was a moment of silence before Mason spoke. "I'm not entirely sure that's true. Clint Randall was an anomaly."

"Are you shitting me? Fuck, Mason, wake up," Tyson argued. "He was a warning. He infiltrated us and...well, you know the rest. He's the first step. The Bad Omens will return and we're the target."

"But why?" I asked as I spread some jam on my toast. I turned, licking a spot of jam from my finger. Mason had turned toward me, his eyes following my finger before they looked away.

"Because they're nasty rats who like taking families down," Tyson said.

"I know that, dipshit. Why Mason? Why not another family? Why not Tides?"

I came around and sat next to Tyson, doing my best to avoid being close to Mason. This was for the best. Keeping my distance so I wasn't a temptation for him, and he wasn't a temptation for me.

"It's a good point," Mason replied.

"You're powerful, Mace," Tyson said. "A threat to other families."

"Sure, but Tides is more powerful than I am. And I have a truce with the others in the province and many across the country. Look at Donelli. Casey's been keeping that alliance secure and with it comes a peace with the others in that province who align with him."

"Tides holds the most power in the province. Shit, maybe even of all the families," I said, taking a bite and seeing Mason's eyes follow the swipe of my tongue over my lips. I was trying my best not to be sexy and flirty, but it wasn't working. He was just as enamored with me as I was with him. This was bad.

Tyson brought his elbows onto the table hard, making me jump and look away.

"We're missing something. And I bet Tides knows what it is," he said.

"Well, we're not getting any answers from him. And I'm not calling him. That ball is in Riley's court and I'm not interfering."

I sat back. "She'll go back to him," I said, watching the way Mason's eyes hardened at my words. "She loves him too much and from the fact that he braved coming here to talk to her and the size of that ring, he loves her just as much." His jaw clenched, his eyes darkening. "It's not the worst thing that could happen, Mason."

"Seriously?" Tyson said. "He's the enemy boss. We do not get along with Greyson Tides."

Wiping a bit of jam from my plate, I licked it from my finger, avoiding Mason's eyes but feeling the way they burned into me. "Well, you'll have to, and it might work to your advantage. Tides is a force, and no one will mess with him. No one but you two idiots. If Riley marries him, he has to work with you. He'll have no choice and with him on your side, the Bad Omens will back off. I guarantee he knows the reason they didn't target him, and you'll have the answer when Riley goes back to Bridgeville."

"Fuck," Mason muttered. I peeked back at him, catching him running his hand through his hair.

"You have a brief reprieve, which might be just enough time for that alliance to form," I continued. "Clint Randall is dead and I'm sure they know Tides was the executioner. They'll back off. Randall had to have told them about Riley and their affair." Mason's jaw tensed further. "They'll sit back and watch, knowing you have your guard up now and that Greyson does as well. I don't know him, but from everything I've heard, he's cold and ruthless. Men like that don't wallow in their pain. He's burying his pain below his work, which means he's even more untouchable now. The Bad Omens play a slow game. They'll wait to see how this plays out and for things to calm. In the meantime, they may even turn their attention to another family."

Mason studied me, his head tilted. "How the fuck did you get so smart?"

"I can play the game with the best of them, Mason. Tyson taught me well. Riley would have been the same if you had relaxed and let her in like Ty did."

His lips pursed.

"She's got a point, Mason. Casey's been training with me since before she moved away. I told you I wasn't letting my sister out of this province without that advantage." He gave me a proud smile, and I returned it.

Mason looked out at the snow, and I could see his mind thinking things through. "So, if this gives us a reprieve, we take the advantage," he said, ignoring our comments on Riley. "Fortify our holdings, put the men on extra guard, and lock down any loose ends. I want everything close to home from now on. No new hires, no new deals until we find out what Tides knows."

Tyson stood. "Got it. I'll head over to the development site—"

"No, head to the other businesses. Make sure the guys know to be extra diligent, especially if any non-regulars show. I'll visit the site. You can meet me over there later and update me."

"Got it." He pulled his phone out and walked away as he instructed the person on the other end to meet him at the club.

I knew Mason had his dealings divested through his territory, which was large compared to others. He not only owned the city but all the surrounding towns and far into the countryside where his home sat. The club was only one business, and he and Tyson had been working on some real estate projects lately. A lot of his investments were in real estate, and I was guessing the site was a new one.

Bringing my dish to the sink, I turned and rested against the counter. The door closed in the distance, signaling that Tyson had left. Mason walked around the island but kept a space between us.

"You saw Riley?" he asked.

"Yeah. She's a wreck. I've never seen her this bad."

The tension in his jaw lessened, a flicker of sadness passing through his eyes.

"She'll be okay, Mason. Just don't expect her to stay away from him. It's too serious, no matter what he did."

"He hurt her," he grumbled.

"Did he? It sounds like he wanted to in the beginning, but then he fell in love. Hard, as hard as she fell. Why else would he risk coming here? He would have to be desperate."

I dared to walk closer to him, feeling the need to offer him comfort. Riley was his world, and he lived for his sister. I knew that even as a child.

"It's time to let her go, Mason," I said softly, bringing my hand to his crossed arms. The strength below them tempted me to rub my hand along his muscles, but I refrained.

His eyes searched mine and I could see the mix of emotion behind them.

"And he killed Randall for her. He saved her, protected her when you couldn't. It's the same thing any man would do for the woman he loved."

"Would he?" he asked, and I could tell he was looking for me to say more, leading me on. But I'd told myself I wouldn't flirt even if it seemed like an impossibility because I wanted to feel what Mason would do to me. I wanted him to break me. Anticipation shivered through me.

"Would you?" I stepped closer to him. His eyes darkened, and he brought his hand to my neck and surrounded it. My heart pounded in excitement as he pulled me against him, and every part of my body came alive.

"I would tear down any man who dared touch you," he murmured. I could barely remain standing, my legs were quivering so badly, but his eyes hardened, and he shoved me away, releasing my neck. "As would your brother."

I tried to regulate my breathing because that move had me so flustered I didn't know what to think.

"Will you choke me like that when you finally give in to your craving for me?" I asked, needing to tease him like he'd just done to me. Tease wasn't really what he'd done. Soaked me was more like it. I could only imagine the intensity he would bring to the bedroom. "Or will you force me to my knees while your fingers wrap around the strands of my hair?"

I shouldn't have asked because I'd promised myself I wouldn't torment him. But a part of me needed to hear his answer, to have him tell me that the heat that was threatening to scald me from the inside out was doing the same to him.

His eyes lit, lust passing through them, and he moved against me, pressing me into the counter. He was so hard I could feel it pushing into my stomach. He was huge, and I bit my lip, trying to silence thoughts of how he really would break me if this ever turned into something.

Putting both hands on the counter so that he me boxed in, he said, "You need to stop this, Casey."

"Why?" I asked.

He gritted his teeth. "Because you're..." He dropped his head, his mouth so close to my ear that currents flicked through me like sparks igniting a wildfire. "Untouchable."

I bit my lip as disappointment smothered the fire in me. The struggle he was having gave me pause and reminded me that I really needed to stop this. He was torn, his loyalty to my brother ran deep, and I was hurting him, even if his denial of his craving for me was hurting him just as badly. I knew my brother, knew how overprotective he was, and knew if Mason touched me like I wanted him to that Tyson would see it as a betrayal. He trusted Mason to treat me the same as Tyson treated Riley. But we weren't the same. Riley had grown up with Tyson. He was as close to her as Mason, and he saw her through the same lens he saw me through—another little sister. Mason and I hadn't seen each other in so long that bond had never formed. Which left us both at a crossroads, trying to deny the instant attraction that was drawing us to each other.

"Okay, I'll stop," I said, suddenly feeling bad for having pushed him. I'd never wanted a man as desperately as I wanted

Mason, but I didn't want to hurt him, nor did I want to hurt my brother.

He didn't move, and I could hear the strained breaths coming from him. He wanted me as desperately as I wanted him, but I wouldn't test him anymore. His green eyes searched mine before they narrowed. "If you don't..." My heart beat wildly, waiting for his next words. "I can promise you my hands will wind so tightly in your hair as I fuck you that you won't know whether to scream or come."

He pushed away, leaving my knees so weak they had turned to jelly. A small mewl slipped from my mouth when it opened. The devilish grin he gave me before he adjusted himself and walked away almost toppled me.

"That wasn't fair," I muttered.

He rolled his neck but didn't turn back. "You started this, Case. Trust me, you don't want to tease me."

"Fuck, yes I do after that."

His laugh echoed through the room as he left me there, trying to calm the quake between my legs. If I'd wanted him before, I craved him like a drug now. But I wouldn't push. I couldn't do that to him. He was fighting it too much, and I knew he wouldn't hurt my brother. I didn't want to hurt Tyson, either. Riley didn't have me concerned. She didn't have the aggressive, possessive streak in her that my brother had. It was Ty I worried about. But I was leaving in a few days and thousands of miles would separate us, giving my hormones time to settle. I just needed to avoid Mason until then, which would be difficult to do living in the same place. And even then, I wasn't certain he hadn't already ruined me for any other man just with the sheer thought of what he'd do to me.

Chapter Five

MASON

Casey was like a drug I couldn't stop craving and it was driving me mad. There was no question I wanted her, and I had a feeling she would destroy me so that no other woman would ever come close to her. She may already have. I couldn't get her out of my head. That question she'd asked had put thoughts in my mind that shouldn't have been there. Dirty thoughts I couldn't erase.

I swiped my hand down my face, trying to clear them from my mind before I opened my car door and headed over to the site manager, who was talking with the foreman. Snow covered the foundation of the high rise that was the newest of my real estate holdings. It sat at the end of the city, where I was refurbishing the run-down establishments to broaden my hold on the city and the prosperity of it. When the businesses were doing well, I did well. There wasn't a piece of Everdin I didn't own, just as with Treemont. I owned it all. My holdings were more vast and more diversified than even Tides' were. It had taken me years to gain my hold on Everdin, but I was calculating, taking risks those who had been in the business longer than I had no longer took. It had started when I was in high school, taking Tyson along with me, and he'd been my wingman through it all.

That was the reason I couldn't give in to my desire for Casey, no matter how her presence was wearing down my resolve. Hearing her talk shop, the intelligent way she evaluated the situation with the Bad Omens and with Tides had gotten me hard. It was almost as sexy as her body. Brains and attitude were sure-fire ways to bring me to my knees and Casey had both. But she was Tyson's sister, and that fact was like a blaring red flag that wouldn't cease waving in my face, even if it slipped to the periphery every time I was near her. It would destroy Tyson if I touched her. He expected me to protect her and treat her just like he did Riley, as if she were my own sister. But where he saw Riley that way, I didn't have that same connection or the same emotion toward Casey. There had been too much distance between us for too long, leaving room for the attraction that sat like a stain between us that we couldn't remove.

I trudged through the snow, seeing the unhappy looks on the men's faces. Leo and Finch followed me. My men were always with me even if I sometimes forgot they were there, and those two were the ones who backed me up any time I was out of the house. Unless Tyson and I went out on a job ourselves like the night we drove from Creekwood to Bridgeville to get Riley. Those times were rare, and being without backup had made my nerves that night even higher than they already were.

"We had to stop yesterday when the snow began to fall," Mike, the project manager, explained. "It's too cold to melt, so we're dead in the water until it warms back up."

"How far does that set us back?" I asked.

"We buffered time for weather into our projections, Mason. This won't hurt the timeline unless we get hit with too much of it."

"Good." I scanned the area, noting how far they'd gotten, before I walked away to inspect the work. I didn't take shortcuts and spared no expense to ensure anything I owned was above par. My renters and buyers expected nothing less from me and it had earned me a reputation as the one to come to when people needed things done. I was a perfectionist.

"Walk with me, Mike," I said, jerking my neck, so he knew to follow.

"What's up, Boss?"

"I need you and the boys on high alert. You question everything and everyone. Nothing happens that you don't know and that you don't report back to me. Understand?"

He scrunched his brows. "Everything all right?"

"I think so, but after the fiasco with Clint Randall, I'm not taking any chances. The Bad Omens have me on their radar, and I want them to see that I'm not one to fuck with."

"No, you're not." He rubbed his chin. "What about Tides?"

"That's another story. One I'll have to deal with, but let me worry about that. Stay vigilant. I want men on the site, even if there's no work being done."

"Got it. Anything else?"

"No, just keep me posted on anything out of the ordinary."

"Yes, Boss."

I gave him a nod and walked away, motioning for Leo and Finch that I was leaving. With no work being done, and the roads still in shitty condition, I had little options as to where to go next. I didn't want to return home, knowing Riley would still be in her room and Casey would be there. Seeing either of them would unwind me. Every time I set eyes on Riley, it killed me. I was a broody man, but she was my sunshine. The months when she'd given me the silent treatment had almost destroyed me. I missed her smiles, her bubbly laugh, the way she lit the room with her personality.

Casey was another situation all together, and I didn't think I could control myself if left alone with her again. She, too, had a sunny disposition, that smile crushing the darkness I stewed in, crumbling the hard exterior I had to carry in the world I'd built. Those hazel eyes of hers held such life that it melted me. I couldn't imagine not seeing them every day. The thought left me frozen, my hand on the door handle as I stood pondering why I'd think such a thing. She'd been back for a day, in my presence mere hours at the most, and I didn't want her to go back to Armina. I wanted her here, even with as painfully as it tormented me.

"Fuck," I mumbled, getting in the car and instructing Leo to drive to the club. I needed to take my mind from Casey. Going to the club wouldn't help, no matter how many beautiful, half-naked women we employed. Nothing would satisfy the need I had for Casey. That was an indisputable fact. But Tyson would be there and if he weren't up to his flirting ways, he'd get my mind from her. If anything, he'd remind me why I couldn't touch her. Our friendship was on the line if he even found out I was even considering it.

Leo pulled in front of the club. It was one of several I owned throughout my territory. This one catered to the richer men, and sometimes women, in the city. I ensured discretion and vetted the women we employed. We treated them with respect and paid them well, paid their medical bills and childcare if they had kids. If it was one thing I'd learned early on, it was that treating my people well made for loyal employees. Turnover was low in any of my franchises, and no one turned on me or fled to another family.

"Boss," Nico nodded to me when I entered the club. The music was low, it was still early, the girls just coming in for the early shift. Unlike Tyson, I preferred to steer clear of getting involved with the women who worked for me, regardless of how sexy or beguiling they were. I didn't want the risk. I was discreet about whom I slept with and extremely picky. With Casey flaunting herself and her desire for me openly, I didn't even venture a look at anyone as I walked through the club. My mind was on her, knowing no other body would satisfy me.

I found Tyson in the back, in a compromising position with two of the girls.

"You two, back to getting ready. Tyson, get your hands off my employees and your cock back in your pants before I ban you from the club." The girls ran off as Tyson griped.

"Well, aren't you a commanding prick today, Mace," he said, zipping his pants back up.

"You need to stop fucking around with them. You already have China sucking your cock, now you have those two giving you a hand-job?"

"Well, the one was, the other was letting me touch her tits."

I smacked him on the back of the head. "I can't wait until you find a woman who finally tames you."

He let out a loud belly laugh. "There is no woman out there who can tame me. You should know that. And since when are you so uppity about it?"

"Since you started making it a habit. I'm serious, Ty. No more, not even with China."

He rolled his eyes. "Fine. You're in a shitty mood. What's going on?"

"Nothing. I went to the site and put Mike on alert. Did you talk to Nico?"

"Yeah, and I stopped by the shop as well as a few of the businesses."

"Good. I want the men monitoring the roads, too. Just in case they decide they can drive right in and fuck with me."

"Got it." He crossed his arms, his hazel eyes that were so like Casey's seeing right through me. "What's wrong, Mace?"

"There's nothing wrong."

"You're on edge—"

"You think so? My sister's got herself locked in her room in some depressed hole she can't crawl out of." I leaned closer, lowering my voice. "The Bad Omens are targeting me and

Greyson Tides might become my brother-in-law. Does that give me reason to be on edge?"

I ran my hands through my hair, knowing the auburn-haired beauty with the irresistible curves, sexy teasing, and gorgeous hazel eyes was the real reason I was so flustered.

"Fuck, when you put it that way, I think we both need a strong drink. If I can't satisfy my dick the way I intended, I can quench my thirst another way." He slapped my back, ushering me to the front of the house.

Sam, the bartender, was setting up. The club opened early, although after last night's storm, I didn't think it would be too busy. We were used to snowstorms this time of year, but they still slowed business down. Sam dropped two glasses on the bar, pouring a shot of bourbon in each.

"It's early for the hard stuff," I muttered, still grabbing my glass and downing the shot.

"Apparently not," he said with a laugh before returning to wiping down the bottles.

"Better?" Tyson asked after finishing his shot.

"No, and now my throat burns. That's not gonna sit well the rest of the day."

"Old man," he snickered.

"No older than you, Ty."

"True, but you show it while I still look like I'm twenty-five."

Sam turned and gave him a side glance, the same one I shot him because as much as he acted like he was that age, neither of us still looked it.

"You might get away with thirty, but twenty-five is a stretch, buddy."

He shrugged, and I wondered if he would ever settle down. He'd always been the player, the wilder of the two of us. I'd taken the lead in the business, managing the money, the investments, calling the shots. Tyson didn't want to be part of meetings or conference calls. He wanted what he considered the fun aspects of the business—doling out the punishments, traveling only to territories where he knew he could enjoy himself when not conducting business, like Armina. He wanted the glory, the power, the women, and the danger that came with what we did. I preferred the structure, the business side of it, the controlled aspects. We were two very different men, and it worked in our favor, providing the perfect balance that ensured our empire remained a feared one. And it was our empire, even if I'd built the wealth and everyone called it mine. Without him, I wouldn't have gotten this far.

"Let's talk about the Bad Omen thing," he said, leaning in. "I think Casey's right and it would be good to assure our allies we're on top of this. The Randall thing makes us look weak. If we don't nip any worries in the bud now, someone might decide to take advantage of what they see as that weakness. It will force us to retaliate and there will be war."

"What do you propose?"

"I visit the most worrisome ones—"

"No. The last thing we need is for you to go in and threaten to rough people up to prove a point. This is more my thing, Ty. With so many unstable pieces—the unknown of when they'll strike next, of this Tides debacle with Riley—I need to look in control. I'll talk to them."

He sat back, crossing his arms and eyeing me. "You take all the fun out of it, Mace."

"I take the risk out of it."

"Damn, what am I supposed to do to keep myself occupied now? You've cut my dick off from these beauties and shut down any ability to relieve that frustration with my fists."

"Go to the gym," I joked, rising and straightening my shirt. "Run a few miles or beat the shit out of a punching bag."

"Not the same as bloodying up a face."

"I'm sure you'll find someone to bloody up. Just make sure it doesn't go beyond our territory until necessary."

"Where are you going?" he asked as I walked away.

"I have a conference call to schedule and calls to make. Someone has to do the grown-up things."

His cackle followed me as I left the building. At least I'd have something to take my mind off Casey.

THE DAY PASSED QUICKLY. I buried myself in work, making a few more stops, then avoiding Casey and locking myself in my office for the rest of the day. When I finally trudged downstairs, I stopped in my tracks. Riley was in the kitchen making dinner with Casey, the two chatting away.

"Ri?"

She turned her green eyes to me, ones that held a glimmer of life again. Her hair was clean and combed, her clothes, although loose from the weight she'd lost, were more than the leggings and raggedy sweater she'd worn for weeks.

"Hi, Mace." Her smile lit my heart, and I walked over to her, brushing her hair back before pulling her into a hug. The way her arms wrapped around me reminded me of the way she would cling to me when we were younger. It had been so long since she'd spoken to me, since she'd let me hold her, distancing herself from me after the Randall mishap. My anger had been brief as I'd sat by her side in the hospital that night, broken from the sight of her injuries. But each day she'd ignored me had been like experiencing the pain of seeing Randall hurt her over and over.

Kissing her head, I gently pushed her back, taking her in. She was pale, her soft features hollow from not eating, the circles under her eyes prominent from weeks of crying and not sleeping. I'd wanted to help, to have her talk to me, but she'd refused.

"She needs to be fattened up," Casey said, her voice drawing my attention.

I let Riley go, but she snuggled against my chest, and I pulled her in.

"I don't need to be fattened up," she mumbled.

"Yes, you do," I agreed, meeting Casey's eyes, the hazel in them a mix of amber and dusty brown. A small speckle of blue sat within them. She licked the spoon she'd been stirring with, and I followed its path, wondering what those lips would feel like against mine.

Keeping Riley in my arms would be a mistake if I didn't stop looking at Casey. I dragged my eyes from her. "So, does this mean you're back?" I asked Riley.

She peered up at me. "I think so. But I still have a lot of things to work out." The sadness filled her eyes again. She let go of me and returned to helping Casey. I left them alone, not wanting to push Riley and needing to distance myself from Casey. As they chatted, I tried not to hear the answers Riley provided about Greyson. I still didn't know how I felt about the situation.

Tyson joined us just as we were sitting down to eat, and I relaxed and enjoyed the meal, the worry about Riley lifting. My other worries sat on my shoulders, their claws digging in and reminding me I couldn't relax too much, or I'd be caught off guard like I'd been with Riley.

Just as we finished dinner, my phone rang.

"Donelli," I answered, rising and feeling everyone's eyes on me as I walked away. Donelli was the head of the power in Armina. Worry sank its claws in further while I waited to hear what he had to say.

"Mason. What's this I hear about the Bad Omens? Is it true? Greyson Tides took out one of their guys? One who infiltrated your network?"

Fuck.

"Where did you hear that?"

"I have my sources. Why is it I'm finding this out only now and not from you?"

Great. When I found out who his sources were, I'd let Tyson relieve his frustration until his knuckles were bloody. "Because it just happened, and I was dealing with the fall-out."

"I want a full briefing. Bad Omens, Mason? This is bad. They're in my backyard. Their territory is the province to the south of mine. And the partnership between my family and yours is not a secret. I expect you or Tyson to be on a flight out here tonight or our alliance is no longer secure."

He disconnected, the silence on the other end deafening.

"Fuck!" I punched the wall, shattering the plaster.

"Mace?"

Turning to Tyson, I saw the three of them waiting for an explanation. Riley's eyes were keen, seeing the side of me I'd always hidden from her, the business I'd never wanted her involved in.

"I need to go to Armina. Donelli wants a full brief of what went down. I'll fly out tonight."

I met Casey's eyes before I walked away, seeing the disappointment in them. It seemed ironic that she would be here, and I would be across the country where she lived. Heading to my room, I heard Tyson's steps as he ran after me.

"Let me go," he said, stopping me.

I shook my head. "No, this is business. You hate this stuff."

"But I can do it when I need to, and I'm close to Donelli. Let me handle this. Riley just emerged and you need to be here with her. If she went back to Tides while you were gone, it would kill you. Stay."

"What about Casey? She's here to see you."

"Nah, she's here for Riley. Besides, she's only here a few more days and I can extend my trip and stay in Armina long enough to spend time with her before I head back."

I gnawed my cheek, thinking it through. The thought of leaving Riley when she was getting better was gutting. The idea of not seeing Casey gave me a completely unfamiliar sensation, but one that was just as powerful.

"Fine. I'll make the travel arrangements and have the jet ready. I want you in contact with me every day while you're there, and don't fuck this up, Ty."

"I'm the face of this family to Donelli. Trust me."

It was the truth. I never traveled to see Donelli. I hadn't in years. Tyson always checked in with the family when he visited Casey. I stuck to calls and video meetings with him. They were the only family I let Tyson deal with because he got along with Donelli and his son, Tony. Donelli had a daughter, Angie, but from everything Tyson told me, she was a spoiled, snooty thing who rubbed him the wrong way.

With a sigh, I said, "Fine. You handle this, but if you fuck it up, my fist will be ready to pummel you when you return."

"When have I ever let you down, Mace? And when have I ever let a threat like that stop me?" he teased before heading down the hall. He stopped halfway, saying, "Keep an eye on Casey. And if you fuck that up, you won't have time to punch me because I'll kill you first."

He meant it as a joke, but there was truth behind it, just like there had been behind my threat. And given the situation with Casey, it was a more serious threat than he intended.

He ran off to his room to pack. I made a few calls to shore up his travel arrangements and assigned two men to travel with him. There was no way I would let him go alone. As much as I trusted Donelli, I wasn't taking the chance, and I knew how quickly relationships could turn when threatened with something as destructive as the Bad Omens.

By the time I had everything in place, Tyson was in the main room of the house, saying goodbye to Casey.

"Where's Riley?" I asked.

"She was tired, so she went back to her room," Casey answered while Tyson gathered his things. "She's fine, Mason."

"Yeah, that's the first we've seen of her in weeks," Tyson said. "I told you Casey had the magic touch."

He gave Casey another peck on the cheek, then slapped me on the back. "Remember what I said. Nobody touches her or I'll kill him and you," he said, low enough for only me to hear. "I'm not playing. You watch her just like you would Riley."

I shoved him back. "It hurts that you would doubt my ability to do that," I told him, holding my hands up to feign innocence.

His punch to my shoulder stung even if it was playful. "I know. I just like baiting you."

"You're an ass, Ty," Casey grumbled, and he flashed her a grin.

"Too bad. You're lucky I don't have you locked down in Armina. I'm gonna have a talk with Donelli about that tattoo. That slut Angie is a bad influence on you."

The eye roll she gave him was exaggerated, but it only caused him to laugh before he headed out the door with the two men I'd assigned flanking him.

"Why did you put these two on me, Mace? Do I look like I need babysitters?" I heard him joke before the door closed.

"Damn right he does," Casey said, her arms crossed. "And he complains about me."

I drew my eyes from the door over to her, my lungs burning from the air that stuck in them. It was like this every time we were alone, which was why I'd been avoiding her.

"It's okay, Mason. I won't push you. I shouldn't have flirted with or teased you. I know how important your friendship is with Ty."

But I wanted her to push me, to tease the way she had the prior night. I wanted my hand around her delicate throat, her body against mine, and it was tearing me up that I couldn't have those things.

Her eyes widened as if she read my thoughts, likely seeing the way my eyes were currently devouring her.

"Mason, what do you want? Because you're giving me mixed signals."

I knew what I wanted, what I needed, but I denied myself, walking past her and through the foyer back into the main room. Grabbing myself a drink, I leaned on the bar. She left me so out-of-control every time I was in her presence.

"I'm only here a few more days. I'll stay out of your way," I heard her say behind me.

The idea of not seeing her was one I didn't like. Just being away from her earlier had taken all my strength and I couldn't figure out why. There was more than just a need to touch her. I wanted to have her, to own her, to make her mine so that no one else could touch her ever again, and I didn't like those thoughts. Watching her at dinner, seeing the smile that had lit the room, the way her eyes danced with her laughter, and how her curls held reddish highlights in the light had left my heart racing.

Turning to her, my ability to think rationally fled. Her long curls called for me to weave my fingers through them, her full lips an invitation to kiss her.

"Don't," I said.

She tilted her head, her brow furrowing. "But—"

"No buts. You stay where I can see you. With Tyson gone, it's up to me to keep you safe." It hadn't been what I'd planned to say, but I couldn't say what I was thinking.

Her face fell, her eyes dropping. "Oh, that makes sense."

"Casey," I said, feeling the need to lift her spirit back up.

Her gaze fell to mine, sending my pulse racing.

"What do you want, Mason?" There was a desperation to her question, the same that was clawing at me to take her in my arms and kiss her. The physical need for her had transformed into a deeper one in the short time she'd been in my presence.

"I want what I can't have," I muttered, taking a swig of my drink.

There was a sparkle in her eyes as her smile grew. She seemed torn for a moment, as torn as I was before she walked closer to me. I needed her to keep the distance, but I didn't stop her as she leaned into me. My body rebelled, and her grin turned sly. There was no way she didn't feel my reaction pressing against her.

"You want me, Mason?"

Fuck, with every fiber in my body, but I couldn't tell her that. The control she had over my emotions and my body was unexplainable. Clenching my jaw to keep my true feelings from showing, I reached my hand out, touching the soft skin of her neck, running my fingers over it and loving how her lips parted in response. The sigh she emitted was one that gripped every part of me and fed my desire for her.

"I can't have you, Casey," I said, smoothing my fingers further up her neck until they were encasing it.

"You didn't answer my question."

My head instinctively lowered, her face tilting toward mine as I pulled her closer, my grip around her neck tightening.

"I want you, Casey. I want to touch every inch of your body, to feel you come undone around me, to taste you, to fill you. I want to hear your cries as I fuck you and watch as your climax shreds you." Her shudder ran through every part of her body.

"Mason," she purred, and I fought my desires.

Moving my hand, I traced the shape of her jaw, then sank my fingers into her soft curls, seeing the dark flicker in her eyes. From every reaction she'd had to my more aggressive moves, I knew she would be the one to break me. No one broke me, no one had ever owned me, but she would...if I gave in, if I betrayed Tyson.

"But you're not mine to take, little girl. You're forbidden, and that means I can't do the things I want to do to you."

She grabbed my neck, pulling my face down, her lips meeting mine. My resolve weakened, and I kissed her back, her mouth sweet and lush. The kiss deepened, my mouth as needy as hers, my fingers threading into more of her hair as I brought her further into me. I didn't want it to end, didn't want to stop, but I had to.

It wasn't right. Against every urge of my body, I halted the kiss, dropping my head and hearing her rapid breathing.

"We can't, Casey." I lifted my head, almost kissing her again. Her lips were red and swollen and I resisted the urge to run my tongue along them.

Soft fingers traced my jaw, her touch sending tingles through me, before she stepped from my hold, her curls slowly sliding from my grasp.

"I know," she said with a melancholy that was palpable.

The pressure of her hand where it remained on my chest had me craving for her to lower it and release the throbbing in my pants, to feel her hand wrap around it before she guided me into her. I pulled her to me again, cursing myself because I knew I was only torturing us both. Letting my hand drift down her body, I slipped my fingers under her waistline, feeling the soft skin of her hip as she arched into me.

"What are you doing, Mason?" she asked.

"Tormenting myself."

She bit her lip as my hand slid further down, past the lace of her panties.

"Tormenting us both," she murmured. "Shit, you need to stop if you don't want me."

"I never said I didn't want you. In fact, I thought I told you the exact opposite." I pushed my knee between her thighs before running my fingers lower. I was so close to sinking them into her, but I was taking a risk and crossing that line I'd drawn for myself. I knew if I touched her any further, I'd lose it and take her.

Slowly, I raised my hand, running it up her stomach until I hit the edge of her bra. Her heart was pounding, her inhale tight and shallow. I slid my fingers below the band, touching the plump flesh of her breast, and she let out a quiet moan. The sound stopped me because I wanted to hear more of her moans, to bring her to ecstasy and smother her cries with my mouth. To be the only one who ever tore a moan from her again.

"Dammit," I cursed myself before yanking my hand away. She had my shirt gripped tightly in her hands and I pried it free, pushing her gently from me. I was so hard I was aching, and I didn't know how I was going to settle myself down now that I'd touched her. "Go to bed, Casey." My words came out hoarsely, a sound that reflected the pain my decision was causing me.

The pursing of her lips didn't help the situation. "You could have just sent me to bed without touching me."

I gave her a smirk, and said, "Don't even think about using your fingers to finish the job, Case."

She inhaled beautifully. "That's just wrong. You get upset when I tease you and you turn around and do the same thing?"

Shrugging, I turned back to the bar and filled my glass.

"Fuck you, Mason." Her voice was playful. I almost dropped my glass when she pressed against my back, her hand reaching around and stroking me through my pants. I closed my eyes, losing myself to her touch. "When you force me to my knees, I want you to hit the back of my throat so hard your cock muffles my moans and gags. I want you to use my mouth and my body until I've come so many times that you erase every man before you from my memory."

She released her hold on me, and I heard her walk away. "Don't think about using your hand to finish the job, Mace."

I snickered at how she'd turned my game on me, throwing my own words back on me. The images she'd embedded in my mind were hard to dismiss and I'd almost come with her touch and the thought of doing just what she'd said.

"Fuck."

I remained at the bar until my body finally calmed down, only then allowing myself to walk into the living room and sit. Casey was on my mind as I swirled my drink, and she didn't leave it until Riley came in hours later. Revealing how she wanted me to teach her the business and temporarily erasing the hold Casey had on me.

Chapter Six

CASEY

I rubbed the sleep from my eyes, staring at the ceiling. Mason was on my mind, just as he'd been when I finally drifted off the night before. That man had become a craving I couldn't quit, no matter how hard I tried. Rolling over, I peeked at my watch. It was late, and I cursed myself, knowing Mason had probably left for the day.

I stretched and made my way to the bathroom. After brushing my teeth, I wandered from the room, heading down the hall to check on Riley. I still had my nightgown on, but since I figured Mason had left and his men rarely came into the house, remaining on guard on the perimeters, I didn't care that it was silky and barely covered my ass, the thin straps always slipping. The only reason it stayed up when they did was because my breasts held it up. I'd debated getting a new one, but I liked the way the material laid against my skin, so light that it was barely noticeable.

Knocking on Riley's door, I peeked in to see her still sleeping. It wasn't surprising. She'd always been a late sleeper. I debated waking her, but knowing what she'd been through, I let her sleep, making my way down the hall. I padded into the kitchen, my bare feet cold on the wood floors. Yawning, I stretched my arms before running my hands through my curls. The sound of glass cracking pulled my eyes from the window, and I turned to see Mason at the counter, his eyes wide and hungry.

Shit, I hadn't expected him to be there, or I would have dressed. He took me in, his gaze ravenous as it drifted down my body. The handle of his coffee cup had fractured before he'd dropped it on the counter, coffee dripping from the edge. He gave it no notice, still devouring me with his intense stare.

"What are you wearing?" His voice was so hoarse it almost hurt to hear it.

"I...I didn't think you'd be here. It's late and...I..." I let the excuses go, my heart racing as he stepped closer, then reached out and slammed my body into his.

"You need to take this off." This time his voice was commanding, weaving its way deep into my body and owning every part.

"Now?" I asked, bringing my hand to my strap and letting it fall. Why did I keep tormenting him like this? I knew better, but, for some reason, I couldn't stop myself. Like I needed to see how far I could take this before I broke him. And that wasn't something I should have wanted, to force his hand and encourage him to go against my brother. But I wanted him to take the chance, to risk Tyson's ire. It was selfish, but in the moment, my concern over it always fled.

"Fuck," he grumbled, his hold on my waist tightening. "No, not here."

"Where?"

He hardened his eyes, his jaw tense. "In your room, Casey. Where the fuck else would you change?"

I leaned into him, and his fingers spread over my lower back. The heartbeat below his shirt grew rapid. The pressure of his hand raised further up my waist, and I inhaled, the anticipation of his touch making my knees weak.

"Casey," he mumbled, his head dropping close to mine. His

thumb caressed below my breast, the feel of it flooding me with heat.

"Mason," I returned, my mind too rattled to think, my body too in flames.

His other hand wrapped around my waist, sliding to my ass, and he pulled me into his hardness. My mouth parted to release a small cry. I was afraid to move, remaining in his arms and waiting for his next move, but as his thumb brushed across my nipple, I raised my hands to his chest, running them up his firm muscles before tugging him closer. I wanted to feel his lips against mine, just as I had the night before. The memory of it remained burned in my mind.

But he stopped touching me, grabbing my wrists and turning me, sending my back smashing into his chest. The air fled my lungs with the impact and as his firmness thrust against me, I tipped my head back to his chest. He squeezed my wrists together, moving them both to one hand, and dropped his mouth to my ear. His other hand ran the length of my body, lifting my nightie and encasing my breast.

"Take me, Mason," I moaned, the torment of that touch setting my body ablaze.

"I can't, Casey." But his thumb brushed over my nipple, this time with no material to block his touch. I whined, knowing what was coming. Knowing this was just a taste of what he could bring me.

"But you are," I argued. "You're touching me and if you don't stop, I'm going to come right here." He already had me so wet, I doubted I could walk without leaving a trail.

"Will you come for me, Casey?"

The sensation those words caused in me was one that fluttered from my head to my toes, then back up and into my clit. I released a whimper, his dick twitching at the sound of it.

"Every time," I said, pushing back into it. I wanted it so badly there was an ache that had settled between my legs, one that hadn't left since the first day I'd seen him.

He dropped his head to my shoulder, his hand lowering in a slow, deliberate caress down my body until he released my wrists and stepped back from me. I teetered, catching my balance and exhaling with the heaviness that now sat in my heart.

"Get some clothes on, Casey." His voice held such sadness that it wounded me to hear it. Turning to him, I could see the struggle there, the desire to go further but the loyalty to my brother forbidding him.

"Why are you doing this? Why touch me if you won't—"

"Because I can't resist you. I want you so desperately it aches. I told you what I wanted to do to you and that craving won't cease. But you're forbidden. A forbidden craving I can't indulge. Now get your fucking clothes on before I sling you over my shoulder and throw you in your room."

He turned from me, walking out of the room and leaving me with a guilt that sat too heavy on my shoulders. I'd done nothing wrong. I hadn't expected him to be there, hadn't thought it was a possibility. Damn if I was going to take the blame for this.

I ran after him, grabbing his arm. He spun to me, his gaze penetrating with the darkness behind them. I stepped back, but he reached out and grasped me by the neck, yanking me close.

"What did I tell you?" he growled.

The anger in his tone left me flustered, but I shook it off. "You're not blaming me for this, Mason. I did nothing wrong."

His fingers caressed my neck while his other hand pulled at the strap of my nightie. "This is doing nothing? You're teasing me again, torturing me."

"The fuck I am. You're torturing yourself. I told you I would back off and I have."

He chuckled, his eyes lightening with the smirk he gave me. "You call those words you said to me last night backing off? You think putting thoughts of that sexy mouth around my cock, those tits bouncing as you drop to your knees, those moans rolling over it while I'm fucking your mouth backing off?"

My legs quivered, the images making me so wet I swore it dripped down my thighs.

"You're playing just as much as I am Casey and it's going to get us both in trouble. I can't have you and you can't have me. Now put some fucking clothes on before one of my men walks in here and I have to kill him for seeing this much of your flesh."

I took a ragged breath, and his eyes perused my body once more, his hand leaving my neck to trace its way down to my shoulder, where he pushed my strap aside. It slid down, exposing the top of my breast, and I watched as his eyes darkened again before they returned to mine. His jaw was clenched so tight I could hear his teeth grinding.

Pulling my strap back up, I brushed past him, returning to my room and sitting on the bed, my legs too weak to hold me any longer. I'd never craved a man like I craved Mason, and I was wishing I had stayed in Armina and never seen him again. I needed to get out of this house and away from Mason's world. My return to Armina was still two days away, but that didn't mean I had to sit around this house.

I took my time showering. Pulling on a pair of jeans and a light sweater that emphasized my chest, I pulled my hair back in a cute ponytail and walked through the house, searching for Riley. I was hoping to drag her out with me and take her shopping in the city. The snow had stopped, and the roads should have been cleared by now. I searched the lower level of the house and didn't find her. Shooting her a text, I looked out the window, seeing one of Mason's men in the distance as he made rounds. A small guesthouse stood to the right, and I remembered Tyson telling me Mason had moved Riley into it after the Randall event. It seemed odd that she was in the main house now, but maybe he'd wanted to keep a closer eye on her. Or maybe he wasn't ready to relinquish complete control of her again.

My phone buzzed, her message indicating she was in Mason's office upstairs. I chewed my lip, not wanting to see Mason, unsure of what my body's reaction to him would be. There was no way to avoid him for the rest of my stay, especially with Tyson away, so with a sigh, I found the stairs and made my way up to the top floor. Mason's office spread the length of half the second floor. Surrounded by windows, it held a beautiful view of the property. I hadn't realized just how much land he owned. The fact that his house held so many windows spoke volumes about how secure he was in his position and his men. He was a target no one could touch out here...although someone had tried and used Riley to break him.

Mason and Riley were deep in discussion when I found them. They were looking at a laptop, Riley studying whatever it was they were concentrating on. Mason's eyes drifted to me, lingering slowly on each curve before meeting my gaze. The lust was there but shadowed behind the steely look.

"I want to go out. Shopping, maybe lunch. I was hoping Riley would come with me."

"No," Mason said, before dropping his attention back to the screen.

That terse answer fired me up, and I snapped at him. "No?"

Riley gave me a questioning look.

"No," he repeated, not looking back at me.

"I don't think so," I said. "Ri, wanna come with me?"

"She's in training and she's not going anywhere. Neither are you."

He still hadn't bothered to look at me.

"Finally letting her in?" I layered my words with sarcasm and his jaw ticked. "Fine, I'm going out. I'll be back in a—"

"Is there something you don't understand about the word no?" This time he did glance at me.

Riley was looking between the two of us, her confusion clear.

I put my hands on my hips and snapped, "I understand

clearly. You're trying to control me like you did Riley, but that's not the way I work. I'm not on a leash." I saw Riley cringe and threw in a quick, "Sorry, Ri. Now, I'm leaving. Assign whoever you want to go with me, but I'm heading to the city for some shopping."

I turned on my heels, hearing him grumble. Walking through the hallway out toward the main rooms, I heard him mutter to Riley to stay as he hastened after me. He grabbed my arm and threw me against the wall, my exhale escaping with the force, but not like the last time he'd been rough with me.

"What is your problem, Mason?" I hissed. "You push me away, then bring me back, only to push me away. I know you're struggling, and I'll respect that, but I'm not yours to control."

He stepped into my space, a dark look in his eyes that reminded me why he was a feared boss. "You're mine to keep safe while your brother's out of town." I saw right through the excuse and felt the stake he was trying to claim on me.

Laughing, I replied, "You can't have it both ways, Mason. I'm not yours if you won't let yourself have me." I yanked my arm from his grip and pushed past him. "Now assign me protection so I can treat myself since I can't treat myself with you."

This time it was his fingers in the strands of my hair, yanking me back to him. The move drenched me, and I melted into his chest. "You're a brat, Casey."

"Well, you did call me a little girl," I played. He tugged harder. "You keep doing that, and you're going to need to finish what you started."

He released me, and I turned to him. His eyes were hooded, but the strain was clear in the clench of his jaw. He had his phone in his hand, and I sighed as he said to whoever was on the other end, "Casey's going out. I want two men on her at all times. Take her where she wants to go, but stay within the city."

The call ended, his gaze intense before he stormed back upstairs. I stood there for a few minutes, trying to calm my body.

He was killing me every time he touched me, every time he even looked at me. By the time I got my coat and trudged outside, my mood had shifted to a melancholy I couldn't shake, and a car was waiting for me.

"WANNA TELL me what's up with you and Mason?"

I jumped, dropping the dress I was pulling from the bag. Riley stood at the door of the closet, her arms crossed.

Stooping to pick the dress back up, I fumbled for words. "Nothing."

"Uh, huh." She waited for more, but I really didn't have more to give her. I didn't know what was up with us, nothing but extreme flirting that was soaking my panties every time I was in his presence.

"Nothing, Ri." I hung the dress and went back to unpacking the few things I'd bought during my uneventful trip to the city.

"Case, Mason is the calmest man I know, and I've never seen him so flustered. You two were talking a long time this morning and there's a weird tension between the two of you when you're in the same room. That whole fight for control about going out today was intense."

"There's nothing going on, Riley. Just some playful flirting."

She snorted, and I threw her a glance before I flopped on the bed, defeated by the day and by Mason. Sitting next to me, she brushed my curls back and took my hand.

"Whatever it is, I'm okay with it. I want my brother to be happy. He's been so worried about me, he deserves to be happy for a change."

"Why don't you tell him that," I muttered.

"Mason's stubborn, and you know he and Tyson are as close as brothers, Case."

"Yeah, Tyson would kill him." I let out a deep sigh, knowing it was the truth, and that's why he wouldn't give in to his desires. Chewing my bottom lip, I decided I didn't like being down. I wasn't a sad person. I was bubbly. "Aren't I supposed to be comforting you?" I asked.

"I'm good. You did comfort me. You woke me up and pulled me out of my funk. Now I'm doing the same for you."

"Let's go out, Ri. Just you and me...and whatever broody henchmen Mason sticks us with. How about drinks and dancing?"

"Drinks and dancing? I think you're mistaking me with your friends in Armina."

Laughing, I pulled her from the bed and ran to my closet. I'd bought a few new dresses and although I was larger framed than Riley, I wore my party dresses tight, so I was sure she could make one work. Grabbing a black one with short sleeves, the most conservative one, I held it up to her.

"You can't be serious," she complained.

"I am. I need to get my mind off your brother, and you need to get yours off Tides."

"I don't need my mind off Greyson."

"You know what I mean. And you need to get out of this house." I gave her my biggest puppy dog eyes. "Please, Ri?"

Rolling her eyes, she took the dress, holding it up. "There is no way Mason is letting me out of the house in this. It makes me look desperate for a good fuck. Is this what you wear dancing?"

"Yes. And it's a surefire way to pick up a few sexy guys."

Her eyes narrowed, the green matching the intensity of Mason's. "Is that what you want? To bring a guy back here and fuck him while it tortures Mason?"

His conflicted expression and words played through my mind, and I wondered what would happen if I did pick someone up. "No, I don't want to torture your brother, but since he's been torturing me, I need some release. Even if it's just dancing drunk on a dancefloor with my childhood friend."

She gave me a doubtful look. "I don't want to pick a man up, Case. I have one."

I almost fell over. Her words were confident and committed. "You're going back to him," I said.

"Yes, once I learn enough about the business. Don't tell Mason yet, although I'm sure he suspects. I...I can't not go back. I love him and being away from him has left this emptiness I can't seem to fill, like a part of me is missing."

I gave her a warm smile, my heart happy for her. Now I understood why she'd emerged the other night without the cloud of depression that had clung to her when I'd first seen her. Pulling her in, I gave her a hug. "I'm happy for you, Ri. I really am and you better make me your maid of honor."

Her laugh was a hearty one, and she hugged me back.

"This is all the more reason to go out," I said, releasing her. "Let's celebrate. I promise I'll be the only one flirting, and I'll keep the guys from you."

"You're bad, and if you think Mason is letting either of us go out tonight, you don't know my brother well enough."

I knew him well enough to judge the size of his dick and to know the feel of his hands in my hair was enough to soak me, but I wasn't about to tell his sister that. Shrugging, I replied, "He'll have no choice. Now get dressed. We can grab some food and drinks first."

She held the dress up, giving me a doubtful look.

"You'll make it work," I reassured her. "Get dressed and break some makeup out. Those circles under your eyes are a turnoff."

Shaking her head, she left my room. I snagged a cute cocktail dress I'd picked up at the same boutique where I'd gotten the black dress. This one had thick straps and the front cut low to give me sexy cleavage. The material was a dark red and clingy. As I pulled it over the black thong I'd changed into, it highlighted my curves perfectly. The bottom hit mid-thigh and, paired with the new heels I'd bought, it made me look good.

Tussling my hair so my curls bounced, I applied a thin layer of makeup. I rarely wore more than a dab of powder and blush, but when I hit the clubs, I put more effort into it. Armina was a party town. When we weren't at the beach, we were partying. I knew Treemont wasn't the same by any degree, but Mason and my brother ran two clubs in the city. I wasn't about to set foot in the one Tyson preferred and where I suspected he'd hooked up with the woman Mason had called him out on my first night there. But the other was a dance club, exclusive and high dollar, like the ones I frequented with Angie in Armina.

"Ready?" I said to Riley as I walked into the living room. Mason stood across from her, his arms crossed and an irritated scowl etched on his face. As his eyes took me in, I'd never felt so seen. They lingered on every part of me, sending a flaring heat through my body, one that matched the lust in his eyes. That lust morphed quickly into anger, and I knew this was going to be a fight. Everything about that look said no one was setting eyes on me tonight but him. It was laced with ownership and a claim that I was his, whether or not he admitted it.

Chapter Seven

MASON

I stared at Casey. She was the sexiest thing I'd ever laid eyes on, and all I wanted to do was pick her up and fuck her against the wall. The dress she was wearing showed her curves, curves I didn't want any other man seeing. It hugged her breasts, pushing them up so that they were calling for me to touch them, to run my tongue over them as I touched her. I'd experienced a taste of that body when she'd walked into the kitchen in that skimpy lingerie, almost breaking my resolve. Feeling her skin had left a craving for more. I shouldn't have touched her, my hand caressing that firm breast, her nipple puckering below my thumb as I'd brushed over it.

She was breaking me more every time I was near her. And now this.

"Does your brother know you leave the house in that shit?" I growled, feeling Riley's eyes on me.

"My brother is as much a player as I am. He doesn't have the right to say anything about what I wear."

Tyson would have dragged her back to her room and locked her in. She was playing with me, testing my need for control.

My laugh came out harsher than I'd wanted. "The fuck he

doesn't. He'd turn your ass around and send you back to your room, which is what I'm about to do to both of you."

"Riley looks like she's going to work. That dress goes almost to her knees."

But Casey didn't. The dress she wore sat so far up her thighs that I could see every detail of those lush legs.

"We're going to Steel. Should we take the two non-talkative bullies you sent with me today?"

At least she'd chosen the classier club, but I still wasn't about to let them go out.

"Mason, I think Casey's right. I need to get out of the house —" Riley tried to argue.

I wasn't budging. "Then go shopping with her tomorrow."

It was Casey who responded. "I just went shopping, asshole."

I flicked my gaze to her, gritting my teeth. She was a handful and had my balls in a frenzy with her attitude.

"I'll wait outside," Riley said. "She's winning this argument, Mason. We won't be gone long. I only want to get out of the house, maybe grab some drinks and some food."

I gawked at her. She'd never disobeyed my rules, never questioned what I'd told her, or rebelled.

"I think you lost your control over her, Mason," Casey said with an annoying smile.

Riley walked away, shaking her head as I continued to stare at Casey.

"Did you do that?" I asked her after Riley left.

"What? Give her the balls to finally stand up to your overprotective rules?"

My fists clenched, and I resisted yanking her head back with my fingers in her hair, something that was becoming my favorite turn-on. She'd moved closer, as if daring me to do it.

"Riley's not yours anymore, Mason. She's a grown woman and another man besides her brother owns her now."

"He doesn't own her," I grumbled.

"Keep telling yourself that, but when she accepts his offer, maybe you'll realize he does."

I rolled my neck, trying to relieve the tension those words caused, compounding what was already there from the sexy brunette in front of me.

"Regardless, you're not going out, not to the club, and not in that."

She gave me a challenging look, her eyes daring as they sparkled in the light. "I'm not yours, Mason. I'm going out with my friend for a few drinks and maybe I'll find a man who can relieve the clenching between my legs that you repeatedly cause and never satisfy."

The thought sent a seething envy through me, one I didn't like, an uncontrollable one that was about to explode. She waited for me to say something, but my emotions were churning too powerfully to even gather my words. The situation had me torn. Left wanting her, wanting no other man to touch her or even look at her, but unable to lay the claim I wanted on her because of Tyson.

She turned, thinking she'd gotten the last word, that she'd somehow put me in my place, but she hadn't read me right because if anything, my need to contain her free spirit was ripping through me. I stormed over to her as she reached the entrance to the foyer, grabbed her by the back of the neck and forced her against the wall, pressing my body into her back. The rapid breaths that were escaping her increased the inferno that was building in me. And when she brought her hands up the wall, her body quivering as she pushed her ass against my dick, it twitched with the need to take her. To throw my loyalty to the wind and fuck her until she came undone around me.

"You are mine, Casey." The words had come out and there was no way to take them back now.

"Then take me, bring me your force and your power. Own me, Mason."

The seductive way she said it ignited the need for her, and I took her arms, guiding them above her head and holding them by her wrists. She sighed, a sound that gripped me, seeping into my soul. I slid my hand up her thigh, the soft skin stirring the craving I had for her. It was like a storm thundering through my body, and ignoring it was almost too painful.

"Please, Mason," she cried, and I moved up her ass, sliding my finger along the line of her thong.

"You're definitely not going out with that on," I said against her ear.

"Then take it off me."

Shit, she was driving me mad. I was driving us both mad because I couldn't keep my hands off her. Dropping my head to her neck, I removed my hand. She let out a whimper that gripped me differently, hurting me with the sound. I needed to stop because I was confusing her as much as I was confusing myself. But I couldn't stop my need for her.

As if she read my internal thoughts, she whispered, "Let me go, Mason. It's for the best. I'm only here two more days and then I'll be gone. I won't come back."

The idea of never seeing her again was gut-wrenching in a way that I hadn't expected, one that went deeper than a physical craving for her body, and I wondered about it.

"I'll avoid you until I leave. I can even stay someplace else."

"No," I said quickly, releasing her wrists. Flipping her around to look at me, I leaned my hand on the wall above her. Her hazel eyes were so sad I wanted to relieve that sadness, to see her cheerful smile again. "You'll stay here. Nowhere else."

Seeing her like that triggered something in me that softened me, and I brushed a curl back, bringing my thumb down her cheek. I didn't know what was happening to me, but the need to touch her was transforming to more because I hated how sad she looked, hated that I'd caused her pain.

Her eyes searched mine, the hazel in them dimmed to a brownish hue, the sparkle gone.

"I don't think I can let you go, Casey."

The inhale she took was ragged. "Then claim me."

I gave her a lopsided grin, pushing away the softness that didn't sit comfortably on my skin. "I already have."

"Am I staying here tonight because I'll be in your room coming around your dick?"

Fuck, she was dirty in an adorable way that continued to break me more each time.

"No."

Her smile dropped, and she shoved away from the wall, her hand pushing my chest back. "Then I'm going out. I'm done, Mason. You have my panties soaked and my nipples aching so badly to be touched that I need to be away from you."

"What the fuck, Casey?"

"What the fuck? Are you serious?" That cute disposition morphed, and a small tigress stood before me, one who only twisted my craving for her. "You are a mess, Mason. Figure out what you want because you have two days and then I'm gone. I won't be back. I'm not going through this again. If I need to fuck every man I meet to get you out of my system, then I will. But I'm not playing this game anymore."

I clenched my jaw, grabbing her by the waist and slamming her against my chest. "You won't touch another man."

She laughed. "See, you want it both ways. Well, you can't have it both ways."

Working from my arms, she sauntered away. "I'm going out with Riley. Don't wait up."

She'd won, just like Riley said she would. I had no grounds to stop her, although Tyson would have my head if he found out I'd let her walk out the door in that dress. The inclination to go so I could keep an eye on them was prominent, but that would only get me in trouble. Resigned to accept that she'd outmaneuvered me, I pulled my phone out and instructed Breck to take two men with him and guard them. I wanted no chance that anything would happen. I still wasn't sure if the Bad Omen threat was looming. And if anything happened to either of them, I'd not only have to deal with myself, but I'd have Tyson and Tides at my throat.

"Dammit," I grumbled, knowing it was going to be a long night.

I TRIED to keep my mind off Casey by diving into work. There were contracts I needed to review for new investments, payroll to approve, and a request from the manager at the restaurant I owned to make renovations to the kitchen. My phone alerted me to the opening of the gates close to eleven and I pulled up the camera, seeing Riley emerge from the car, but not Casey. Breck followed her in, and I grabbed my phone, bolting down the stairs.

"Where the fuck is Casey?" I asked, meeting them as they came into the living room.

"She wanted to stay," Riley answered with a shrug. She looked exhausted, and I could see the night had been too much for her. Damn Casey for pushing her. She wasn't ready yet, and it showed.

"Go to bed, Ri."

She lifted on her toes and gave me a small kiss on the cheek. "Don't go too hard on her, Mace," she mumbled so that only I could hear her, then walked away, her shoes in hand as her bare feet made soft slaps on the hardwood.

I turned to Breck, my fists bunched. "What the fuck were you thinking, leaving her there?"

"She didn't want to come back. I tried to convince her, as did Riley, but she was adamant. Shep and Finch stayed with her. She's still being watched, and she's safe. They won't let anything happen to her."

But Breck was the only one I'd told to ensure no one touched her.

"Let's go," I said, shoving past him.

"Boss?"

"We're going to get Casey. Tyson will chew me a new one if he finds out she stayed. He'll be pissed enough that she talked her way into going out tonight." It was an excuse, one I used to cover the fact that she had me pissed off. That I was afraid another man's hands were on her, doing what I wanted to do to her. And that she was letting him to get back at me.

While Breck sped through town, my mind played all the scenarios out, my heart thumping harder with each one. She'd thrown the truth in my face before she'd left. I couldn't own her and deny my need to touch her at the same time. It was twisted, and it wasn't fair to her, but that didn't mean I wanted some other man's hands on her.

My teeth were grinding by the time we arrived. I tore from the car as Breck pulled up to the front, bypassing the line of people still waiting for entry. Breck ran to catch up while the bouncer let me in. There were a few complaints from the line, but this was my club. If they complained too loudly, I'd shut it down for the night. If I found anyone touching Casey and had to put a bullet in him, I'd close it down for good.

I rolled my neck, feeling the tension as I felt for the gun I'd snagged from the glove compartment and tucked in the back of my pants. The music was blaring, the smell of alcohol strong, the crowd rowdy. Breck pointed to where my men stood, their hands clasped in front of them, their eyes vigilantly surveying the crowd, but Casey wasn't with them. I scanned the club, spotting her on the dance floor. With three men surrounding her. My blood boiled as the man that was holding her waist pulled her closer.

"Fuck," I muttered, storming through the crowd, my eyes

riveted by the flirty smile she gave him as the one behind her closed in on her. I saw the glance over her shoulder that she gave him, but the other tugged her, jerking her body hard. She pushed against him as the third one blocked her in. They were circling her body like predators, ready to attack. Her staggered moves alerted me that she'd had entirely too much to drink. My men noticed her vulnerability at the same time I did, hastening toward her, but I was ahead of them. They would pay for letting her get that drunk and for letting another man put his hands on her.

The guy behind Casey grabbed the bottom of her dress, hiking it up. There were too many people for anyone to notice, but I saw it. I shoved people aside, making a beeline for her, my men following behind me. The clench of my fists was so fierce, the skin stretched uncomfortably. When I reached them, I punched the one behind her in the side of the head, pounding him until he was on the floor.

People scattered, the other two men reacted, but not before I pulled my gun. I yanked Casey from them, ignoring her complaints. They looked like they wanted to fight, and I invited it, keeping Casey in my grip even as she struggled to free herself. The one on the ground stumbled to his feet.

"Don't even think about it, shitheads. You fucking lay another hand on her and my staff will end the night cleaning your guts from the floor." I nodded to Finch and Shep. "Get them the fuck out of here and teach them a lesson about touching women who don't want to be touched."

"The fuck she didn't," one mouthed off. "The whore was begging for it."

Rage blinded me and my control precariously teetered, ready to topple and unleash what tether remained on my rage. "On second thought, take them to the alley, now."

Any complaints stopped the second my men pressed their guns to their backs. They shoved the three through the club and out the back entrance into the alley. I dragged Casey behind me, ignoring her grumbling.

"What the fuck did you call her?" I said, as the door slammed behind us.

I motioned for Breck to let him go and the cocky shit had the nerve to get in my face.

"I said the whore was begging for it."

I released Casey and slammed the end of my gun into his face. His words elicited fury from the depths of my body, and I drove my foot into his head when he hit the ground. Cocking my gun and shoving it against his temple, I said, "Apologize to her."

"What the fuck—" his friend started until I glared at him. He seemed like a rational guy until he moved to attack me. Finch blocked his attempt with a strike to the eye and raised his gun to his head. Shep had already immobilized the one I'd punched first, his knife against the guy's throat. Shep preferred playing with knives and he was my go-to guy when I needed to extract information from someone. I planned to let him have some fun with these three after I finished making them suffer.

I turned my attention back to the one on the ground.

"I thought I told you to apologize to her," I growled, removing my gun from his temple and shooting him in the kneecap.

His scream mingled with Casey's.

"Mason, stop, please," she begged, but my need to make the fuckers pay was fueling me. My control had slipped, which rarely happened, but once it did, it was difficult to rein back in.

"Nobody talks to you that way and nobody touches you," I roared, before I cocked my gun and pointed it at his head. "Apologize, or I put more holes in you."

"I'm sorry," he whimpered.

"Dude, he apologized, let him go. We didn't mean any harm."

I rolled my neck, bringing my sight to the one in Finch's grasp. He tried backing up, but Finch's grip on him was tight.

"Dude?" My laugh was feral, and I had the urge to just shoot all three of them in the head and be done with it. But they deserved a slow death for what they'd been planning to do to Casey. "Do you know who I am?" I snarled.

He shook his head, the one in Shep's hands doing the same. The third man was still writhing on the ground.

Two of my club security came through the door. They were large, with muscles that kept people in line. The music seeped through until the door closed, confirming that things had returned to normal. This club was private, and those who frequented were locals. The locals knew who I was, and they knew to stay quiet and to fear me. But these three weren't local.

"Tell them who I am, Case," I said, without looking away. She said nothing. "Tell them!"

"Dammit, Mason, let them go. It was harmless."

I glanced at her, knowing my eyes were lethal. Hers were bloodshot, the liquor slurring her words and impairing her ability to stand well. I turned back to them, growling, "Where are you three from?"

"Dankirk," one said, his voice quaking as I pointed the gun at him. His buddy was on the ground still, writhing in pain. All three were bloody, but not bloody enough for what they'd been doing.

I laughed. "Krill's town." I saw the recognition of the name. The Krill family had a powerful hold on Dankirk, and they were indebted to me for keeping it that way. I pulled my phone out, hitting Krill's number.

Krill answered on the second ring. Even at this time of night, he knew not to ignore my call. "This better be important."

"Some of your trash wandered into my city and touched my girl. Should I dispose of them here or let my boys escort them home?"

"You have a girl now, Brinks? 'Bout time. Send the fuckers to me. I'll ensure they're taught some respect. Have your boys leave them at the junction. We'll take it from there."

"I thought you would."

I disconnected and rammed the butt of my gun into the one who had escaped my fury, knocking his front teeth out. With the black eye Finch had given him, it made a colorful addition. Casey screamed, but I grabbed her, throwing her over my shoulder as she kicked and grumbled at me. My men had heard my slip up, calling Casey my girl, but I was hoping they'd figure I'd said it because she was Tyson's sister and not question it.

"Give them a proper escort back to Dankirk. Krill's men will meet you at the border to take care of the trash. Shep, be sure to give them a taste of what's in store on the way."

There wouldn't be much life left in the three by the time they reached the drop-off point, but I was certain whatever life remained, Krill would ensure it was excruciatingly painful.

I didn't bother to look back, hearing the scuffle and knowing no one else in the club would raise a finger to help the scum. This was a private club, and I'd find out who let the assholes in.

Breck left with me, his hand on his gun the entire time. Casey continued to punch at my back and kick for me to let her down, but I kept her there, my hand firmly planted on her ass to keep her skirt from rising any further. I threw her into the backseat, locking her in before I climbed into the front with Breck.

I peered back at her when she grew silent. She was fuming, even as drunk as she was. Crossed arms, beautifully pouting lips, and flared nostrils accompanied the hazel eyed glare she was giving me. She remained that way the entire ride back. Breck stayed quiet, knowing my mood. The situation had me wired, the anger still spilling through my veins. By the time we pulled up to the house, I was like a live wire.

Casey threw her door open and stomped into the house. I followed, catching up to her in a few strides and slamming the door behind me. She'd made it through the foyer and into the main living space by the time I took her arm and stopped her.

We stared at each other, the heat intense.

"You're an asshole, Mason," she slurred. "You can't go around punishing people like that. They didn't do anything."

"Didn't do anything? They were touching you! If I'd been any later, they would have had you in a corner raping you." Even though I knew my men would have stopped them, the thought still burned through me.

"Don't exaggerate—"

"Exaggerate?" I towered over her. "He had your skirt up, your ass showing, and his dick would have been out if I hadn't beaten the shit out of the fucker. And don't get me started on the one who was making a move toward your tits."

She stepped into me and poked at my chest. "You didn't want me and you're angry because someone else took what was yours."

I couldn't deny it, although the way they were going about it had me hot. The fact that she was too drunk to know better, too trashed to realize what they were doing and to fight back had me hostile.

"You had your chance, Mason. I wanted you...fuck, I still do, but you turned me away."

"I had to turn you away."

"But you want me." Her eyes were large and inviting, her chest pushing into mine so that her breasts swelled above her dress.

"Of course I want you."

"Well, here I am," she said, throwing her arms out. "Take me then. You took away my other options, forced me home. Now fuck me."

The invitation was a bold one, an opening that few men could resist, that I may not have resisted if she hadn't had one too many drinks, if the alcohol wasn't impairing her thinking, if there wasn't a risk that she'd wake in the morning and regret it. Or that I would.

"No. You're trashed, Casey. Go to bed."

"Go to bed," she mocked. "That's all you ever tell me to do."

"And that's what I'm telling you now. Go to bed and sleep the alcohol off."

"Why? So you can turn me down again?"

She turned away, but I grasped her arm, pulling her back to me. "Yes, but I can promise you, Casey, if I ever give in, I want you sober when I fuck you. I want your cries to be pure, to be raw, and when you come for me, I want it to be me who breaks you and not the alcohol."

I let her go, wondering if she was teetering from the alcohol or from my words.

"Now get your drunk ass into bed and sleep it off."

I left her there, not wanting to look at her anymore because all I could see were the hands of those men on her tan skin, the skin I wanted to keep for myself. The skin she'd offered me repeatedly and yet, I'd denied myself over and over. My resolve was wearing thin, and I didn't know if I could make it another day without giving in. And if I resisted, I wasn't sure I wouldn't follow her to Armina and take her there.

My head was pounding, my mouth dry and nasty. When I stretched, it only exacerbated the situation. Hangovers were my nemesis, and I avoided them, knowing my tolerance level and where surpassing it would leave me obliterated. And last night I sped right past it and plunged my way into a drunken stupor.

"Idiot," I muttered, trying to sit up.

I flopped back down, throwing my arm over my eyes to stop the room from spinning. The urge to vomit was climbing in my throat, increasing as the events of the night returned to my memory.

"Oh, fuck."

Mason had found me and beaten the shit out of the guys who'd been hitting on me. The same guys who kept buying me drinks, handing me a strong one when Riley's early exit had distracted Mason's thugs.

My stomach churned, and I stumbled out of bed, making it to the toilet just as the burn of all my drinks surged forward. I laid my head on the toilet, hating that I was so sick.

"That's a sexy look."

I peered up, seeing Mason's outline in the moonlight that lit the room. The same light I'd thought was dawn waking me to slap me in the face for my stupidity.

I didn't have the energy to say anything back, my stomach knotting as the bile burned its way up my throat. I lost my hold on it, closing my eyes. It spilled into the toilet, splatters repelling back into my face. I felt the cool touch of Mason's hands as he pulled my hair back and waited for me to stop. When I could function again, I leaned back, hitting his legs and resting against them. My eyes closed to the sensation of his fingers pushing a strand of hair from my mouth.

Tears welled, but I kept my eyes closed to hold them at bay. I didn't want to admit how stupid, vulnerable, and embarrassed I felt over what had happened.

"You know, when you invited me to come fuck you, this wasn't what I had in mind."

I laughed, which only stirred my stomach, sending the remaining contents of it spilling as I grasped onto the toilet. His hands never left me, his presence steady and comforting. Reaching up, I flushed the toilet, and collapsed back against him, wiping my mouth with the back of my arm.

"Done?" he asked, and I nodded, too exhausted to move.

He reached down and scooped me up, the gentleness of it a dichotomy to the way he'd tossed me over his shoulder hours earlier. I rested my head on his chest, the strength of it comforting until he laid me on the bed, pulling the blankets up over my rumpled dress. His green eyes held concern and an emotion I couldn't pinpoint.

I turned from his gaze, hating how weak I looked. He walked away and the tears I'd been fighting released, a few slipping quietly down my cheek. I heard the water running, then his footsteps returning. The mattress moved as he sat next to me, laying a damp cloth on my forehead. His thumb brushed a tear from my cheek, and I glanced back at him.

"I'm sorry," I whispered.

"I know. Get some rest." He went to rise, but I grabbed his wrist.

"Stay, please."

His brow creased.

"I'm not in any condition to seduce you," I joked. "I just..."

His eyes searched mine, and he rose from the bed, turning his back on me. Sighing, I rolled to my side, taking the rag and holding it like it was a piece of him. But the door didn't open. The bed shifted, and he turned me into his chest. His clothes were still on, but I didn't complain, loving how perfectly I fit against him. His arm wrapped around me, and I rested my head and hand on his chest.

"They put something in your drink, Case," he said so softly I almost didn't hear him. "They were predators, ones Krill had on his radar. His men dealt with them, and I dealt with my men for letting them near you."

I tried to raise my head, but he held me tighter. "Your men didn't do anything—"

"They left you vulnerable and let..." His muscles tensed. "Go back to sleep, Casey."

I let it go, knowing he'd needed to reprimand his men. This business was a deadly one, and they'd let me dictate the night. Mason was right to be angry at them and at me. I'd been stupid and his reaction was the same as Tyson's would have been. Leaning further into his hold, I closed my eyes, listening to Mason's steady heartbeat and loving the strength of his arms, the way his fingers softly caressed my shoulder. I vaguely wondered if he'd been here the entire time, watching over me as I slept. Worried about me.

I drifted off to Mason's touch and the fleeting thought that this night had changed the seductive flirting we'd been doing into something more, something real.

WHEN I WOKE, Mason was gone, but what I'd thought was a hangover before had compounded. I rolled over with a groan, squinting my eyes at the sun that was blinding me through the crack in the curtains. Curtains that had been open when I'd crawled into my bed. Mason must have closed them to let me sleep longer. The act was a sweet one, but then everything about what he'd done last night had been sweet.

There was a light tap at the door and my belly flipped in anticipation before it reminded me it was still queasy. Riley peeked in.

"Wow, you look like death," she joked, coming into the room.

"Says the woman who hadn't showered in days when I first saw her."

"Touche." She pulled the curtains open, and I hissed, shielding my eyes from the glare.

"It's after eleven. Get up. Mason had one of his guys run to get bagels this morning to soak up the alcohol."

My stomach churned violently, and I shivered at the thought of food. Riley pulled my blankets off, shaking her head when she saw I was still in my dress.

"You're a mess," she teased.

"I feel like a mess. Is Mason here?" I asked, trying to sit up and hoping it wasn't obvious that I really wanted him to be.

"No. He took me out to the club and a few other places this morning to get a feel for the business."

"Which club?" I asked, raising my brow. I knew about the risqué one my brother preferred to oversee, but I wasn't sure if Mason would bring Riley in on that aspect yet.

"The one we went to last night. Although he told me about the other one. Yuck." She flopped next to me, the movement of the mattress turning my stomach. "You don't think Greyson has one of those, do you?" She bit her bottom lip, her expression reflecting the worry the thought had caused her.

"You know he's a lot older than us, right? I mean, what is he? Forty something?"

"Yes," she replied dreamily. Leave it to Riley to fall for an older man. I was no better. Mason was eight years older than me, but that didn't come close to the age difference between Riley and Greyson.

"Then that means he's seen a lot more tits than yours, Ri."

She elbowed me. "I don't have to think about it, Casey."

"Yeah, you prefer to think you found a forty something year old virgin?"

Her laugh told me he was anything but and the blush that filled her cheeks said everything I needed to know about the personal side of Greyson Tides.

"Mason told me what happened," she said, quickly changing the subject.

I lifted myself from the bed, trying to steady my walk as I breathed in my hand to see just how heinous my breath was. I jerked my head back, trying not to gag. Brushing my teeth became my priority when I reached the bathroom.

"And what did he tell you?" I asked between brushes.

"That those assholes drugged you and no one noticed until he got there."

Until he rescued me, I thought. And suddenly the incident took on an entirely different light. Mason had rescued me, protecting me from the assholes I'd naively flirted with in my attempt to get even with him.

"Case?" Riley was staring at me, and I realized I'd stopped mid-brush, the toothpaste dripping down my lip.

I returned to the sink and spit and rinsed before gurgling an extensive time with mouthwash. Content that my breath was up to par, I returned to the room, rummaging through my clothes for something comfortable. I didn't care what I wore today. I only wanted to curl up on the couch and binge-watch something. Mason had seen me with vomit in my hair, so there was no sense in caring if I looked like a slob at this point.

I snagged a sweatshirt and a pair of leggings, along with clean undies and a bra, before heading back to the bathroom.

"Casey."

I turned. "What do you want me to say, Ri? That I fucked up? That I got trashed because I was angry at your brother? That I didn't want to go out, but I wanted to get even with him for turning me down?" I stopped, biting my tongue and realizing I'd said too much.

Her emerald eyes studied me with no judgement. "Did you tell him that?"

Sighing, I let my anger go. "No. No, I didn't."

She stood and came over to me. "You might want to. I can't tell you he'll admit his feelings, but I can say he's a mess, and I think it has to do with you."

I shook my head. "It's Tyson. If I was any other woman, he would have taken me up on it by now."

"Ew, that's just gross every time I even try to picture it."

"That you try to picture your brother having sex is gross on its own, Riley," I teased.

"You're nasty. Anyway, you're not any other woman, Case. You're you and you're Tyson's sister."

"I know."

She gave me a kiss on the cheek. "You're already like a sister to me—"

"You'd text me more if that were true."

Punching me playfully, she said, "I'm serious, Case. You're like a sister to me and if you and Mason end up together, that just makes it even better."

She waved her hand in front of her face and headed to the door. "Your breath no longer smells like death, but you stink like a bar."

"Thanks, that makes me feel better."

Laughing, she paused, her hand on the knob. "Maybe you'll even be my sister-in-law...if Tyson doesn't kill him first."

My jaw dropped, but she'd left the room before I could process what she'd said. Mason and I had barely touched each other, and she'd already married us off. The thought sent a shiver through me that sank deep into my soul like it belonged there. I shook it off and showered, washing the stank of the club from my skin and the lingering touch of the men Mason had beaten from me.

When I emerged from my room, I found Riley munching on pretzels in the kitchen.

"Don't they have a television?" I asked, spying the bagels Mason had gotten for me. I tried hiding my smile because they were from a local bakery he and Tyson would take us to when we were kids. He'd always teased me about my love for their bagels, and it surprised me that he'd remembered such a trivial thing.

"There's one in the basement. That's where they have the movie screen set up and the fun stuff. This is just for show, so they look mature."

I glanced at her, seeing the knowing smile she gave me when I picked out a bagel.

"Look mature? Your brother is the second most deadly boss in this province and my brother is just as feared. The only one who outdoes them is your old man."

Scoffing, she said, "My old man?"

I stuck my tongue out at her before sipping on some water and waiting to see how my stomach would handle it. I was so dehydrated that I wanted to gulp it down, but I didn't want a repeat of the previous night.

Bagel in hand, I wandered out of the kitchen on a hunt for the television. "Come spend the day doing nothing with me," I called to her as I searched. "It's my last day here."

"I would, but Mason sent Breck to pick me up. He wants to take me shooting."

I stopped in my tracks. "You with a gun is a bad scenario, Ri. You're likely to shoot Mason before I can get him in my pants."

"Eww, dammit Casey. Stop putting those images in my head. I don't care what you do with my brother, but I don't want to know about it."

I wandered back to the kitchen. "Fine. Where the fuck is the basement?"

She rolled her eyes. "That's a nice mouth you've got on you."

"That's what he said," I added, laughing at my joke.

Her snort was loud, and she burst out laughing with me. We'd always been silly, and I missed hanging out with Riley. It didn't matter how much time passed between our visits, we were always the same when we were together. Just two goofy friends, oblivious of the dangerous world our brothers sheltered us in, me ignoring it and her unaware of it until now.

I TALKED Riley into hanging out with me until Breck found us and hauled her away to wherever Mason was waiting for her. The rest of the day, I curled on the leather sofa watching movies.

Riley hadn't lied. The basement reflected the relaxed side of Mason and my brother when they weren't playing the parts of dangerous gangsters. Video games and pinball machines lined one wall at the far end of the massive room. A pool table sat in the middle. There was a bar against the other wall, a full range of alcohol, and even a stocked fridge. The other half of the basement was a movie theater, complete with reclining leather seats and a long leather sofa in the front. I tried not to think of either of them getting busy with women on the sofa I was now comfortably occupying. A streak of jealousy stung me when I thought of

Mason on it, my mind envisioning a scene a little too vividly until I shooed it away.

Neither of us was innocent, and it wasn't like we were together. I couldn't even get him to fuck me, let alone anything more serious.

I was mid-movie, lost in the fantasy world on the screen, when Mason picked up my legs and sat on the couch next to me, laying my legs over his lap. I peeked over at him.

"I'm covered in blankets, my body hidden below layers of clothes, and now you decide to touch me?"

He gave me a coy grin that sent a torrent of flutters through my belly. "I told you, you're too easy. I like a challenge, Case."

"And the sloppy, unkempt looking girl with no makeup and an 'I've been vomiting' pallor is a challenge?"

He shrugged. "It's cute."

I flopped my head back, realizing I didn't even have my hair down. I'd thrown it up in a messy ponytail, which had since started loosening so that curls lay in chaos around my face.

"Did you eat?" he asked, rubbing my ankles beneath the blanket.

"Just the bagel this morning." I peered back over at him. "Thank you, by the way."

"For what?"

"For everything."

"It was nothing. I would have beaten the shit out of them if they'd touched Riley, too."

"And the bagels?"

He looked back at me, his green eyes hooded in the dark room. "Were for you. And I hope you know, I don't hold hair back from puke for just anyone." The wink he gave me sent my heart pounding, and I swallowed a little too loudly.

He narrowed his eyes. "Do you make that noise every time you swallow, or does it depend on what's going down your throat?"

My mouth gaped, my heart rate doubling. "It depends," I answered, hearing the shake in my voice.

Laughing, he picked my feet up and rose. "I had Finch pick pizza up. Your stomach okay with that?"

I nodded as he leaned over me, his hands on either side of my head. "Riley's out with Breck still. I have her learning the ropes at the club. Stay here and I'll bring something down for you."

His face hovered over mine and I reached up, placing my hands on either side of it, but he drew away, my heart dropping. "None of that, Case."

Disappointed, I looked away, staring at the screen. His thumb tilted my face back to him. His eyes were intense as they dropped to my lips and trailed the path his thumb took as it brushed over them.

"Then what?" I asked. "We go back to teasing until you send me to my room alone and dripping while you stalk off just as unsatisfied as I am?" He glanced back up and the hunger in his eyes left my knees weak. His fingers traced my neck and when he lifted them, I kept them in place, leaning into them. "I leave tomorrow, Mason. It's one night. One night that won't hurt anyone. One night no one needs to know about."

He moved his hand, embracing mine and pinning it against the couch. Bringing his face closer, his lips swept across mine and my heart leaped to life. "Can you do just one night, Casey?" The torment in his voice sent my heart stuttering, the emotion behind it palpable. "Because I'm not certain I can."

His words tore through me, leaving an ache in my chest, one that went too deep, and I thought he might be right. One night wouldn't be enough.

"But it's all we have," I said, hearing how raspy my voice sounded.

He stood, letting my hand go and leaving me with a strange emptiness. My eyes followed his path until he was gone. I sat up, drawing my knees to my chest and hating the uncomfortable feeling that still sat in it. The movie ended, the credit music playing as I stared blankly at the floor, trying to work out the emotions that were sifting through me.

By the time Mason returned, the credits had ended, the next in the series starting. I'd paid no attention to it, still rattled like I was each time I was with him. He stood over me, handing me a plate with a piece of pizza on it and a ginger soda. Sitting on the other end of the sofa, he sipped on his glass of liquor.

I eyed the soda, knowing there had been none in his kitchen. It was another caring gesture, another glimpse at the soft side of him that he'd given me last night.

"Figured it would help your stomach," he said with a shrug, looking uncomfortable as if I'd caught him doing something he didn't want seen.

Deciding to let it go and take it as the sweet gesture it was, I nodded to his drink. "Your meal looks a bit skimpy."

He smirked. "Like I prefer my women."

I pursed my lips, not liking how that comment left a stir of envy in me. He took a sip, keeping his eyes on me like he was waiting for my reaction. Placing the soda on the floor, I picked at my pizza, dragging my finger through it and scooping up a long string of cheese. I brought it to my mouth, holding my tongue out and letting the cheese slowly stretch onto it before putting my finger between my lips and sucking the sauce off.

His grip on his glass was so tight I thought it might shatter, that ravenous look returning to his eyes.

"I thought you preferred your women in sweats and leggings?" I said, swirling my tongue around my finger.

"Fuck, Casey," he grumbled.

I took a bite of my pizza, making sure to lick my lips with deliberate slowness. "If that's not the case, I can go upstairs and change."

He grimaced, his expression hardening, and I knew the game was over again. I'd gotten a moment of revenge for his earlier teasing, but that was all I'd get. He wanted control again. He stood, setting his drink down and grabbing the plate from my hands. "That's enough," he said.

Huffing, he sat back down, taking my legs and yanking me down so they were in his lap again. He snatched the remote, mumbling about my poor taste in movies, and started flicking through the options. It seemed odd that he hadn't left the room.

"I hear that one's good," I said as he flipped past a romance. He shot me a look. "If you want me to stay down here, I'm not watching that shit."

"You're staying?" I asked, unable to hide the excitement in my voice.

"If you behave." He stopped on a sci-fi, and I shook my head. "What?" he asked. "You're not going to behave?"

With a laugh, I replied, "No, you put a dorky sci-fi on. Should I tell the guys that's what you're watching?"

He glared at me. "There's nothing wrong with my choice. It's better than your shit."

Shrugging, I sat back, content to watch whatever he wanted as long as he continued to rub my legs the way he was. By the time the movie was half over, his hands had risen to my thighs. I didn't think it was an intentional move, there was nothing sexual about it. Instead, it was comforting, almost loving. I glanced over at him, catching him looking at me rather than at the movie. He held my gaze when any other man would have looked away.

Pulling my legs from him, I sat up, maneuvering so that I was sitting on my knees next to him.

That flash of lust returned to his eyes. "When I want you on your knees, I'll tell you," he said, sending butterflies through my stomach.

"But you won't," I said, leaning closer. "You won't let yourself and tomorrow I'll be gone."

He reached up, brushing a curl from my eye. I saw the desire in his eyes, the same that was simmering inside of me, waiting for us to take this further, the same that wouldn't turn to a blazing fire because doing so would send my brother off the deep end and drive a wedge between him and Mason that might never be repaired. Tyson held grudges and he would never look at Mason the same if he had a one-night stand with me. Although I was certain from Mason's remark earlier that, just like me, he wanted more than one night. It would never happen because Mason wouldn't risk it. As much as I didn't want to put Mason in that position or hurt my brother, I craved for Mason to take the chance and let me experience his touch. But I knew my brother's expectations for Mason were too high and Mason's attempt to meet them and ignore what was growing between us was just as high.

"Will you miss me when I'm gone?" I asked, wanting desperately for him to say yes. Needing to hear the words even if it risked hurting us both to hear him admit it.

"I can't miss what I haven't tasted."

My stomach flipped, warmth spreading through my thighs.

"And what if someone else tastes me?" His teeth clenched, the muscles in his jaw tense. I was pushing him when I shouldn't be, but fear was driving me. A fear that there was more to us and if we let this chance go, we would lose something we would regret for the rest of our lives. "What if there's a man in Armina waiting for me to return? Waiting to take what you won't, to own what you claim is yours, but won't let yourself have?"

His eyes darkened, and he leaned into me, his fingers draping down my cheek before he took my chin in them, his grip firm. "Then I'll have to make a trip to Armina to put the mutt down. No one touches my girl."

I inhaled so deeply that the air burned my lungs. "But I'm not your girl." I sat back, drawing my knees to my chest and resting my head on the couch, seeing the vulnerability in his face for a fleeting moment. "You won't let me be," I whispered.

"Is there another man waiting for you in Armina, Casey?" he asked, his hands pulling my ankles back to his lap.

I shook my head. "Is there a woman you're turning me down for, Mason?"

His lips turned upward to form a crooked grin that made me want to pull him over and kiss him. "And what would you do if there was?" he asked, raising his brow.

I pulled my legs back, ignoring how he tried to hold on to them and crawled back over to him. His eyes perused me, a devious smile taking over his grin. "I think I told you what I thought about you on your knees. The same goes for you crawling."

I straddled him before he could stop me, pressing down against the firmness. The thought that I was glad Tyson was still in Armina with no chance of walking in on us like this flittered in the back of my mind as Mason's hands moved up my hips, pushing my sweatshirt until he was touching my skin.

"First, I'd tell her you were being naughty with all your flirting and touching."

"And then?" His laugh muffled his words.

I pressed my hands into his chest, sliding them up his muscles as I leaned closer. "Then I'd have one of your men throw her in the trunk and drop her outside the city before I returned to claim you."

"Claim me?" He tilted his head, studying me intently. "No one claims me, little girl."

"I'm not a little girl," I said, my lips so close to his that the slightest move would bring us together. "I'm all woman, with enough experience to know how to break you, Mason."

Desire flared in his eyes, and his hands squeezed my waist tighter. "No one breaks me, either."

"No?" I moved forward, my lips meeting his. He pulled me into him, moving his hands further up my back.

The kiss was deep and sensual, with an emotion behind it that was mingled with lust. His touch was soft this time, no aggression behind it as he slid his fingers under my bra, unhooking it, then cupping my breast. A moan freed from me, and he pushed me down so that I was grinding into his hardness. My body was a roaring flame that was about to ignite into an inferno. But he ended our kiss, dropping his forehead to mine.

"No one breaks me, Casey." His fingers brushed my nipple.

"No one but me," I murmured.

He tipped his head up, removing his hands, and leaving my body cold without his touch. He placed them on my face, holding it while he searched my eyes for something I couldn't name.

"One night, Mason." But I heard the doubt in my voice because I now knew what he feared more than my brother's anger. One night wouldn't be enough...for either of us.

He shook his head, the conflict returning to etch in the lines around his forehead. Sighing, I went to move from him, knowing I needed to be away because the craving I had for him was too hard to deny, too hard to resist if I didn't move. But his hands lowered to my arms, holding me in place. I could see the internal struggle. It was the same I'd recognized early on and forgotten to respect. I was hurting him again, and I hated myself for it.

Raising my fingers to his face, I traced the shadow of stubble along his jawline. "It's okay, Mason. Let me go like you want to. I'll stay away the rest of the night and leave early for the airport, so you don't have to see me again."

The hurt in his eyes confused me because that's what he was telling me he wanted. "Let me go, Mason. It's only one more night, then you never have to see me again." Saying the words hurt, like a knife slicing my heart with each word, because I wanted to see him again. I wanted to see him every day, to have his touch be the only one I ever felt again. I reeled back at the thought, realizing what it meant and how complicated this had become for me and possibly for him.

He dropped his hands, and I climbed from him, fixing my bra

and pulling my sweatshirt down. He didn't move, but his eyes never strayed from me. I could see him fighting himself, trying to call the hard boss back to cover his emotion.

"Goodnight, Mason," I said, picking up my plate and the soda. "I'm sorry."

I left, unable to look back at him because the silence was a heavy burden, and I didn't think I could bear seeing how I had broken him without even meaning to.

MASON

The soft padding of Casey's feet faded the further she was from me. Resting my head back, I ran my hands up my face and through my hair. The myriad of thoughts and emotions filling my mind were almost too much. The way she'd felt in my hands and the sensuality of that kiss had left me questioning what this had become. Our flirting had turned, the events of the prior night changing something between us, something in me. The Casey who had needed me last night to hold her hair back, to hold her while she slept, the one I'd watched sleep, worried that the drugs they'd given her would cause a reaction, and the one snuggled up in sweats watching fantasy movies was not any woman I'd ever allowed myself to be with. I took what I needed from women and kept it physical, but Casey made me want more. I wanted to hold her, to be her strength when she was weak, to curl on a couch and rub her feet. To see the vulnerable side of her with her curls slipping free of her ponytail.

I knew the feeling that was sinking into my soul, claiming my heart. It was a sensation I hadn't allowed myself to embrace since I'd been in my early twenties. I'd made myself hard and untouchable. Casey broke down my resolve, my barriers, and I wanted her to. I liked the way she made me feel, especially when she wasn't throwing herself at me. That was the woman who I now desired in a completely different way than the initial craving I'd had for her.

Picking up her blanket, I held it for a moment, smelling the scent of her floral soap on it. I cleaned up and shut everything down before returning to the main floor. One night. That was all I had left with her. I wondered if she could return and never see me again. The thought was wrenching, and I shoved it away, not liking how weak it made me.

"Hey there," Riley said, coming into my office where I'd plunged into administrative things I had accountants and lawyers for, but that kept my mind from turning to Casey.

I glanced up, giving her a smile. Riley never ceased to make me smile, except for the time she'd shut me out. Her smile was contagious, her sweet personality enough to soften even the hardest of souls. And maybe that was why Greyson Tides had fallen for her. Maybe she'd softened the bastard.

"You look flustered," she said, sitting on the loveseat on the other side of the room, crossing her feet under her.

"Nah, just tired of staring at this stuff."

She was perceptive, seeing past my façade. Even when I'd been sheltering her, hiding my secrets, she'd never failed to see when my mood was off, when my gruff disposition was faltering. She leaned forward, resting her elbows on her knees. For a moment, she reminded me of our mother. Although she and I had our father's eyes and hair, Riley had my mother's soft features and her gentle disposition. Riley had been young when our parents had passed, but I had distinct memories of them, nineteen years of life with them. Their deaths had hit me hard, but I'd already made my name in the underground scene of Treemont, learning to hide my emotions, to remain heartless. Things that had been helpful when life had derailed us, leaving me as Riley's guardian. A nine-year-old under the care of her teenage brother who hadn't known what he was doing but had managed.

I'd done everything in my power to protect her, to ensure I didn't lose her like we'd lost our parents. I'd overprotected her, even as she'd grown older, because that's all I knew.

"Mace, I know what's going on."

I clenched my teeth. "And what's going on, Ri?"

"Between you and Casey."

I glared at her, but she didn't flinch.

"Don't give me that look. It's hard not to notice and you better be glad Tyson's in Armina, or he would have picked up on it already."

Tyson had texted me earlier, checking in on Casey and letting me know he had things handled with Donelli. I didn't have the balls to tell him I wasn't handling things with Casey and that those assholes had almost raped her at the club. It didn't matter that I'd taken charge and handled it, he'd be on me in seconds for letting her go in the first place. The fight would be a bloody one, but no bloodier than it would be if he found out I'd touched her.

I sat back with a sigh. "It's that obvious?"

She snickered. "Obvious is an understatement. The heat between you two is intense. Why don't you give yourself a break, Mace? Casey would be good for you."

"And how do you know what would be good for me, Ri? A few days in my world and you suddenly know?"

She recoiled like I'd hit her, then recovered. "Don't give me that macho shit. I know you well enough to know you haven't let yourself do more than fuck a woman in years. To know you keep a distance."

"Watch your language."

Her laugh was louder this time. "Seriously?" She stood and walked to the desk, leaning her hands on it. "I'm your sister, Mason. You may not have brought me into your world, but I know enough from having you and Tyson as my permanent bodyguards to know how you both work. I can cuss like the best of them. And I also know enough about you and Tyson to know that he fucks every woman he can because no woman has come close to cracking that playboy shell he wears. And you, although more discriminating and controlled, indulge only in one-night stands because you don't let anyone close enough to know what's underneath that guarded exterior you wear. No one but Casey."

Crossing my arms, I gritted my teeth, hating how she'd just nailed us both in those few short words.

"I also know you enough to see how she's cracked that hardened shell you built after our parents died." I flinched, my eyes creasing. "For once, let your control go and take a chance—"

"I don't take chances. That's why I rule the dynasty I rule." I stood, towering over her. "That's why I have the power I have, the money I have. Why people fear me."

"And why you're alone." She gave me a sad smile. "I'm going back to Greyson. When you're done training me. I won't be here for you to protect, to depend on you."

"Neither will Casey," I snarled, my anger at the thought of her returning to Tides coming out in the bite of my words. I'd suspected it was coming, but that didn't mean I had to like it.

"Maybe not, but you don't know that. You have one more night. Take the chance."

"I can't, Ri," I said, the futility of my circumstance wearing me down again. I flopped back in my chair, letting my anger go, and stared out the window into the dark night. "Tyson's my best friend. He's as protective of her as I am of you, and I know exactly how I'd react if he touched you."

"Yuck," she said, and I peered back at her, giving her a questioning look. "Ty's like you, like another brother to me. But that's because I grew up with both of you. Casey didn't."

"Doesn't matter. He'd never forgive me."

She walked around the desk, tussling my hair before giving me a kiss on my head. "Maybe he will if he sees what I see."

"What do you see?" I asked as she left the room.

"Take the chance, Mace," she called on her way down the stairs. "You have one night left."

I SAT for a long time after Riley left, my mind running wild. The situation I was in didn't give me any option where I ended up unscathed and where Casey didn't end up hurt. If I gave in, Tyson would hate me forever, ending our friendship, cutting me off, or even taking her from me. That was the worst-case scenario, I knew that, but I worked with little risk. The worst cases were what I lived by.

If I resisted, my decision would leave me with a craving I could never satisfy, one I wasn't sure would ever cease. Casey would still end up hurt. She was hurting now because I'd turned her down again. I saw it in her eyes each time. And tonight had been bad. The emotion there had gutted me. The resolve and a sense of surrender replacing the seductive fight that had filled her before.

One night. Those two small words held so much power. I had one night and if I took it, I could finally have her, touch her, taste her, own her like I wanted to. One night and maybe we could make it just that. Nothing more. One night to give in to our desires, and Tyson would never need to know.

I rose, shutting the lights out and heading downstairs. I took two steps toward my room, then turned, changing direction as my heart thudded more with each step I took toward Casey's room. Pausing outside her door, I thought about the implications of opening it and doing what I'd wanted to do since the moment she walked back into my life.

The door handle turned, and I entered the room. She looked up, her eyes wide as I shut the door behind me. Her mouth parted, the book she was reading slipping from her hands. As she rose, the book fell to the floor. The oversized sweatshirt was the only thing she had on, leaving her legs bare and the sight of them stirring the need in me.

"Mason, what are you doing?"

I kicked my shoes off, seeing understanding cross her eyes. "What I should have done the first night."

I grasped her by the back of her neck, pulling her to me, and this time I didn't stop myself from kissing her. Her soft lips met mine, her surprise fading quickly as she opened her mouth, my tongue quick to dance with hers. I tangled my fingers in her hair, pulling her closer, feeling her heart pound below her clothes. Smoothing my hand over her thigh, I played along the edge of her lace panties, my fingers sliding under them. Her breath hitched as I dipped, feeling the smooth skin that turned me on even more. She moaned when I slid them further, slipping almost low enough to feel how wet she was but stopping myself because I knew I'd lose it if I did. And I wanted to savor this, to take her slow because if this was my only night with her, I was going to make it last.

Sliding my hand back, I cupped her ass, pushing her further into me. Her hands threaded through my hair, pulling my head down as I continued to devour her mouth.

"Mason," she murmured against my lips. "You don't want this."

I bit her lip, tugging it between my teeth as I drew back, giving her a scolding look. Releasing her hair, I moved my hands up her sweatshirt, encasing her breasts, my dick so hungry for her that it leaped at the feel.

"Shut up and let me have you, Casey."

Her eyes narrowed, and I pinched her nipple, causing those beautiful lips to part again.

"But..." I worked her shirt off, throwing it to the side, then brought her against me.

"It's one night. One night to do everything I've been fantasizing about since the moment you set foot back in Treemont. One night that no one needs to know about. One night to own you the way I've desired since I saw you."

She let out a small *oh*. I leaned my forehead against hers. "Do you still want this, Casey? Tell me what you want and if you don't want me, then I'll walk out and never touch you again."

Her hands ran up my chest, gripping the buttons of my shirt and sending my pulse racing. "I want you, Mason. I want you to take me, to own me. I want you to ruin me for every other man out there, to leave your mark so deep in me that I can never escape it. I don't want one night, Mason."

Her words were like a match lighting the flames in me and sparking that feeling that had been nagging my heart since I'd held her in my arms as she slept.

"But if one night is all we get. Then I'm yours for tonight. Take me, touch me, fill me, own me. I'm yours."

Her acceptance burned through me, and I ran my hands the length of her body. I kissed her again, her mouth greedily meeting mine as she fumbled with my buttons. Grasping her wrists, I yanked her hands behind her.

"Get on the bed, Casey."

A small gasp escaped, and her eyes sparkled with excitement. I released her hands and watched as she crawled onto the bed, her curvy ass beckoning me to give up my control and just fuck her. I wiped my hand down my face, denying myself as she turned and propped herself on her elbows, drawing her leg up seductively. She knew what she was doing to me, how her body broke me.

I took her in, the ample breasts that were fuller than any woman I'd been with except those who'd had them enhanced. These were all natural, perfectly proportioned to the rest of her body. And I wanted every inch of it. Her words came back to me. She wanted me to ruin her for any other man, and I wanted that. I wanted no other man's hands on her skin again. It was mine, all of her was mine.

I unbuttoned my shirt, peeling it off while she watched me with a hunger that matched my own. Crawling over her, I let my hand drift up her body, a body I was ready to use in every naughty way I'd been craving. I pulled her hands up over her head, holding her wrists together before I kissed her again, pulling her body into mine. She sighed, a sound that sank deep into my core, the feel of her breasts against my skin enhancing the sensation.

Dropping my head, I dragged my tongue down her neck, cupping her breast and swirling my tongue around her nipple before sucking it into my mouth. She groaned, her body arching slightly.

"Mason," she purred, and I smiled before pulling her nipple between my teeth and gently scraping it as I released it.

Letting her wrists go, I hovered over her. "I thought you wanted me to ruin you, Case? Did I mishear you, little girl?"

The hazel of her eyes turned a dark amber, and she bit her bottom lip.

"None of that yet. I'll put those lips to use, but I'm not ready for anything but this body right now."

Those tempting lips parted, a quiet moan falling from them before her hands ran over my chest, tracing each of my tattoos. The touch was firm and confident, my heart thudding in response. My stomach tensed when she dropped her fingers to my pants, reaching in and grasping my hard-on. I bit back my groan, not ready to give her control yet. I had plans for her before I satisfied myself. Her grip was just as confident, and a pang of jealousy hit me at the thought of why she was so assuredly stroking me. I grabbed her arm, yanking her hand away and pinning it to the bed.

Her eyes questioned me.

"None of that yet, either."

"And what if I want to ruin you for any other woman, Mason? To own you. To break you."

It was a bold statement and one I thought might not be far from the truth. She was breaking me and may have already destroyed me to the point that I couldn't return. I didn't want to think of the repercussions of that thought.

"Is that what you want, Casey?"

She brought her free hand up and pulled my face to hers. "Yes."

Her answer weaved its way into my being, tugging at my soul and shattering the hardened case around my heart. This was dangerous, a risk I shouldn't have taken because I knew where it would lead but as she leaned up and kissed me, I realized it was a risk I wouldn't regret, one I embraced fully because I needed Casey in ways I'd never needed anything in my life.

I loosened the hold I had on her hand, my fingers wrapping around hers as our kiss deepened, the lust turning into something more sensual. As our lips parted, I searched her eyes, seeing that same emotion that was twisting my need to fuck her so that I wanted something that would leave us both fractured. There was no turning back now, no way to avoid what was happening, and so I stopped fighting it.

I let my kisses linger until my mouth found its way down her body, my tongue licking her stomach until it reached the edge of her panties. Lifting myself from her, I stood, taking the time to peruse her body once again before I tugged at the delicate lace, dragging it down her legs until she was completely naked. Looking over her again, I thought there was no part of Casey I didn't desire. Every inch of her called to me and my dick twitched at the thought.

"Spread those gorgeous legs for me, like a good girl."

She'd leaned up on her elbows again, and my eyes followed the path of her legs when they spread for me. My chest tightened. She was completely bare except for a small trail, and I licked my lips in anticipation of tasting her. Grabbing her ankles, I jerked her closer, letting my hands run the course of her legs, my tongue following until my fingers sank into her. She was soaked, and I groaned, gritting my teeth and resting my head on her thigh. She moaned, the muscles in her legs quivering as I pushed deeper before slipping out to play with her clit. Her moans increased, and I gave in, grabbing her thighs and sinking my tongue into her. She tasted like the finest wine, and I lost myself to the taste, flicking my tongue over her clit and plunging my finger back into her. Her hands entwined in my hair, her back bowing when my tongue replaced my fingers, lapping up the arousal that pooled around my face. I continued to torment her until her thighs tightened, her hands pushing my head further as she came undone. A cry fell from her lips that reached in and grabbed my body so hard I almost came with her.

Raising my head, I took in the flush of her skin, the deep breaths as she calmed from her climax. It was an image I engrained in my memory, one I never wanted to forget. Wiping my face against her thigh, I stood, sucking my fingers into my mouth to savor another taste as her eyes met mine. They were glazed over with ecstasy, the look beckoning me to finish taking her.

"My turn," I said, unhooking my belt and dropping my pants. She propped herself back on her elbows, pulling her knee up further and licking her lips as I pushed my boxers off. "Keep that tongue ready because I'll put it to use later," I said, stroking my cock and readying myself to finally take her completely. "For now, be a good girl and pull those knees up. I'm going to fuck another orgasm from you."

I climbed over her, pressing my tip at her entrance, her wetness surrounding it. "Fuck," I muttered, dropping my forehead to hers. She shifted her face, kissing me, her legs wrapping around me. I broke the kiss off sooner than I wanted when her heels dug into my back, pushing me further into her. She felt perfect, and it took all my strength not to drive into her. I wanted to watch her as I filled her one inch at a time, and it was worth my patience. She held my gaze, the intensity gripping me as tightly as she was. Her eyes rolled back, a moan falling from her lips, one I smothered with a kiss, a desperate need to fill her completely consuming me. She felt too good, so tight around me that I couldn't stop myself. My patience gone, I penetrated her fully. Her legs wrapped tighter around my back and urged me on. Her cry was intoxicating, encouraging my need to ravage her completely, and I lost control to the need that had hounded me for days.

She met each thrust, her pelvis driving into me, her kisses growing more desperate. My hands roamed her body, taking in every inch I could that wasn't occupying my greedy dick. Her head fell back, and I sucked her nipple into my mouth, flicking my tongue over it and slowing my thrusts, needing to have her fall apart again for me. Her body quivered with each slow plunge I made, and I could feel her tightening around me, her climax so close I could sense it.

"Are you going to come for me again, sweetheart?" That nick-name was one I'd never used, but as she broke, her orgasm hitting her so hard that I almost lost my hold on my release, I knew it was hers.

Her cry was feral, and I captured that sound with my mouth, unable to resist the clenching of her muscles around me and plunging deeper into her, my moves driven by the need for release. "Fuck, Case, I'm gonna come." Her legs gripped my back tighter, pushing me further, my climax so close it was pounding through me. "I need to pull out," I muttered, knowing if I got her pregnant, that would be a nightmare that would only complicate what I'd already done to Tyson.

"No, fill me Mason."

I groaned, my dick not listening to my mental scolding and driving into her harder. "But—"

"I'm on the pill. Now fuck me harder and fill me."

Those words obliterated my hold on my release. I hadn't come bare in a woman in ages, never trusting their word and pulling out or using protection, which always dimmed the experience. But this was ecstasy, freely spilling into Casey with no restrictions, no hesitation as my climax raged through me. It pummeled me until, with an exhausted sigh, I lifted my head and looked into her eyes. They sparkled with a satisfied gleam. Her fingers traced my face, and I turned into her hand, kissing it.

"Now what?" she asked with a coy smile.

I couldn't help returning her smile before kissing her. "Now, I keep you up the rest of the night because if we only have one night, I'm going to use this body every way I've been imagining, and that won't give you any time to sleep."

Her giggle was rewarding. "Good. I can sleep on the plane. Tonight, we fuck."

I shook my head. "Why does that word sound so dirty when you say it?"

She shrugged, pulling my head down and kissing me. I gave over to the sensation of it as it wove its way through my body, claiming me, corrupting me, breaking me so that I could confidently accept that one night would never be enough.

CASEY

My alarm startled me, and I jumped as awareness shook the heavy hold of sleep from me. An arm slipped over my stomach as I fumbled to silence it. Mason. He pulled me into him, my back hitting his warm chest and causing my curls to flop into my eyes. I couldn't help but sigh, remembering how he'd taken me over and over, bringing me to ecstasy more times than I ever remembered. It had been the most wonderful night of my life and one the alarm reminded me would never happen again. Tyson had scheduled the jet to take me home instead of letting me fly commercial like I'd done on my way out, but for the first time since I'd left Treemont, Armina no longer felt like home. Being in Mason's arms, the strength of them, the way his face nuzzled my neck, his morning firmness digging into me felt like home.

I traced the tattoo on his forearm, his kisses against my neck reminding me of the confused tangle of emotions that had surged as he'd taken me.

"I need to get up, Mason. Riley will be looking—"

"Riley knows exactly where we are. Trust me, she won't come looking."

That surprised me, but then again, Riley knew how I felt, so it made sense that she'd confronted Mason on his feelings.

"But my flight—"

"Shush." He let me go, climbing over me and grabbing his phone from his pants. I took the moment to admire him. He was the sexiest man I'd ever been with. The muscles that lined his back enhanced the tattoos, which flowed down to where his tight ass sat. He turned, and I looked up to see his raised brow and a crooked grin that would break any woman's heart. I could sense the heat rising in my cheeks, but I ignored it, deliberately letting my sight drift down his tattooed chest. I licked my lips, and he gave me a tsk as he brought his phone to his ear.

He liked to think he could control me, but I had a feeling he knew just as well as I did that he didn't. I crawled from the bed, dropping to my knees. He inhaled just as someone answered. Taking him in my hands, I let my tongue circle his tip, looking up to see the irritation in his eyes.

"I need Casey's—"

I dropped on him so far that he hit the back of my throat, eliciting a loud gag from me. He put his hand over the phone, growling at me, but I didn't let that stop me. I was enjoying myself, not only because his dick was glorious, but because I was in control.

"Boss?" I heard on the other line, descending again and loving how he dropped his hand to my head, twisting my hair around his fingers.

"I'm here," he managed, although the authoritative voice he usually had was diminished. "I need...fuck."

I giggled, pulling back, my tongue sliding along his shaft. He stopped my head, shoving back into my mouth. A loud gag surged from me before I took control and sucked my way back up his length.

"Delay the fucking jet..." His hand stilled me again, his pelvis thrusting so far it ripped another gag from me as it hit my throat. "Fuck...I'll let you know when she's ready."

He hung up and threw his phone, yanking my mouth from him.

"That was wicked, Casey."

I licked my lips, grasping his shaft.

"Open that sexy mouth again and finish what you started."

I opened, loving that his aggressive side was coming out. He'd been soft last night, but I was craving the side of him that had pulled my hair and choked me when we'd been flirting. He shoved my face forward, plunging into me hard as he used my mouth until I could feel him growing closer. He'd shown me the prior night that he could go multiple times with little coercion, and I was looking forward to seeing what he'd do to me once I satisfied this need I had to taste him.

He had his fingers wrapped so tightly in my hair I was sure he'd ripped strands out, but I didn't care. The act was turning me on so much, there was a chance I'd end up coming with him.

"Shit, Case." There was a tremble that layered his voice, and it left me even wetter than I was. He yanked me from him, and I tried to catch my breath, lines of saliva spilling from my mouth, a long one still attached to his dick. He smirked, his eyes lit to a devious shade.

"You gonna swallow for me, sweetheart?"

Parting my lips, I reached my hand to my head and urged him to pull my hair tighter. He shook his head, his smile growing before he plunged back into my waiting mouth so hard my gags were like a flurry of noise that filled the room. With one deep feral grunt he came, spilling down my throat so that it seeped around him. When he finally freed himself from my mouth, he released my hair and stumbled back.

"Holy fuck, Case. Do I want to know how you know how to do that so fucking well?"

I wiped my mouth with my finger before licking it clean and

rising. Shrugging, I grabbed my sweatshirt and cleaned my chest off, his eyes following my every move. He looked stunned, his eyes creasing until he clenched his jaw.

"I don't, do I?"

Shaking my head, I gave him a grin. "Why did you delay my flight?"

"Because it's my fucking plane, and I wanted to come in your mouth."

"Well, you did, but I still had time to make my flight."

He arched his brow, stepping over to me, his hand running up my body and encircling my neck. The moan I released was animalistic.

"You like it rough, sweetheart?"

When he called me that, it twisted my insides into knots. "Definitely."

He yanked me closer. "I delayed the plane because I'm not done fucking you. You played a dangerous game, distracting me while I was on the phone."

"Are you going to punish me for it?" I gave him my most innocent look.

"Punish? Nah, I leave that for shitheads I need to fuck up with my fists. You, I'm going to torment until you're begging for me to let you come."

A weird whine slipped from my lips as his fingers tightened on my neck. His other hand ran down my hips before moving between my legs.

"Are you wet for me, Case?"

"Soaked."

He penetrated me with two fingers, his groan loud and mingled with my cry.

"Good, because you're gonna ride me until I'm ready to forgive you and rip that climax from your body. That plane doesn't leave until you've come around me enough to ensure you won't be using that mouth or that pussy on another man when you're away from me."

I leaned into him. "Are you claiming me?"

"Oh, I claimed you last night, Case. Now I'm marking my territory."

He pulled my mouth to his, kissing me with such intensity that my knees buckled. Picking me up, he walked us to the bed and sat, wrapping my legs around him. He was hard again, and I lifted, guiding him into me and sighing loudly when he filled me to the hilt. He dropped his hands to my hips, grasping them tight. There was nothing that compared to the feeling of having him inside me, nothing but the way my heart soared when he was touching me.

I dropped my head, smashing my lips into his and loving how his hands left my waist to encase my breasts. His touch was firm, and it coaxed my building climax, calling to it so that I was pushing down on him, needing him as deep as he could reach. He stopped me and I grumbled as he flipped me to my back roughly. My stomach knotted in anticipation. Grabbing my wrists, he held them over my head, hovering over me. I pushed my pelvis toward him, wanting him inside of me again, but he only chuckled and nipped my lip.

He pushed my legs apart further with his knee, and his hand slid down my waist until two fingers sank into me. I bucked, pushing them further as a deep moan escaped.

"That's it, sweetheart. I want to feel you coming all over my fingers."

"I thought you wanted me coming around your dick," I said, my voice hoarse.

His thumb brushed over my clit before his fingers began fucking me the way he had moments earlier. I thrashed at his touch, writhing as my climax closed in on me like a train barreling down the path and ready to derail.

"Oh, you will. This is just my warm-up."

He dropped his mouth to my chest, tugging my nipple between his teeth, his fingers making just the right move and sending me crashing, my climax tearing through me so hard that I screamed.

"That's it, Case. Come for me."

His mouth smothered mine, and he drew his fingers from me, his firmness filling me quickly. The death grip he had on my wrists kept them secure, and my body jerked from the force of his thrusts. I was on fire again, my waning release given no time to fade as pleasure riddled my body. His hand slid over my breasts, still damp from my orgasm, and he released my lips, dipping his head to lick the dampness from my skin. His moan cut me to the core, beckoning my release with the same power his thrusts had. The longer he played with my nipples, the fiercer my need to break until his pace increased and I lost it, my body convulsing. He slammed into me so deep the intensity of my climax doubled, and I cried out, fighting his hold on my wrists because I wanted to touch him, to sink my nails into his back, to tug at his hair while the waves of rapture worked their way through me.

I dug my heels into his back, forcing him deeper and hearing his grunt. He released my wrists, his teeth tugging my nipple before letting it go, and I wrapped my arms around him, feeling the shake of his muscles. He lifted his eyes to me, before pulling me so that I was astride him.

"I told you I wanted you riding me, Case. Now ride me like you own me." The rasp of his voice was sexy and when he brought the fingers that had been in me to his mouth and sucked them clean, I almost shattered again.

Almost. But I took control, riding him, dictating our rhythm and losing myself to the touch of his hands on my waist, on my breasts, on my ass, and the possessive glimmer in his eyes as he watched me until I could take no more. My climax tore through me, and I felt him lose control, his release hitting him just as mine drowned me. He pulled me down, his lips crashing into mine, and we rode out the pleasure that was soaring through us.

The fierce beats of his heart were a calming sound that soothed the sudden fear that overcame me and caused me to cling to him. Our one night had turned into more, seeping into the next morning, and I didn't know how I could return home now. Didn't think it would be possible for our one night to be just that. Because what I saw reflected in his eyes when I rose from his chest was the same emotion that was currently paralyzing me. Love.

MASON WAS on his phone when I finished dressing. We'd showered together, and he'd taken me against the shower wall as the water pounded over us. It was almost like if we stopped touching each other, we'd have to admit that it was time for me to leave. We were already several hours late.

"She's fine, Ty. She wasn't ready to leave yet." I cringed, hating that he'd deceived my brother. He hadn't lied to him, but he'd left out the reason I hadn't been ready.

He glanced up at me, the sexy grin nowhere to be seen. Instead, his eyes were creased, his jaw tight. Worry sat on his expression along with guilt, and I dropped my eyes.

"She's right here," he said and handed the phone to me.

I took a deep breath before bringing it to my ear. "Hey, Ty."

"You changed plans on me, Case. Is everything okay?"

"Mason told you everything was fine."

Mason brushed my hair from my neck, kissing it while his other hand cupped my breast. The sensual way he was caressing it gave me goosebumps and made it hard to think.

"That asshole wouldn't tell me if it wasn't because he knows I'd kill him."

"You sure about that?" I asked as Mason's hand slid down my

leg, lifting the hem of my dress. Shit, he was going to pay me back for going down on him while he was on the phone. My hand shook. "I'd place my wager on him, Ty."

"Fuck you would. Your loyalty is with me, Casey. You remember that." There was a playfulness to his voice, but his words cut deep until Mason's fingers pushed my thong aside and rubbed my clit. I squeezed the phone tighter. He had pushed the sleeve of my dress down, his hand kneading the flesh of my breast and when his finger penetrated me, I bit my lip so hard it bled.

"Case?"

I wanted to curse, but Ty would freak out. "I'm fine, I…" Mason pulled at my nipple, his finger sliding from me and rubbing my clit again. "I just stubbed my toe," I said through gritted teeth.

Mason chuckled in my ear, then nibbled on it as his finger sank back into me.

"You're a disaster. That's why I want you to be careful. Mason's sending extra men with you, and I'll meet you at the airport. Donelli gave me three of his men to escort us back."

"Why so many?"

Mason added a finger, and I almost choked on the cry that I stopped. His touch had my body on fire, and I didn't think he was faring any better. His length was so hard against my back that it was beckoning me to use it.

"Donelli's worried about the Bad Omens. There were sightings in the northern part of the province." I would have been concerned if Mason wasn't edging my orgasm on. "Maybe you shouldn't come back, Case."

"What?" I tried to move, but Mason held me tighter, his fingers fucking me so hard now that it was difficult to concentrate on anything but the pleasure he was bringing me.

"I'd rather have you under our watch."

"Donelli's as protective of me as he is of his daughter. He won't let anything…" Mason pulled his fingers out and their absence left a dull ache between my legs, but he squeezed my breast, returning his attention to my clit and that feeling disappeared quickly. "He won't let anything happen."

"Are you sure you're okay?" he asked. "You sound off."

"My toe is throbbing." I couldn't tell him it was really my entire body that was throbbing and about to fall apart for Mason. "I'm going to put some ice on it. I'll see you in a few hours."

"Fine. Love you, sis."

"Love you, too, Ty."

I managed to hang the phone up just as Mason thrust his fingers back into me, leaving my legs shaking. Resting my head against his chest, I let the phone slip from my hand.

"Come for me, Case. One last time."

As if my body was his to command, my climax shredded through me, leaving me a quivering mess as he held me through it. It lit every part of my body on fire, from head to toe, my knees giving out so that I would have toppled if he weren't holding me.

"Fuck, you're beautiful when you come for me, Case."

He freed his fingers, letting me go, and I glanced over at him, trying to keep myself balanced. His eyes were dark as he brought his fingers to his mouth and licked each one clean. "And you taste like heaven."

Butterflies tickled my stomach, growing to a massive stir of wings when he stepped to me and wound his hand around the back of my neck, pulling my face to his.

"I wish you hadn't worn this skimpy dress," he mumbled, nipping at my lip.

"It's the style in Armina."

"It's too cold here, and too tempting for me to avoid fucking you one last time." His words held a softness to them that lessened the forcefulness he'd intended them to hold. He wanted his hard exterior back, but it had teetered with me, disappearing one too many times, and so I heard the desperation that underlined those words. The one that told me that panicked sensation in me that was screaming for me not to leave was screaming for him not to let me go. Our one night had never been just a one-night stand. We were both too invested, the emotion too entwined with the desire.

His eyes searched mine, and I kissed him, needing him to leave his touch on me permanently. Needing him to claim me one last time before circumstance forced us apart. I pawed at his back as he wrapped his arms around me, grasping my ass and lifting me. The wall hit my back when he slammed me into it, but his kisses didn't give me time to react. They were so needy that it broke me. I didn't want to leave, and the pain in my chest told me why. He pushed my panties aside and entered me, hitting me so deep that I cried out against his mouth. Our moves were laced with emotion that neither of us could admit. Each thrust was a desperate attempt to hold on for just a few more minutes, every moan mingled with the sense of impending loss that hung over us. His strokes were long and forceful, calling to the climax that was building again in me and as he came, it flooded through me, meeting his with an intensity that left me riven.

Mason dropped his head to my shoulder, pushing his pelvis into mine once more as the remains of his release filled me.

"Don't let me go," I whispered, knowing those words were more than a simple plea to hold me longer.

We remained entangled until I let my head fall back against the wall, knowing he could fulfill my plea no more than I could let him. We both had separate lives, and I wasn't ready to give mine up. There was also Tyson to contend with, and neither of us was ready to confront that situation.

I let my legs slide down his body, and his hands released my ass. He tucked himself away, then fixed my skirt in a sweet move that only increased that ache in my chest. Sweeping a curl from my cheek, his emerald eyes stared intently at me, emotion behind them that matched my own but would remain unspoken. The gentle look morphed, his eyes hardening, that mischievous glint returning to them.

I leaned over and gave him another kiss, then walked toward the bathroom to clean up. Discomfort flared through my wrist as he caught it and turned me back to him, sending my body crashing into his.

"Don't even think about cleaning that out of you." The pinch he gave my ass would have made me jump had he not shoved my body into his dick, which twitched as it slowly came back to life. "My cum stays there. I want it leaking out of you the entire flight home, so you remember who owns this body." My breath caught at the possessiveness of his words. "I want it sticking to your thighs the rest of the day, marking you for any man who even dares look at you."

"And you think they'll know your cum is on my thighs?"

"Damn right they will." He gave me a lopsided grin, and I took his face in my hands. I wanted to tell him why my chest was hurting so badly, but I knew I couldn't. It would only break him more.

"I'll let it mark me and leave it there so when I finger myself to thoughts of you tonight, it'll remind me of you thrusting into me each time I plunge my fingers further."

"Fuck, that's an image that won't be leaving my mind all day. Maybe you can send me some pictures of that."

Shaking my head, I kissed him once more. His hands encircled my waist and pulled me so tight against him I thought my bones would snap.

"It's time to let me go, Mason."

He touched his forehead to mine and released me. Losing his touch was a sensation I would never forget and as he picked up my suitcase and opened the door, gesturing for me to move, I realized just how lost I was to him. So lost, I didn't think I could ever find my way back.

Chapter Eleven

MASON

My eyes trailed Casey as she walked down the hall, the swish of her ass in the short dress threatening to make me hard again. It also tempted me to force her back to the room to change into something less revealing. There was no way any man could avoid taking in those curvy legs, legs that were too bare for Treemont this time of year. I didn't know if she was doing it to torment me one more time or if she was just that ready to return to the sunny weather of Armina. I was hoping it wasn't the latter.

My night with her had led to a morning filled with her body and her cries. One night hadn't been enough, just like I'd suspected, and now my craving for her had transformed to a burning hunger I couldn't satiate no matter how many times I'd taken her. And with that endless need came something I was having a hard time grasping,

While she'd been getting ready, I'd called Breck to have the plane prepped and a car outside for her. That had been just before Tyson's call, the one that had left a pang of guilt thriving in my gut the entire time I'd talked to him.

Dropping Casey's suitcase next to the door along with her

purse, I noticed Riley standing in the doorway to the main room, her arms crossed.

"Took you two long enough," she teased.

Casey blushed, a look that only enhanced her beauty. Her hazel eyes sparkled in the light that flooded in from the windows.

"Don't worry, your secret is safe with me," Riley said. "But I wouldn't wait too long to tell Tyson. It'll only make it worse."

"It was one night," I said, trying to ignore the way Casey's smile deflated.

"Mm hmm, keep telling yourself that." She walked back through the kitchen and Casey looked over at me, her brow furrowed, the sparkle that had been in her eye now dulled.

Just looking at her sent my heart racing. It was more than the original attraction, the need to have her. This went deeper, and I didn't know how to dig myself out of it.

The front door opened, the sound, and the cold air that rushed in with it, making her jump and breaking her gaze from mine. The light sweater she wore was too thin, and she rubbed her arms.

"The car's ready. The pilot adjusted the flight plan to fit the new schedule," Breck said. His words were like the weight of a hundred cement blocks layering on my shoulder. I wanted to tell him to leave, to force Casey to stay, to let the world burn around me just to keep her with me. Last night had left me with a taste for her I knew I could never be without, and my heart clenched at the thought.

She met my eyes again, a sadness there that I felt in my bones. It was pounding through me like bullets tearing me into pieces.

"Thanks, Breck. She'll be out in a minute. Casey, go tell Riley goodbye."

She nodded, and after another moment, made her way to the kitchen. Breck was gone, returning to the car, leaving me alone and thinking it was something that had never bothered me before. There was an empty feeling in my chest now, one I'd only experienced when Riley had disappeared. Only this was different, leaving me gutted and wondering if it would ever fade.

Casey returned after a few minutes, walking over to where I was still standing, too confused to move. She stopped in front of me, and I glanced up at the doorway, looking for Riley before I met Casey's eyes again.

"It's okay. Riley and I said our goodbyes so you and I could have our own."

She lifted her hand to my face, her fingers draping over my cheek before I grabbed her hand, pressing it into my skin. My chest was burning, the emotions I hadn't wanted when I started this game pummeling me.

"Mason, I—"

I pulled her to me, stopping her words with my mouth, knowing what she was planning to say, the same words that were bouncing through my head like a ricocheting bullet ready to wrench my heart in two. "Don't, Case," I murmured against her lips. "We can't."

Our lips parted, her eyes glistening with tears. I knew she was too strong to release them. Bringing my finger to her eye, I caught one that escaped just as she swallowed the rest back. She moved from my arms, and I could see the change in her as she hardened herself to the emotion, the same way I was because there was nothing else to be done. The situation was too risky, our lives too separate, a distance there, placed by miles and her brother, that we couldn't surmount.

She ran her hand down my chest and gave me a smile. "Goodbye, Mason."

She planted a quick kiss on my cheek before walking past me toward the door. I didn't turn around, knowing if I did, I would never let her go. The door shut, a car door closed, and eventually the sound of tires took her from me. I didn't know how long I stood there, the pain ravaging me before I could toughen myself to it. Casey had lowered my defenses, shaking the foundation I'd built to shelter my emotions and remain in control.

"Why did you let her go?" Riley asked from the doorway, her eyes sad as I peered over at her.

Raising the guardrails I kept around my heart, I rolled my neck, finally moving from my spot. "Because it's something that should never have happened."

It hurt to say, and her expression told me she didn't believe me. She pursed her lips as I walked past her into the kitchen to make coffee. I really wanted a stiff drink, but it wasn't noon yet and downing shots would only confirm to her that Casey had gotten to me.

"When I'm done working out, I expect you to be dressed warmly. We're going shooting, but not to the range."

"Mason—"

I slammed my cup down, seeing her jump from my periphery. "Just do it, Riley."

Leaving the coffee, I stormed past her and back to my room. I didn't want to be around her because Riley was the only person who knew the vulnerable side of me. She was the only one who could break through my cold exterior...until Casey. And I didn't want to be vulnerable. Weakness was an opening for my enemies and with the Bad Omens still out there waiting like hunters for their prey to show weakness, I couldn't afford it.

I sat on the edge of the bed, ignoring the sight of the rumpled sheets and dropping my head to my hands. A dull throb was hammering in my chest, and I scraped my fingers through my hair to numb it, unsure if it could ever be numbed. But it needed to be, or I stood the chance of losing more than just Casey. My head needed to be in the game, no matter what my heart wanted.

I needed to find a distraction, something to take my mind from her. Standing, I removed the clothes I was still wearing from the prior night, the scent of her drifting past my nose as I threw them in my hamper. Changing into my workout clothes, I hit my indoor gym, taking my frustration out on the bag until my knuckles were bruised and bloody. The pain dulled the ache in my chest, helping me focus, but not enough. The treadmill took a beating as I pounded the ache away with each mile until sweat drenched me and I was ready to face the truth of the mess I'd gotten myself into. Ready to push past the memory of Casey's touch, of the sweet taste of her, of the way her smile cracked every defense I'd built, of the way her sunny disposition grated against my cold indifference until I needed that smile, that taste, that touch like a craving I couldn't run from, no matter how many miles I burned through.

I stopped the treadmill, catching my breath and dropping my head to the console. I was angry at myself, angry at our situation, and I invited that anger in, letting it coat everything until I could push her from my mind...except I couldn't because what we'd shared left her permanently ingrained there.

"Fuck!" I punched the console, cracking it so badly that the lights faded.

Stomping back to my room, I called Leo, who was on duty in Breck's absence. "Let the men know I'm taking Riley shooting on the grounds."

"Yes, Boss."

"And have someone buy me a new treadmill."

"Boss?"

"Don't ask, just do it."

I disconnected, running a shower and washing the remains of Casey's touch from my skin. By the time I met Riley in the living room, I was back in control, but thoughts of Casey lingered like uninvited ghosts. Breck had texted an encrypted note saying she was safely on the plane, and I let Tyson know, asking him to text me when she landed. With each mile further she flew from me, the acceptance that she was gone sank further into my being, leaving only the hollow sensation in my chest to remind me of what I'd lost.

TYSON RETURNED at the end of the week. I had Riley learning self-defense from Breck and Leo while I assessed her moves. She was quick, and I could see she'd been doing more than playing with dolls when I'd been improving my fighting skills with Tyson all those years. Breck knocked her from her feet, and she fell hard on her ass.

"Don't bruise her, Breck. If I send her back to Tides bruised, he'll start a fucking war with me."

She threw me a dirty look.

"He's right, Ri."

I looked over at Tyson as he rounded the corner. My heart dropped, the guilt I'd stored away resurfacing.

"Why so moody, Mace?" he asked, grasping my shoulder.

I shook off my reaction, saying, "Just didn't expect you here. How was the flight home?"

"Eh, uneventful. You know that sexy flight attendant Chill hired?"

"The one with the long legs?" I asked, knowing exactly who he was talking about. She'd flirted with me the entire time I'd been on the plane last. I'd considered fucking her just to shut her up, but I drew a line with employees, a line Tyson never heeded.

"Fuck, yeah. I let her ride me this time, but she's not worth the fuck. Barely worth the condom I wasted."

I was hoping he could feel the daggers in my eyes. "No screwing around with the women who work for us, Tyson. What part of that rule do you find so hard to follow?"

"All of it, especially when you hire beauties like that."

"I don't do the hiring," I grumbled. "Keep your hands off the flight attendant and all the girls at the club. Damn, I can't wait until you find a woman who can tame you."

He laughed, gesturing to his crotch and saying, "I told you, Mace, there is no woman worthy of taming this."

Shaking my head, I turned my attention back to Riley. Exhaustion was showing in her delayed reactions, and I'd have to end her training soon.

"How was your time with Casey?" I asked, hoping my voice was calm because saying her name sent palpitations through my chest.

"Good. She was a little less spirted than she usually is, though. You know how she usually annoys the shit out of me with her gibbering and that damned cheery personality?"

"Yeah." He often returned from his trips complaining about it, but I'd never thought much of it. This time I wanted to shake him because I missed that cheerfulness and the witty comebacks.

"She was off. Did something happen while I was gone?"

I swallowed, nerves tumbling through me. This was my chance to come clean, to admit what I'd done and what I was feeling, but I couldn't do it. Fear was something I rarely acknowledged, but it was hounding me not to confess because I knew what it would cost me. I would lose Tyson and with him, Casey. He was too protective, and what he would see as betrayal would be my undoing.

"Not that I know of," I lied, hating myself for it. "Maybe she was worried about Riley. You know she's returning to Tides, right?"

"Casey told me. That's a nightmare. How are you going to handle that?"

Glad the conversation had shifted, I answered, "I'll have to wait and see. If he wants my sister that badly, I want something in return."

"A bargaining chip?"

"Exactly."

Riley huffed as she hit the mat again.

"I think that's enough, guys. My sister needs a hot shower and some time with her feet propped up."

She gave me a thank you with her smile and waved to Tyson.

"Hey kiddo. I see you're playing with the big guys today. Need me to rough them up for you since they weren't being nice?"

Her laugh lit the sections of my heart I had fortified behind my defenses. They were places reserved only for my sister and now for Casey. With Casey gone, only Riley would access them again.

"I need to talk to you," Tyson said, his tone serious. "About Donelli."

I turned to him, not liking the way his demeanor had shifted. "Breck, you and Leo see Riley home. Tyson and I have business to discuss."

"Yes, boss."

I heard Riley complain, but I continued my path to the small office of the boxing club. Petey, the manager, had his feet propped on the desk and I pushed them off, kicking him out and closing the door behind him. Tyson owned the club. It had been one of our first building projects when we were coming into our reign over Treemont. He hired Petey to oversee it because the man was extremely loyal. We'd dug him out of an unpleasant situation, taking out a man who raped his girlfriend, and letting Petey put the final bullet in him before we dumped his body under the foundation of the gym.

"The families are worried, Mace. There's tension and they're at each other's throats."

"The Bad Omens?"

"You could say that. I think they're stirring the bad blood, but Donelli is nervous. They caught a Bad Omen just north of his city."

I sat in the chair, crossing my arms. "Bad Omen don't get caught, Ty."

"Exactly. They think this guy was a mark."

I sat up. If they were using marks, it was a bad sign. Marks were people hired by a family to pretend they were part of the family. They were decoys, martyrs who took the job because the family would guarantee whatever it was the mark had traded his life for. No one used them anymore, not since the turf wars were out of control, way before my time. If the Bad Omens were using marks, we would have no way of knowing who the real killers were. "A mark? Why would they think that?"

"He had their tattoo, but he was too green. Barely knew how to use his gun."

"Fuck," I muttered, running my hands through my hair. "That's sloppy." And the Bad Omens were anything but sloppy. Either they were playing games or there was something we weren't seeing.

"Donelli thinks he's next because he has an alliance with you. I argued that the other families do as well, but he says he's closest to their territory, so he'll be first hit."

And I'd let Casey walk straight into that danger. "Did you tell Casey?"

He gave me a funny look, squinting his eyes. He'd expected me to ask about Donelli, but my concern had been for Casey, and I'd blurted the question out. Not a smart move.

"Yes," he said warily, "I damn near dragged her home with me, but she argued that bringing her back would leave Donelli questioning our trust in him. Convinced me to leave her so it wouldn't damage the relationship. I agreed, but told her I'd pull her at the first sign that anything was going down."

Once again, Casey's sharpness impressed me. She was on point. If we pulled her out from Donelli's protection, he'd see it as a slight against him and question our motive.

"So, they're using marks," I said, trying to turn Tyson's attention from my misstep of asking about Casey. I tried not to think of why the thought of her there raised my hackles. Donelli had kept her safe all these years. There was no reason to think he wouldn't continue to. "I don't think we should assume we're any safer from that than any other family."

"Agreed."

"Let's secure the city limits, increase rounds on the house and all the businesses. Make sure the men know marks are involved. Donelli has eyes on Casey?"

"Yeah, he assured me she has two men on her at all times. One watches her building, the other her apartment, they escort her everywhere."

The need to have that number doubled screamed through me, but I kept it silent. "Good. Riley's been sticking with me and when she's not, I have Breck and Leo assigned to her."

"They can't follow her into Tides' territory, Mace."

"No, she'll be safe once she's there. No one's touching him now, not when he took Randall out so efficiently. They won't risk his wrath any more than they have, and sending Randall into Bridgeville was a call for war. Having him touch Riley was a call for annihilation. I'm just not sure they realize that. He's biding his time until he has them where he wants them."

Tyson ran his hands through his hair, his hazel eyes reminding me so much of Casey's that I had to shift my sight from him. Standing, I slapped him on the back. "Let's go home. You look like you could use a drink, and I know I could. You can tell me all about that flight attendant."

"I wish there was more to tell," he muttered as we left. "My dick's still not satisfied."

"Is it ever?" I teased, nodding to Petey, then motioning for my men to follow us.

He continued to prattle on about his hook up while my mind whirred with the news he'd delivered and the fact that he'd left his sister in the hornet's nest where neither of us could get to her.

Chapter Twelve

CASEY

Armina had always felt like home to me. I loved everything about the city from the ocean air that smelled of salt to the way the waves pounded against the shore to the feel of the sand between my toes and the way the sun always touched my skin with a warmth that was gentle on my soul. But that had changed the day I'd left Mason, leaving a part of myself there that I couldn't seem to find again. He was on my mind constantly and no matter what I did, there was no cleansing it of him.

"You're no fun tonight, Casey," Angie whined. Angela Donelli was the daughter of Vince Donelli—spoiled, rich, beautiful, and sexy. I tolerated the competition when I went out with her because I was just as sexy, and for every two men who swarmed to her, I had my own to choose from. "That man was hot, and you waved him away like he was nothing."

"Have at him," I said, taking a sip of my drink. I was milking my drinks tonight, afraid that drinking too much would corrupt my rational thinking. The memory of the last time I'd gotten drunk was fresh in my mind, as was the way Mason had taken care of me. I didn't have him here to protect me or hold my hair back, and the thought left a strange longing in my heart.

Angie forced my drink in my hand. "I brought you out to have some fun. Now that your overprotective brother is gone, you can return to your normal slutty self and take your pick of the hotties here. I have my eye on that one," she motioned to a tall blonde man with greedy blue eyes, "and you can have any of the other twenty men who have hit on you since we got here."

But I didn't want those other men. I only wanted one and as much as I told myself he wasn't mine, that it was only one night, I couldn't convince myself to believe the lie.

"What is wrong with you, Casey?" She had her hands on her hips, her long blonde hair flipped over her shoulder, her brown eyes expecting my explanation.

"Nothing, I'm just not in the mood. I guess I miss Tyson," I lied too easily.

"That controlling prick? He's an ass—"

"He's my brother, Angie," I warned. They didn't like each other, and both made the animosity clear when they were stuck in the same room together.

"I know, but he's still overprotective and overbearing."

"And he's two thousand miles away."

"Good," she huffed. "While you sit in this corner and pout about your brother, I'm gonna let that sexy specimen of a man have his way with me."

She pulled herself from the couch and teetered over to the guy, her flirty confidence earning a deviant smile from him. Billy came over and sat next to me. He was one of the regular guards Donelli assigned to me. There were four other men watching us, one moving closer to Angie, his keen eyes watching the interaction.

"She never learns, does she?" Billy said.

"Nope. You think this one will deal with the pat down and interrogation just to get a piece of her?"

"She's got high standards, Casey. That one is the mayor's son. We already vetted him the minute he started eyeing her. Now, if she'd gone for the one to the left of him, the one who won't stop staring at her even though another man's hand is already on her ass, well, that would have been another story."

"What's his deal?" I asked, giving up on my drink and plopping it onto the table in front of us.

"He's got a habit of taking advantage of women, especially younger ones, which is why I'm surprised he's even considering Angie. She's too old for him."

I turned and looked at Billy, my mouth hanging open. "Too old? She's twenty-five."

"Yeah, he likes them illegally young."

"Eww, that's just gross." Angie looked like she was still in college, so I could see the confusion in her age. "Don't you guys do something about men like that? You know, keep the streets clean of the scum?"

He chuckled. "Boss wants us to track him now that he's back in the open. He went underground after he got paroled. If he makes the wrong move, we'll make sure he never resurfaces again."

If it was one thing I'd learned from my brother and from working with the Donelli family, it was that women and children stayed safe. The only women who were ever victims of the family were ones who turned against them. And men who hunted women quickly became prey.

"Why aren't you out there tonight? We're usually vetting the men who flock to you, too."

I shrugged. "Not in the mood tonight, I guess."

"That's not a bad thing. You and Angie party too much, Case. Don't let the boss know I said that."

"Your secret is safe with me." It was the truth. We partied a lot, and I hooked up as often as Angie did. She was the only friend I had in Armina, and while she was intolerable at times, spoiled and opinionated, she was still fun to go out with.

"Have you ever been in love, Billy?" I asked, knowing it was the alcohol loosening my hold on my thoughts.

"Yeah, once or twice."

"Not the normal puppy love, you cry for a few days then move on post break-up kind of love. The soul shattering kind where you know there is no one else who will ever satisfy you the way this person does. Who fills your heart, body, and soul and makes you realize you were never complete before?"

"That's deep. I can't say I've been there."

"It's not a good place to be," I mumbled.

"Why not? Sounds like it's a fantastic place to be."

I remained quiet, thinking about how numb I was to everything without Mason, how just those few days with him had left me completely out of control and craving to be near him again.

"It's not. It hurts too much," I finally replied, rising from my seat. "Take me home, please."

He said nothing further, and I knew he wouldn't share our conversation. He was a good guy, one I was glad the family had assigned to me these past few years.

Billy motioned for my other guard to follow and escorted me home. I sent a text to Angie to let her know I'd left, although I knew she wouldn't even look. She was likely in one of the private rooms riding the mayor's son by now.

I stared out the window, watching the lights pass by, hating how my chest carried an ache that wouldn't subside and wondering if it ever would.

DAYS PASSED AGONIZINGLY SLOW, like peeling wallpaper from the walls of a dilapidated home. No matter how many passed, the ache didn't disappear, but only seemed to grow. I thought of texting or calling Mason. I had his number. Tyson had given it to me years ago, in case I couldn't reach him. But every time I thought about it, I worried it was the wrong thing to do.

He hadn't called me. Maybe he'd moved on, his heart not carrying the same never-ending emptiness that mine held.

What if he was trying to forget me and talking to me would only worsen things? And there was a chance that if I did text him, Tyson would see it. I was certain he'd kept my brother in the dark, just as I had. Otherwise, Tyson would have called chewing me out by now.

Riley called me a few weeks later to tell me she was returning to Greyson in a few days.

"I get to pick the bridesmaid's dresses," I teased her.

"Bridesmaid's?" she asked.

"You're saying yes, right?"

"I am but Casey, I've been away two months. He may have moved on—"

"Stop it. That man is still pining over you, just like you are him. He didn't risk Mason's wrath by coming to Treemont just for a fling."

"Maybe," she said, sounding nervous.

"Ri, I'm serious. He killed for you. That kind of man does not fall out of love that fast...if ever." My words hit too close to home, reminding me of Mason, the pain in my chest growing tenfold.

"I'll see in a few days."

"Are the guys going with you?"

"What?" She sounded terrified. "Are you mad? There's no way I'd take either of them with me. Especially Mason. He's liable to get overprotective and shoot Greyson." I had to chuckle because it was the truth. It was the same thing Tyson would do. "No, I'm going alone. I've already talked it through with them and we have a plan in place."

"Okay, but be careful. There are ramblings of the Bad Omens out here. It's not good. Everyone is on edge."

"Are you okay, Case?" she asked.

"I am. I've got guards and I never get to go anywhere alone.

It's a wonder they don't have them stationed in my apartment. Thankfully, they don't."

"You sure you don't want to come home? I'll need help planning this wedding."

The ache in my heart filled momentarily with her words. "From me?"

"You're the closest friend I have."

"Of course I'll help you. Just let me know when and I'll drop everything to be there."

"You'll have to see Mason," she said in a whisper.

My heart stopped, my hands growing clammy, my stomach in knots. "I know, it'll be fine." I chewed my lip, not wanting to hear her answer to my next question. "How is he?"

She stayed quiet for a moment and my mind filled in so many answers that I had myself in a worried frenzy by the time she answered. "Burying himself in work, hiding behind that hard exterior he wears. I think he misses you. I've never seen him so flustered, especially around Tyson."

"Shit."

"Yeah. What happened between you two, Case?"

"You know what happened!" I hissed, my cheeks blushing even though I was the only one in the room.

"I know that! It still grosses me out, though!"

I laughed, telling her it was okay.

"I meant besides the sex." The way she said sex sounded like she was holding a rotting corpse far from her body while her other hand held her nose shut.

"I...I don't know." But I did. It was the unspoken word that we'd avoided the day I left.

"Do you love my brother?" Leave it to Riley to get right to the point.

Sighing, I answered honestly, admitting what I'd been trying to hide from since the day I'd walked away, never looking back because I knew he hadn't. "I think so."

"You think so?"

"Fuck, Riley. Yes. Yes, I love him. And I hate it because he's all I can think about. It's consuming and no matter what I do, I can't climb back out of the hole I've been stuck in since I left."

"Well, that explains a lot. Damn, you two were just supposed to have sex, not fall in love. No wonder he's so off-kilter."

"Wait, what are you saying, Ri?"

I waited, my heart pounding erratically.

"I think Mason is in love with you, Case."

Hearing it sent a flush of warmth through my chest, then tingling through the rest of my body. "You do?"

"I know love, Case. Trust me, I know how much it hurts and how good it feels. And I know what it's like to have it be all-consuming. That's why I'm going back to Greyson."

I picked at a loose thread on my shorts. "What do I do, Ri?"

"I don't know. Come home?"

I looked out my balcony window at the beach in the distance. Could I leave this place? I loved it like I now realized I loved Mason. "I don't know if I can do that."

"I know. Just think about it. I need to go. Your brother is dragging me to that titty bar they own again. When I see the way Tyson acts around those women, it makes me wish I didn't know that aspect of the business."

"Does Mason act that way?" I had a feeling after hearing him scold Tyson the first night I was there, that he didn't, that he was the more grounded of the two.

"Ha, no. My brother made it a point to explain that he doesn't mingle with his employees or anyone associated with their business affairs. It's risky, and Mason doesn't take risks."

We said our goodbyes, my mind whirling with thoughts of Mason and the idea that he was just as devastated without me as I was without him. Riley's mention of Mason not taking risks reminded me that he had taken a risk. Me. And it was one that could cost him everything.

The conversation stuck with me, my heart soaring each time I allowed myself to think that Mason loved me, that we could have something together. Then it would plummet again when I thought of the obstacles, namely my brother.

I WAS SITTING in the office Donelli had for me at his mansion when his son, Tony, came in. Tony was full of himself and constantly hit on me. I had no intention of even considering fucking him, no matter how hot he was with his head of thick blonde hair and dark brown eyes. He was so similar to Angie that they could have been mistaken for twins, even though he was five years older.

"Looking sexy as usual today, princess," he said in that smooth tone he had. He'd nicknamed me princess a few months after I started working for his father, and it always made me wonder if it was a name that came with commands in the bedroom.

"You say that every day, Tony. What do you want?" I said, not bothering to look up from my spreadsheet. I was far from sexy today. A pencil poked out from my head where I'd used it to secure my hair after I couldn't find a hair tie in my bag. Ripped shorts accompanied a tank top that was a size too big. And my black flip-flops with the kittens on them topped the look off. The only thing that looked sexy on me was my manicure.

I usually tried to look the part of the put together accountant for the Donelli family, but I'd been in a funk this week and hadn't bothered to do my laundry.

"My father wants to see you. You and I are eating lunch with him."

Shit. I couldn't see Vince Donelli looking like I'd spent the morning on the beach. "Damn, is Angie here?"

"Yeah, she's out sunbathing by the pool. Why?"

"When does your father expect me?"

"In twenty minutes."

I got up, muttering thanks, and dashed from the room, ignoring his call for an explanation. I was halfway down the hall when I rounded the corner and smashed into a solid chest. Hands came out to steady me, hands that held a familiarity to them that I didn't want to admit. I looked up, meeting Mason's green eyes, my chest heaving painfully until I found my words.

"Mason?" His name was barely audible, a breath of life that lit my soul.

He gave me a crooked grin. "I was just coming to find you."

"You were?"

He released my arms, his fingers grazing my bare skin.

"That's quite a look, Case. Sexy, but in a disheveled way."

I bit my lip.

"What are you doing here?" I said, trying to regain my ability to function.

"Brinks," Tony said, coming around the corner.

"Tony," he acknowledged back with a respectful nod.

"Good to see you, old man."

Mason raised his brow. He wasn't that much older than Tony, so I knew Mason was biting back an insult. "Likewise. I hear we're having lunch together."

"Yeah, my father has some things he wants to discuss with us." He threw me a wink, then sauntered away. "Twenty minutes, princess. I'll let Angie know you need help finding something more appropriate for lunch with my father and to make sure it's something that lets me see those sexy tits."

He didn't turn back to see the way Mason's jaw ticked or the knuckles that were clenched so tight I could hear them popping.

"Mason, I—"

He glanced over at his man and the one Donelli must have assigned to watch him before grabbing me by the arm and dragging me down the hall to my office. The dark fury in his eyes spoke volumes as he threw me in and slammed the door shut. He was on me before I could react, shoving me against the wall and pinning me.

"Are you fucking Tony Donelli?" he sneered.

I laughed, the thought that he was jealous of Tony too funny not to.

Grasping my waist, he snarled, "You find that funny, *princess?*"

"I'm not fucking Tony. Nor have I ever fucked him. He's been trying to get in my pants for years and calling me princess for just as long."

He relaxed, but only slightly, his grip on my waist loosening as he ran his hand down my ass. "Has anyone touched you since you left?" There was an underlying plea to his question.

"No."

"No? Not a single hand on this body?" His hand slipped under my shirt, moving below my bra. I moaned at his touch, having missed it for too long.

"No, just my own," I teased.

His grimace turned to a coy grin, sexy and irresistible.

"And who were you thinking about while you were touching yourself, sweetheart?"

I sighed, relaxing into his touch. "You."

My answer triggered something in him, and he pulled me to him, kissing me ravenously, his kisses demanding and unrelenting.

"Mason," I mumbled, not wanting him to stop, but knowing I was running out of time.

I pushed him back, seeing the hurt in his eyes. Needing to reassure him, I grasped the lapels of his jacket and asked, "And has any other woman touched this body since I left?"

His grin was adorable, a moment when his guard was down. "Not a single one. But I can't say these hands haven't stroked my cock a few times while I imagined filling your mouth as I came."

Heat spread through my lower body, and I inadvertently crossed my legs. He pushed me back. "You wanna come, sweetheart?"

Did I ever, but my time was limited, and I needed to change. "Yes, but I have to go get ready for lunch. This isn't appropriate for Donelli."

"I'll keep Donelli occupied. Don't worry about him. You just worry about how you're going to keep from screaming when you're coming around my fingers."

His words soaked me, and I lost any thought of fighting as he unhooked the button on my jean shorts and pushed his fingers into me. I threw my head back, but his other hand forced my neck still. "Look at me when I'm breaking you, Case."

He rubbed his thumb up my neck as his fingers drove into me, then back out to tease my clit. The heat in my body was rampant, flames licking at me with the intensity of his stare as he watched me fall apart. He ran his hand down my neck and over my chest, pushing my shirt up and pulling my breast free from my bra. All the while, his fingers continued to plow into me.

"That's it, Case. Break for me. Show me who owns you."

His words sent me over the cliff, my orgasm hitting with such force that I bit my lip to restrain my cry, feeling the skin break.

"You're so beautiful when you come," he muttered, leaning in and licking the blood from my lower lip. His fingers left me, but the convulsing between my thighs was still steady, increasing as he sucked his fingers into his mouth and groaned. Dropping them to my waist, he pulled me against his erection, saying, "See what you do to me, sweetheart? You have me so hard, I'm gonna think of nothing but sinking into you the rest of the day."

"Whose fault is that?" I asked, stroking my fingers over it.

He grunted, snatching my hand away and pinning it over my head. "Don't play with me, sweetheart. I may just fuck you here and let you sit through that meal with my cum leaking from you."

"And I may just like that," I played.

He dragged my bottom lip between his teeth, then scraped his cheek over mine, saying, "I missed you, Case."

My heart soared, and I noticed how full it felt with him here. The thought of him leaving was terrifying because I didn't want that emptiness to return.

His tongue traced my neck before he pushed away from me. Rolling his neck, he adjusted himself, his eyes hooded once again. "Do what you need to do, and I'll stall Donelli. But if that asshole calls you princess again, I'll kill him."

"You can't kill him. Nobody knows this is going on...whatever this is."

His brow creased. "Whatever this is?"

I drew in a sharp inhale, hearing the hurt in his voice. "What is this, Mason?"

He shoved me against the wall again, stealing my breath with the intensity of his eyes. "This is me owning you, Casey. Don't ever question that."

"Is that all it is?" I asked, needing to know.

His eyes softened, his fingers brushing my cheek and pushing a loose curl back. He didn't answer until he'd moved away from me, adjusting his suit jacket and taking the door handle in his hands.

He glanced over at me, saying, "No, that's not all," before he left, leaving my heart pounding with a mixed sense of hope and disappointment as I listened to his footfalls echo down the hall.

Chapter Thirteen

MASON

Touching Casey had been a mistake. This entire trip had been a mistake, but Donelli had insisted I come instead of Tyson, which worried me. Tyson was the liaison in Armina. If Donelli wanted to see me, that meant he was wavering in his loyalty to me. Either that or he needed something that Tyson wasn't in the position to agree to.

Riley had left for Bridgeville two weeks earlier. My men and I had dropped her at the border with a new car, a loaded pistol, and every fighting skill I'd ensured she learn before she left me. It still hurt to admit she was gone. Riley had been my life until she hadn't, and when I'd brought her home from Bridgeville, I swore I wouldn't let her go. I'd broken my oath to myself, and now she was in Greyson's hands. My one instruction was that she text me the minute she was there…something she'd failed to do, leaving me waiting for hours. My mind had been a mixed mess of nerves and images until the phone rang, Greyson's voice coming through on the other end instead of Riley's.

"Her terms were steep, Brinks," he'd said, and I'd clenched my fists, ready to take my plane to Bridgeville and land it in the middle of his damned city. "But I accepted."

The relief had flooded through me as I heard Riley fighting playfully for the phone in the background. He scolded her, making my hairs bristle. What they did was their business, but I didn't want to know, and I certainly didn't want to hear.

"I'm fine, Mace," she said, and I could hear the smile in her voice.

"I want a text from you every day. You tell Tides if you miss a single day, I'm coming in there with my guns loaded."

"No, you won't. But I'll text you anyway. I love you, Mason."

"Love you, too, Ri."

That was the last time I'd talked to her, but she'd dutifully texted me every day since. Her text buzzed as I headed down the hall. Glancing at it, I sent her a quick note back, glad to have my mind off Casey for a few seconds.

Casey was another story entirely. While Riley leaving me had hurt, there was a deeper void that hadn't healed since Casey returned to Armina. Seeing her today had filled the void, but I knew it would return. Touching her had been unavoidable, especially after the interaction with Tony. The little prick. Hearing him call her princess had my blood boiling, and I knew it would take everything I had not to deck him when I saw him again.

Angie, Donelli's daughter, slammed into me as I entered the main hall. She was holding a pile of clothes and a pair of heels in her hand, but it wasn't enough to hide the skin her skimpy bikini left exposed.

"What the fuck?" she asked, snapping at me. Her brown eyes were bright in the sun that seeped in from the open balcony of the room. They quickly perused my body before her red stained lips turned upward. "Well, well, does daddy have a new henchman?"

I hardened my eyes, not caring that she had no clue who I was. I knew everything there was to know about the spoiled party girl. I had a file on all the families I dealt with that included their children. Knowledge was the kingpin in my business.

"You ever call me a henchman again and I'll make sure your father cuts your credit line off, Angela."

Her brow creased, the only imperfection on her beautiful features, although her attitude marred that beauty. It didn't matter to me that her breasts were pushing the tiny triangles of her suit, or the strings on her bottoms showed her thin hips and emphasized the waist that dipped in seductively to what I could only imagine was a perfectly flat stomach, her long legs high-lighting calves that looked like she spent hours in the gym sculpting them. I knew too much about her to consider laying a hand on her, not that I would now because Casey's body was the only one I wanted to touch. Angela Donelli may have tempted me in the past, and had I not known what a bitch she was, I wouldn't have thought twice about fucking her. But I knew exactly who she was, and even though he hated admitting it, she was more Tyson's type than mine.

Besides, I had a gorgeous hazel eyed beauty who I planned to take my sexual needs out on until my plane departed.

"Who are you?" she asked, her tongue coming out to lick her top lip. Damn, she was a temptress, and I wondered how many men she went through in any given month.

"No one you want to know." I stepped around her, feeling her eyes on me as I continued my path, two of Donelli's men taking the lead and escorting me to the dining room. I waited several minutes, admiring the view of the coast beyond the windows, before Donelli arrived.

"Mason Brinks," Donelli said, walking in and giving me a firm handshake. "It's been too long."

"It has, Donelli. I need to make a point of coming to your province more often. It certainly is warmer here."

"Indeed, yet you send your partner out all the time, as if you don't like us. I don't believe you've been to see me in years."

He sat down at the head of the table, motioning for me to sit at the other end. Pushing his mid-sixties, Vince Donelli had once been as feared as Tides now was, but as Tides' power grew and the Bad Omens settled in his backyard, Donelli's once secure hold over the other families in the province buckled. One thing I appreciated about Donelli was his open mind. He saw an opportunity in the waves I was making among the families. I challenged the old establishment, and he understood that to survive he needed to change, so he made an agreement with me. It was one we'd had for well over a decade and one the other two families in the province quickly imitated. I kept peace between the three, helped them when needed, and my reputation kept the Bad Omens from their backdoors...until now.

"Tyson prefers to represent us," I explained, taking my seat. "It gives him an excuse to check up on Casey."

"Ah, yes. My men told me you made a point of finding her when you got here."

"Tyson likes to keep an eye on her when he can and since this visit is mine, that mantle passed to me."

A server placed a wineglass in front of me, but I stopped him from filling it. Donelli took a long sip of his red wine. "I forgot you weren't a wine drinker. You should try it, Mason. What was it you preferred? Scotch, if I remember correctly?"

"Excellent memory." I watched as the server moved to the bar on the far side of the room, returning with an empty glass and a bottle of scotch. I surveyed his every move, just as I knew my men were doing.

"Why the formalities, Donelli?" I asked, not comfortable with the way he was positioning me as the inferior power in the room. If anything, we'd always been on friendly terms. He'd watched over Casey for us and treated her almost as well as he treated his daughter. There had been nothing but good rapport between our families. I knew how quickly that could change, but I'd never had my doubts about Donelli's loyalty before.

The doors burst open, and I stood, hand to my jacket, my men all grabbing their guns.

"Stand down, Mason. You act as if you don't trust me," Donelli said as Angie sauntered into the room, oblivious to the tension in the air.

She'd put more clothes on, but her tits still hung exposed under the tight black jumpsuit she wore. It was snug in every area that would tempt a man, her red manicured toes peeking from below the billowing bottoms that rested over her open stilettos.

"Daddy, why are there guns pointed at me?" She breezed by me, walking over and kissing her father on the head, deliberately leaning down to flash her cleavage to me.

"Just a mix-up, pumpkin. You should be careful barging into closed rooms. I've warned you about that before."

She eyed me, her gaze casting the same hungry scan of my body as she'd done in the hallway.

"So, this is the infamous Mason Brinks. If I'd known when you bumped into me in the hall, I would have stayed and flirted longer."

I gritted my teeth, not interested in playing her game.

"Mason, this is my daughter, Angela—"

"Angie," she corrected, walking toward me. My jaw tensed and I glowered at her, causing her path to falter. "You are intense. I like that intensity. Do you bring that out in the bedroom?"

"Angela, behave," Donelli scolded. "Sit. We're going to have a pleasant lunch with none of that behavior. Where is your brother?"

"Flirting with Casey again," she said, dropping into the seat next to her father and batting her eyes at me. "She's going to deck him if he makes another play for her."

A flare of jealousy sliced through me, and I ground my teeth further, hoping Donelli didn't notice.

"Sit, Mason and relax. Angela doesn't bite."

"Tony does from what his last girl told me," she prattled on, clearly oblivious to my tension.

I snapped my suit jacket and sat, my eyes keen to the interaction between Angie and her father. She was still rambling about her brother's escapades, as if this weren't a meeting between two bosses. I wasn't sure why she was part of this or why Casey would be. Tony might have made sense, although from everything Tyson had told me, he was more interested in the party life than taking over for his father. With every word she spoke, my envy mounted. Just when I thought I would lose it, Tony strolled in with Casey by his side. Thankfully, they'd used a side entrance instead of the main doors where Angie had entered and caught me unawares.

Casey looked ravishing. She'd changed and the pile of clothes in Angie's hands earlier now made sense. Casey was a completely different body type from Angie's long, thin frame, but the dress she wore fit perfectly, enhancing every curve I missed touching. The neckline was too low, revealing her full breasts and making me want to rip Tony's eyes out. A slit ran from her mid-calf up to her thigh, her curvy leg protruding with each step and tempting me to run my tongue along it.

Where I'd thought she was adorable in the outfit she had on earlier, she was sexy in this.

"It's a good thing I'm tall," Angie said. "Otherwise, that dress wouldn't look nearly as good on your short, thick frame."

I swiveled my attention to her, seeing the jealousy in her eyes. I'd wanted to strangle her before for daring to flirt with me, but now I wanted to tear her to pieces. Donelli shot her a look but didn't scold her, giving me the impression that this was normal behavior for her.

Her comment didn't faze Casey, who replied, "Does this even cover your ass with those giraffe legs? My tits are a little squished since they're so much bigger than yours, but I guess I make it work."

Angie glared at her before giving her a nasty smile. "I guess some men like that thick look."

"Enough Angela," her father warned her before giving me an

apologetic look. This may have been an official meeting, and I should have held my tongue, but she'd hit my last nerve.

"I do," I said to Angie, taking a swig of my scotch and loving how her expression morphed before she recovered. "I prefer my women thick. They're better in bed."

Her mouth gaped, and I glanced over at Casey to see her lips lifting to a wicked smile. Donelli chuckled and shook his head. If it had been any other boss, this conversation would never have taken place.

"Their tits are bigger, too," Tony said, ruining the moment as he sat next to Casey. The urge to pull my gun out and plug him full of holes was one I was having a hard time controlling. Especially when he scooted closer to Casey and put his arm around her. "Casey's got amazing tits, don't you, princess?"

The fire that burned in me was a red-hot searing heat that needed release. Casey shoved his arm away just as his father said, "Tony, have some respect. Is that the way your mother raised you?"

"Nah," he replied with a laugh. "Ma would have smacked me upside the head for that."

"Someone should," I sneered.

He thumped his elbows on the table and studied me. "You just as overprotective of my princess as her brother is?"

"You could say that," I managed, silencing the growl that wanted to accompany my words. "And she's not your princess."

"Not yet," Angie remarked.

Both Casey and I swung our attention to her. She had a smug look on her face, but she said nothing to expand on her comment.

Donelli cleared his throat. "Well, now that you've set that up so well for me, Angela, there's no warming up the room."

I pulled my attention from her and looked at him. He sat back, folding his hands over his stomach. I ignored the salad that was placed in front of me, my appetite suddenly diminished.

"What's going on, Donelli? You didn't invite me here just to have lunch with your charming family, did you?"

I crossed my arms, leaning forward in my chair.

"Always the observant one, Mason. That's why I like you. You're sharp and calculating, someone no one wants to fuck with."

"So I've been told."

"I'd like to fuck with him," Angie mumbled.

"You're not my type," I retorted without turning my eyes from Donelli.

He let out a booming laugh. "See, that's what I mean. You could cut glass with that glare and that tone." He leaned forward, placing his elbows on the table. "But you slipped up, Brinks."

I noticed the change in his voice, the way he used my last name as if we were rivals. The tension in my jaw was tight, but I didn't let it show.

"I don't slip up."

"No? Then why is it Greyson Tides killed your Bad Omen?"

Fuck. This wasn't good. "What are you implying, Donelli?"

"That you fucked up and Mason Brinks doesn't fuck up. You let a Bad Omen into your territory and now—"

"And now what?" I said, standing.

His brown eyes evaluated me, beady and insightful.

"Do I have reason to question your loyalty, Donelli?" I left the question to hang in the air, my eyes never leaving his. The atmosphere minutes before may have been light with only my tension to darken it, but now the tension in the room was thick. I could feel Casey's nerves, her eyes on me. She was used to this world and the dangers it posed, unlike Riley, but she'd never seen me in it. People feared me for good reason, and if Donelli doubted that, I'd leave his territory with his head.

He knew it, but he was playing a game, showing off for his children and his men, puffing his chest out to ensure they respected him. And I didn't like games.

"Sit, Mason. And explain to me why I'm just finding out you have a sister, one who is marrying Tides."

I hid my shock, forcing my mouth from gaping. No one knew about Riley. She was a secret I kept safe so that no one had leverage over me. It was something Tyson should have done with Casey, but my deal with Donelli kept her safe enough.

I adjusted my jacket and sat, my posture stiff. This was a deciding moment, one that could turn the conversation if played just right.

"I keep my personal business private, and my sister is personal. The Bad Omen we were hunting forced my hand, and I needed to ensure she remained safe and unharmed if they come after me again. Having her marry Tides ensures that."

He raised a brow. "You arranged her marriage?"

"In a way." I'd need to talk to Tides as soon as I could before word got back to him, but I had a feeling he'd back my claim up. If he really loved my sister, he'd understand my motive for the deception.

"Smart. An arrangement like that ensures you two are aligned, strengthening your hold over the province." He swirled his wine before taking a sip. "No one touches Tides and having him kill your Bad Omen sends a sign to them that he's still not one to be fucked with. You handed him the reins and, in doing so, cemented your place in the hierarchy, just below Tides where you've always stood."

"Only now, I'm on the same notch as him because my sister shares his bed." The thought made me cringe, but I pushed it aside. I didn't want to think of Tides touching my sister, especially at this crucial moment.

"Well played, Mason."

"So where does that leave us?" Tony asked, shoving a piece of bread in his mouth. His uncouth hand was touching Casey again, and the anger burned through me.

"It leaves you exactly where you are, only my alliance with

Tides now reinforces your power because it links every one of my allies to him."

"Actually," Donelli said, folding his fingers. "I need more."

My jaw tightened, the tension returning to my shoulders. "More?"

"More. The Bad Omens have turned their attention from the east for now. While they bide their time, they've been active in my province. The families to the north have spotted their activity, as have we. I'm sure Tyson told you about the mark we killed."

"Yes, but the Bad Omens have been in your backyard since they formed. They're to the south of you in the next province and they've never bothered you before because they know you're under my protection."

"Correct, but that was before they broke through your defenses. Now they seem intent on playing with me, and that leaves me in a dangerous position. I need more than your word. I need a sign, so they won't even look my way."

Shit, I didn't like where this was heading and if he dared even assume that I wanted anything to do with Angie, I'd walk out.

"My son has taken a liking to Casey." This time, my jaw did drop before I had time to catch it. That wasn't where I'd expected him to go. Casey's gasp was audible, but I didn't dare turn my attention from Donelli. "I would offer my Angie to you, but she likes to play too much and I'm not ready to give her up."

"That's a shame," she muttered, and I dared to look at her. "I could have changed your mind on my type. You'd be surprised what these long legs can do—"

"Angela!"

"Fine," she huffed, but still seductively licked her lips again.

I wondered what was going through Casey's mind but didn't want to look over at her because doing so would break my composure.

"This isn't about you, my dear, this is about your brother. As I said, Tony has taken a liking to Casey, and I propose we use that to secure the relationship between my family and yours just like you did with Tides."

Fuck.

"What?" Casey asked.

"He's saying you become mine, princess. Come on, you know you want it."

My tension was erupting, anger seething through me.

"I don't want it." I could hear the distress in her voice.

"It's not up to you, Casey. This is a business arrangement," Donelli said as I continued to grapple with how to handle this situation.

"Just think, we'd be sisters," Angie gushed in a completely opposing way to the snide insults she'd flung at Casey earlier.

"I'm not sure how I feel about this," I said. "Tyson—"

"Does Tyson run your business?" Donelli asked, challenging me. "Are you not the head of the family?" He leaned further in. "Was I wrong about that?"

"No," I snarled. "Don't question my power, Donelli."

"Then Casey marries Tony."

This was turning so fast I was losing control. My mind was a flood of thoughts and emotions, my body so heated with anger and jealousy that my hold on my glass of scotch tightened the further the discussion went.

"I can't—" Casey started.

"You can, princess. Just think, you'll be sharing my bed and my name. You'll be my girl."

My glass shattered, and I stood, shaking the glass away. "She's not your fucking girl. She's mine. And if you touch her or call her princess again, I'll shove that hand so far up your ass you won't walk straight for months."

Silence fell, the echo of Angie's fork dropping against her plate the only sound. Casey's mouth had fallen open, her eyes filled with emotion.

"Your girl, Mason?" Donelli asked.

"Yes, she's mine. She won't be part of any deal because she's not free to be taken."

I drew my eyes from her and back to Donelli.

"Why didn't I know this?" he said, furrowing his brow.

"Because no one knows."

His lips tightened. "Everyone out, leave us now," he said, rising and waving his hands.

"But daddy, I'm hungry," Angie whined.

"Eat in the fucking kitchen. I want you and your brother out now!"

Tony rose, grumbling about how Casey was his. I threw him a look that shut him up as Casey rose to go, too.

"You stay, Casey. Everyone else leave us."

Angie brushed by me, making sure her hand slid over my arm.

"He's mine, Angie," Casey said, crossing her arms, her breasts further emphasized by the move. Her words sunk into my heart, waking it once again.

"No wonder you were no fun at the club. That hottie could have been yours, and the one that was hitting on you looked like he would have been worth risking this one's wrath."

I glanced at Casey. "You went to a club?"

She rolled her eyes.

"We'll talk about that later," I snarled, not liking the fact that she'd gone out or that other men had been hitting on her.

Breck and my men didn't move, flanking me as I yanked Casey toward me and tucked her next to me. She let out a complaint, but I quieted her with a stern look. I didn't know where this was heading. If Donelli wanted to take her from me so her son could have her, he was in for a fight. The two men he had in the room flanked him as he stood, following his path around the table.

"You hurt me with your mistrust, Mason," he said, moving to the bar to pour himself more wine. He picked up a fresh glass and filled it with scotch before bringing it over to me. "I won't hurt her. I will, however, question why you have so many secrets."

"We all have secrets, Donelli. I'm sure you have plenty of your own."

"True." He took a sip of his wine and looked between the two of us. "Why is it your brother didn't mention this when I passed the idea of Tony and you by him the last time he was here?"

"What?" Casey said, confusion in her voice. She glanced at me.

"This is the first I've heard of it, Case. Although I'm surprised Tyson didn't mention it."

"Don't be. He was very adamant that no one touch his sister. I didn't divulge how many men have, Casey."

A growl slipped from me, and she shot me an annoyed look. Donelli only laughed, making his way back to his seat. "I guess that means lunch is off, as is any chance that our families will merge. At least until Angie tires of flaunting herself to every man she meets," he grumbled.

"Was this the only reason you asked me to visit?" I asked, wondering why Tyson hadn't mentioned it.

"No. I wanted to hear your explanation about your sister."

"And I satisfied you with the answer."

"Did you?" he asked. "The Bad Omen are still a threat and one I do not want at my back door. Find a way to get rid of them." He sat back in his chair and let out a long sigh. Exhaustion rested in his posture. "Between us, I'm weak. I no longer have the resources you do. My daughter cares only about my money and the things I indulge her with, and my son is an idiot looking to get laid. There is no one to take over until I get his head out of his pants long enough for him to step up."

"What do you want from me?" The stress was leaving my shoulders. Donelli wasn't a threat; he was only trying to protect his family from an enemy none of us could predict.

"Your assurance that if they strike, you will protect me. I've been loyal to you since you first flexed your muscles against the old school bosses like me. I know when to embrace change and to respect motivation like yours. And now you have Tides in your corner. No one can touch you."

I wished his words were true, but someone had touched my sister and almost killed her twice. I wasn't invincible, and I didn't know if Greyson even was. That was something I wouldn't admit, however.

"You have my word. If they attack you, they attack me. But we're hours away, Donelli. I can only do so much from there."

"And you'll do even more now that you have a greater chance of loss here." He looked directly at Casey and my chest tightened. He'd played the right card—I'd kill anyone who threatened Casey's safety and run them down and fuck her in their blood. I didn't want to leave her here, but I was in a bind. If I took her home, Donelli would consider it a sign that I wouldn't hold up our agreement. Plus, I had Tyson to contend with, and I was damned sure Tony was already calling him to tell him the news. Vengeance for taking Casey from him. I'd deal with him when I finished dealing with the Tyson mess.

Donelli rose. "You may want to have a conversation with your partner when you return, Mason. He about ripped my head off when I suggested Casey marry my son. I can only imagine what he'll do when he finds out you've been touching her."

"Leave Tyson to me. I can handle him." Although I wasn't certain I could. "I'm taking Casey with me until my plane departs."

He pursed his lips, looking like he wanted to retort, but he knew better.

"Oh, and Donelli, if Tony touches as much of a hair on her head now that he knows she's mine, I'll show him just why the families fear me, regardless of my alliance with you."

I didn't wait for his response, turning and dragging Casey behind me. She didn't protest, likely knowing it wasn't the right time. She'd never seen me in a business setting, and I wasn't one to fuck around with.

Breck opened the car door for me, and I shoved Casey in, climbing next to her as he got into the driver seat, Leo following. My other two men tailed us as we took off.

"Mason," Casey started, but I glowered at her, not wanting to talk until I calmed down. Too much had happened both professionally and personally in that meeting, and I needed to digest it. Our secret was out, forced out into the open in an unexpected moment, and now I'd need to deal with the repercussions. Tyson was the main one, but leaving Casey here left her vulnerable to anyone who found out about us. Donelli's men guarded her, but I didn't trust his men. His hold on the territory was shaky and the only reason he hadn't fallen was an agreement between me and the other two bosses who held territory in this province.

If either of them found out about Casey, they could turn on me and take her as collateral, just like what had happened with Riley. The thought gutted me. I'd have to leave her soon, but I was damned sure it wouldn't be long. As soon as I worked things out with Tyson, I would bring her home, whether she liked it or not.

CASEY

I didn't know what to think as the car sped down the road and Mason brooded next to me. Seeing him like he'd been with Donelli had given me a glimpse of the side of him people feared. I'd never been privy to any of the meetings between Donelli and Tyson. That was the part of this life I remained sheltered from, and I preferred it that way. I could handle interacting with them, padding their books, partying with them, but I didn't want to be around the violence, the indifference, the killing I knew went along with it.

Glancing over at Mason, I noticed how tight his jaw was, the tension clear in the veins in his neck. He stared straight ahead. What had started as an erotic meeting earlier had turned into pieces of wreckage neither of us could repair. Our secret was out and now we would face the consequences. He would face them because I was sure he would leave me behind. Not that I could go with him, no matter how much I wanted to now that I was next to him again. I couldn't. My life was in Armina. I looked back out the window, admitting that as much as my life was here, my heart was in Treemont, and I didn't know how to reconcile the two.

Mason's phone buzzed, but he ignored it, something I was

certain he never did. We both knew it was Tyson and neither of us was ready to talk to him. I wondered why my phone wasn't blowing up until I remembered my purse was still in my office. It was for the best. I didn't want to hear Tyson rant about what we'd done. Didn't want to hear him threaten to kill his best friend because that's what he would do, and I knew him well enough to know that in a heated moment, he would attempt it. Tyson was hot tempered, and I imagined that was why he and Mason made such a perfect team. Mason was controlling and even-tempered, and that balanced my brother's rash impulsiveness. But there would be no way to balance this, to assuage the betrayal Tyson would feel. Mason had crossed an invisible line Tyson had drawn without ever using the words, a code he expected Mason to follow like he followed it—our sisters are off limits.

When the car pulled in front of my apartment building, Breck opened my door, Mason climbing out the other side. The other men exited the cars, their hands ready to access their guns, their eyes combing the area. Donelli's men pulled up, joining them. They were the same two who escorted me everywhere, my personal security team. Mason had never been to my apartment, so he nodded to Donelli's men, and we followed. I could have led, but I knew after he'd placed me behind him at the house that he wouldn't let me more than a few inches from him. Although I appreciated his need to protect me, this had been my life for years before he'd come back into it. I knew what to look for and I knew how to use the gun I carried in my bag...the bag I'd left at Donelli's.

Donelli's men took positions at each end of the hall.

"Damn," I mumbled when we reached my door. I had nothing on me, not even my keys.

"What?" Mason griped, a frown marring his sexy features.

"I left my purse at the house. I'll need to get the spare from Donelli's men."

"No, you won't," he replied, motioning to Breck.

"And how do you suppose we—"

Breck had the door opened within seconds, lodging a small metal pin-like device back in his pocket as he gave me a proud grin.

"Well, aren't you handier than I suspected," I commented, returning his smile.

"I can't give away all my secrets at once," he said with a wink.

Mason's other man walked in first, followed by Mason, his gun drawn.

"Don't you think this is overkill?" I muttered.

"No," Breck answered, making me wait with him. "It was a necessity when you were Tyson's sister, but now that you're the boss' girl, it's expected."

The second man came back out, Mason motioning me in.

"We'll be out here, boss."

Mason nodded to him and Breck ushered me into my apartment and closed the door behind me. I wasn't sure what Mason's mood was. He was hard to read when he was like this, cold and unapproachable. He placed his gun and phone on my table, then removed his suit jacket and stretched it out over a chair. Rolling his sleeves up, he glanced at me.

"Take that dress off. I don't want you wearing anything of that cunt's again." I sucked the air between my teeth at the vitriol in his tone. His phone buzzed again, and he flicked his gaze to it. The muscles in his jaw were rigid, and he rolled his neck, turning his eyes, which now held a dangerous glare, back to me. "Now, Casey."

Tipping my chin up, I huffed to my bedroom, lifting the dress over my head as I walked and tossing it on the floor.

"And where do you think you're going?" he asked, following me.

"Away from your possessive ass to change like you demanded I do."

His arm came around me, halting my track before I could

make it to my closet, and slamming my back into his chest. "I didn't say to put anything else on."

Currents flooded through my body as if he'd touched me with a live wire. His hand slid along my stomach and up to my bra, caressing my breast through the thin lace. The air froze in my chest, and I dropped my head against him.

"Is this what you wear under your clothes every time you see that spineless fucker who touched you?"

The pounding of my heart increased. It was so loud that he had to have heard it.

"Sometimes," I mumbled, unable to think with his touch and his mouth against my neck.

He brushed his hand down, squeezing my ass and lifting my thong with his finger. Making a tsk sound, he said, "That's going to change."

I tried to turn my head, but he pushed me down on my bed. "You can't—"

A slap that reverberated through my body hit my ass, and warmth spread between my legs. That I'd enjoyed the sting of his hand seemed naughty. That I was craving more seemed even naughtier. He yanked my ass back, smoothing his hand over the tender spot.

"Oh, I can, sweetheart." He pushed my thong aside, his fingers skating through the wetness he'd caused before plunging into me. "And I will. This body is mine, which means all your sexy panties are only for me."

"Mason—" I tried to complain, to voice how controlling that was, but he had my body too riveted by his words and his touch.

His fingers left me, and he yanked me back against his chest, pushing the strap of my bra down and cupping my breast. "How many men did you flirt with at that club, Case?"

So that was what this was about. It had nothing to do with Tyson. The controlling prick in him didn't like that I went out when he wasn't there.

"None," I said.

His slap to my ass jerked me forward, and I moaned.

"How many men flirted with you, sweetheart?" He smoothed his fingers over the sting.

"I don't remember."

"I'd suggest you remember quickly." Another slap sent me arching into the hand that had my breast, and he tugged at my nipple, his tongue sliding up my neck. "How many and which ones did you flirt with?"

"Three—"

Another slap burned my skin, this one slightly harder, but still just as pleasurable. Hard enough to remind me I was his. Every part of me was alive with sparks of pleasure. I was one smack away from coming and as he shoved me down, his fingers burying deep inside of me, my orgasm shredded me.

"That's it, sweetheart. I'm the only one you come for, the only one who touches you, the only one you wear sexy panties for." His words twisted around my climax and intensified it.

He pushed my head down into the mattress, removing his fingers, the sound of his zipper merging with the sounds of my uneven breaths.

"Did you like his touch on your skin, *princess*?" He growled the word as his tip sat against my dampness.

"No," I managed, my body burning with the inferno he'd lit.

Another slap jerked me forward, but he held me in place, pushing his hardness another inch into me.

"I said no," I whined, my voice shaking.

He rubbed the sting away, saying, "I know, but your ass looks sexy with my handprint on it."

"Asshole," I muttered.

He yanked me back, filling me completely, my cry a feral one that joined his grunt.

"You're my girl, Case." His every word accompanied a thrust.

"No man touches what's mine. No man gives you nicknames. No man even looks at you without feeling my wrath."

"Fuck, Mason, you can't stop men from looking at me." My voice sounded distant, a weak attempt to maintain some control over my life, no matter that I wanted to give it all over to him.

He bottomed out, hitting me so far it ripped another climax from me, one that gripped me as tight as his hands gripped my hips. "I can do what I want, sweetheart, and you'll let me."

And I would, because I was his. Every part of my being was owned by Mason because I wanted him to own it. Not because he'd taken it, but because I'd given it to him, willingly and completely.

His thrusts became more rapid, his hold on me tighter, and he broke, spilling into me, his growl so loud it thundered through the room. When he finally let my hips go, I dropped forward, completely depleted.

I heard his zipper and turned my body, peeking up at him through my curls. He gave me that sexy smirk I adored, his eyes scanning my body.

"Where are you going?" I asked, disappointment taking hold.

"My plane departs soon, and I have to deal with your brother. That little punk called him the minute he left the room."

Tyson. Shit, that was a dilemma I wasn't ready to think about, not with the afterglow of my orgasm still buzzing through me. If he weren't so overprotective, the situation might not be as delicate. Mason was the only one he trusted, and this would kill him.

Mason dropped over me, his arm encircling my body and bringing me against him. I wrapped my fingers over his shirt, ignoring the way his eyes dropped to the twisted fabric, giving me a disapproving look.

"What are you doing, *princess*?" He layered princess with a sarcastic seduction.

"Keeping you here."

"Not gonna happen."

I entwined my legs around his back, pulling him down further. "Yes, it is. And you're going to call me your princess when I'm coming around your dick again." I took his bottom lip between my teeth, dragging them over it until he was groaning. "And again when you're spilling into me. Maybe then I'll let you leave."

He studied me, a gleam in his eyes. "Damn, you're sexy when you're giving orders."

"Good. Now take those clothes off and fuck me again."

He shook his head before pulling me in for a kiss. My body flared to life again, his kiss burning through me. I struggled with his buttons, needing to feel his skin against me, but he stopped my hands, pushing them down, then untangling my legs from his back.

A small mewl slipped from me, and he gave me a crooked grin. "Hold on, *princess*."

I watched him walk from my room to the table. He picked his phone up, his expression shifting to concern. He didn't have to tell me how many missed calls from Tyson there were. With a sigh, he walked back in as he swiped the screen and hit a number. He brought the phone to his ear, then yanked down my underwear, which he'd never removed before he'd so erotically taken me.

"Delay the flight. I have something I need to deal with."

He hung up, pocketing the phone before unbuttoning his shirt. Having forgotten just how sexy he was, I rose to run my hands over his tattoos. He dropped his pants, his dick springing free and hitting between my breasts.

"I'm gonna need to find out what those beauties feel like wrapped around my cock, sweetheart, but for now..." He threaded his hand through my hair and lowered himself, forcing me back. His kiss was gentle, almost emotional with its depth and I closed my eyes, letting the feel of his lips on mine, his tongue entwining with mine, his skin warm against my own, take me away. The rough, dominating man who'd brought me to ecstasy with his smacks to my ass and his dirty words was gone, replaced with one who reminded me of the space he'd claimed in my heart. Every touch lit me on fire until the blaze was too hard to control, soaring through me with a force that left me crying out and his mouth capturing my cry.

Mason made love to me as only he could, reclaiming me as our unspoken emotions drove our moves. I gave myself over to him completely, my heart and soul open and ripe for the taking, willingly offered and vulnerable with the wave of climax that crested within me until it flowed through me just as he came, our joined release heated and shattering, leaving us clinging to each other.

I rested my head against his chest, hearing the rapid heartbeats, his hold on me so tight it seemed like he feared letting me go. Just as I feared his leaving. He lifted his head, and I brought my hand to his cheek, feeling the strength below. Leaning into it, he searched my eyes. There were no words spoken, but I saw the love there, his gaze so heavy it seemed to burrow deep in my soul. He turned his head, kissing my hand before he released me, hovering over me and giving me one last passionate kiss.

I watched as he dressed, sitting and pulling a blanket up to cover me. He picked up my lace bra, the one I'd worn earlier that left little to the imagination it was so sheer.

"This only gets worn when you see me. No sexy lingerie for anyone else. Understand, princess?"

Rising, I snatched the bra from his hand, looking at it, then at him, tilting my head as I took him in. My mob boss was back, my passionate lover tucked behind his façade.

"Only if you keep calling me princess."

He yanked me against him, pulling the blanket from me. "It's my nickname now, no one else's. And if the prick calls you princess again, you call me. I'll be on a plane in seconds to beat the shit out of him."

My giggle was light, and he smiled, kissing me again. I lifted the blanket back up and followed him out, watching as he put his suit jacket on and slipped his gun back in his pants. I reached up and fixed his tussled hair, running my fingers through his thick ebony locks. The green in his eyes had shifted to a sage hue, their intensity warming me to the core.

His fingers brushed over my face, and he took my chin in them. "I don't want you here anymore, Case. You're too far away, and I can't protect you out here."

"It's never been a problem before. Donelli keeps me safe." But I knew the real reason. He wanted me with him, and I wanted to hear him say it. To give me a reason to give everything I knew up.

But he didn't give me the reason I wanted to hear, keeping it undisclosed, like saying it would change things more than they already had. "Donelli can't keep you safe. He's vulnerable, and he admitted that. I have no choice but to leave you here as a sign that I still trust him, but I'll find a way around that. For now, you stay. It'll give me time to face Tyson, but once we work it out, I'm bringing you home."

"With you?" I asked.

"With me," he answered. He released me, walking toward the door but stopping at the scarves that hung on my coat hooks. He fingered them, saying, "Riley has a set of these. I haven't seen them in so long. They were our mother's." He peered over at me.

"And those were mine. My parents went with yours on that trip, remember?"

"I'd forgotten," he said, letting the purple one slip through his fingers. I had three of the scarves, the brighter colors. Tyson had taken the other three darker ones when she'd died a few years back.

"I wear them sometimes. The softness reminds me of her." I took the purple one from him, running it against my cheek. "This one is my favorite, the one I wear the most." Taking his hand, I placed it in his palm, folding his fingers around it.

He looked at me, his brows furrowing.

"Take it. It'll be like a piece of me until you can have all of me."

His fingers gripped the scarf tight. He brushed my hair back from my cheek, then kissed me once more, the kiss so emotional it left me weak. He ran his fingers over my cheek, lingering on my bottom lip before his eyes darkened again, his moment of softness gone as quickly as a summer rain. "No more going out to clubs. In fact, you keep close to Donelli. And always keep your gun and your phone on you."

"They're at Donelli's in my purse."

He pulled his phone out and dialed. There was a second of silence before he said, "Casey left her purse there. Have one of your men deliver it. I don't want her without her phone."

There was a muffled acknowledgement on the other end, and he hung up.

"You have my number. You call me or Tyson at the first sign of anything."

I nodded, not liking how hard his expression had become, his tone deadly serious.

"A few days, Casey. That should be enough time to sort things out with Tyson. Then you're mine, completely."

My heart leaped into my throat, and I let out a strangled cry. The corner of his mouth lifted to form a sly grin as he tucked my scarf in his pocket. He said nothing more, leaving me to stare at the door and missing his presence the instant he was from my view.

Returning to my bedroom, I avoided looking at the bed and instead cleaned up. The shower should have been soothing, but I hated every drop of water that hit my skin and washed Mason's touch from me. As I was toweling my hair dry, there was a knock at the door. I peered out, seeing Runt, one of the bodyguards Donelli assigned to me. His name always made me chuckle because he was anything but a runt. If I had to guess, I'd say he was the largest of them.

"The boss sent this over," he said, holding my purse out to me. He wore a mischievous smile, and I was sure he knew what Mason and I had done.

"Wipe the smirk off your face, Runt. It's not the first time I've had a man over."

"No, but it's the first time it's been someone like Mason Brinks." He shook his head. "Is it true your brother doesn't know?"

I rolled my eyes. "You guys gossip more than women I know," I teased, closing the door on him.

I could hear him laughing on the other side. My phone showed a barrage of text messages and missed calls from Tyson. The last one read, *Call me and tell Mason to get his cock out of you and come home so I can make sure it never touches you again.*

Great, not only was he pissed, but he was throwing threats around. I dropped my purse on the table, glancing at the chair where Mason's jacket had been. There was a strange emptiness in my chest, that same one that had been there when I'd left Treemont. It had lingered until today, Mason filling it.

My stomach twisted in knots as I dialed Tyson. I wasn't sure what to say, but he didn't give me a chance to say anything.

"What the fuck are you thinking? I'm gonna kill you both. First him, then you!"

"Shut up, Ty."

"Don't tell me to shut the fuck up, Casey! Mason's a dead man. How long has he been fucking you? Have you both been lying to me this entire time?"

"Ty, I—"

"Fuck! You have. I'm gonna pulverize him. And if he ever touches you again, I'll lock you up in the nearest convent so you can never spread your legs again."

The phone went dead and with it my heart crashed. Tyson had never been angry at me. Sure, he scolded me for some of my choices in men, for the clothes I wore, but he'd never been so ugly to me. I sat in the chair, my legs trembling too much to stand, my hands shaking so that I nearly dropped the phone.

Mason's plane had already left, and he'd be in Treemont in a few hours. Enough time for Tyson to stew in his anger, enough time for him to become deadlier than he already was, and stupid enough to do something he'd regret once he calmed down. I didn't need to call Mason to warn him; he already knew what awaited him. Phone still in my hand, I considered calling Tyson back but my brother was hot tempered and there was no reasoning with him when he was like this. Besides, he wouldn't listen to me, no matter what I said, because it was Mason he blamed and not me. It was Mason he would expect an explanation from but would never give him a chance to offer one up.

I stared out the door to my balcony, feeling helpless for the first time in my life and knowing whatever happened when Mason stepped off that plane would change my life forever.

The soft material of Casey's scarf caressed my fingers as the jet approached Treemont. I'd spent the hours contemplating everything that happened, from the events at the Donelli house, to taking Casey again, to the scarf that still held her scent, to the barrage of missed calls I'd ignored when I'd been with her.

I looked down at the last text message, my gut twisting.

You're dead, fucker.

Typical Tyson style—act first, talk later. This was the reason I'd hesitated to act on my attraction to Casey. Why I'd resisted her for so long. Tyson wouldn't understand. He'd see my act as a betrayal. I was the one who was supposed to protect her when he couldn't and instead, I'd touched her. He wouldn't listen to any reasoning I attempted, no matter how profound it was. And it was profound. Casey had changed me, prying open a heart I'd closed off after my parents died. I couldn't resist her if I tried. And if Donelli hadn't asked to meet with me, I would have found an excuse to see her. Being without her was painful, but being with her completed me in ways I couldn't have ever fathomed.

I'd taken her hard, smacking her ass and relishing how she'd responded, the moans she'd elicited that had made my dick ache. But the second time, I'd made love to her, crashing with her into an oblivion I didn't want to escape, one I knew no other woman would take me to because no other had. She'd tamed me, claimed me, captured me, and now she owned me. All of me.

The plane touched down, and I hardened myself to what I knew I would face when I arrived at the house. Tyson would want a fight. It would be physical and bloody, and I prayed it was one we both survived.

Breck stepped out first, ensuring the hangar was safe. My car was waiting, two of my men standing ready. Tyson emerged from the car, his eyes lethal. He strolled over to me, the tension in his shoulders almost palpable, his fists clenched so tight I could see the pronounced veins in his hands.

"Boss?" Breck asked, understanding immediately.

"Stand down. This is between me and Tyson. No matter what happens, you are not to interfere. Tell the other men."

I walked toward Tyson, detesting the hatred that sat in his eyes. We'd had our fights in the past, always over small things, petty things, and nothing a simple brawl couldn't settle. But this… I didn't know if we would ever settle this.

"You fucking bastard," he snarled.

"Tyson, hear me out."

"About what? How you stuck your cock in my sister? How you backstabbed me, then lied about it?" He swung, and I blocked him, but not before his other fist caught my jaw.

I staggered back, rubbing my jaw. "I don't want to fight you, Ty."

"Well, too bad, because I want to tear you to pieces." He lurched at me, his fists pummeling as I defended myself, trying not to hit him until he gave me no choice. We beat each other until we were both teetering, and I feared he would turn the fight to his favor with a weapon if I didn't stop him.

"Tyson, listen to me!"

"No! You're an asshole. That's my sister! How would you like it if I fucked Riley?"

The thought was sickening, but mostly because Riley thought of him as a second brother. "I'd rather you than Tides!"

"Fuck off, no you wouldn't! I trusted you, you piece of shit. And what did you do? You used my sister like a whore."

His words sent a red-hot streak through me, and I attacked him, throwing him to the ground, my punches quick, his just as fast and violent.

"Don't you ever call her a whore again," I growled.

He got me in the kidney, and I rolled from him, in too much pain to move. He was no better, his face just as battered as mine.

"Why?" he asked as we laid there panting. In his voice, I heard the defeat. "Of all the things you could have done. If you wanted to hurt me, why use her like that?"

"I didn't use her," I wheezed. "I love her, Ty." The words fell from my lips like they had been waiting for me to say them, reserved only for her because the depth of emotion that filled me when I said them was one I'd never experienced.

He looked over at me, his expression unreadable. His eyes held mine for what seemed forever before he picked himself up and walked away. I laid there, hearing the car drive away and wondering if he'd ever forgive me and if he'd ever see past his anger to realize the truth in my words.

THE CUTS and bruises on my face healed, but the pain in my chest, along with the guilt that was swallowing me piece by piece, only intensified as the days passed. Tyson moved out. His clothes and essentials were gone from his room by the time I arrived at the house. Breck informed me he was staying in the apartment we kept in the city. I didn't bother calling him, knowing he needed the time to cool down. And he didn't reach out to me. The silence stung me and after a week of shaming myself for falling for Casey, the guilt turned to anger.

Tyson knew me better than anyone, better than even Riley did. He should have known I wouldn't use Casey, that I wasn't a player like he was, that if I admitted the words that I had finally released, words I had yet to admit to her, it was serious. Yet he kept his blinders on, seeing only the betrayal of what I'd done and not anything good about it. What was so wrong with me making Casey mine?

My phone rang as the car took me to the gym where I knew I'd find Tyson. He'd been avoiding me for over a week, and I was ready to put this behind us. Casey was still in Armina and with every day that passed, the need to bring her home gnawed at me.

"This better be good, Donelli. I'm in the middle of something."

"You need to work on that temperament, Mason. It does you no service."

"Fuck off, Donelli. What do you want?"

"I need a favor."

They were words that carried a lot of weight in my business, especially since I'd done him several favors.

"And what do I get in return for this favor?"

"My loyalty."

I laughed. "I have that already. I need something more."

"My son may have leaked your relationship with Casey to her brother, but no one else knows because I shut him down and kept my mouth shut."

So that's why I had heard no rumblings.

"You have time to deal with your little mess because I kept the wolves from your door."

I gritted my teeth, hating that things had gone down this way, that I hadn't just confronted Tyson when he'd returned home, told him the truth then instead of having it revealed so that it left me vulnerable. Enough so that Donelli was using it to exploit me, leaving me no choice but to do his bidding. Tyson and I came as a pair and if there was friction between us, the other families would see it as weakness, an opportunity to strike while our rift had my attention diverted.

Greyson had assured me he would keep it quiet, and I was certain none of my men would talk, but that didn't mean Donelli wouldn't. Not only did that leave me weak, but it left Casey exposed. Now Donelli was her only protection until I could bring her home. I cursed myself for not forcing her to return with me.

"What do you want?"

"I need your help with my Angela."

Cringing, I hesitated to know what kind of help he needed with the bitch. My distaste for her had grown infinitely after her comments about Casey's weight. She was the last one I wanted to deal with right now.

"Why?"

"Tirenti has a son, older prick who treats women like shit. He's the last person I want anywhere near her, but he's taken a liking to her."

"I fail to see why that's my problem."

He was quiet for a moment. The car had pulled up to the gym, but I motioned for Breck to wait. He left the car, Leo following, the two then standing guard while I talked.

"Tirenti wants my Angela to marry him."

My laugh was vicious. It was perfect for the wench. I'd seen Tirenti's son. He was a massive oaf who fucked everything in sight. Tirenti was a boss who ruled his territory with a firm grip, but his son terrorized every woman in it. When rumors of rape had surfaced, I'd threatened Tirenti to rein him in or lose my alliance with him. I didn't tolerate that kind of behavior from anyone I associated myself with. Without me, his hold on the drug market there would have faltered and Stirk, the boss to the north of him, would have swooped in and buried him. As it stood, I held both of them in my network and Tirenti knew it. I could unleash Stirk on him within a matter of minutes.

The thought of Angie having to marry that brute was entertaining. It would be nice to see her put in her place. She was a brat who needed taming, and Tirenti's son wouldn't tolerate her spoiled attitude. He'd likely have her submitting and on her knees before the wedding ended.

I wiped my hand down my face, remembering that Donelli had Casey. That he'd taken care of her for years and had been working with me for longer.

"What are you asking? You want me to talk to Tirenti?"

"No, I've tried. He won't budge," he said. I could tell he was keeping something from me.

"Why won't he budge, Donelli?"

Silence again, and with each passing second, my ire increased.

With a sigh, he said, "Because she opened her big mouth and insulted the idiot."

I stifled my laugh. She'd gotten herself into this mess. "So, when you said he'd taken a liking to her, you meant he wants to punish her and marrying her ensures he can do that without repercussions?" And he'd be punishing her in more ways than one. Not only was Angie a brat, but she was also a party girl who was fucking and drinking her way through life. Tyson had filled me in on her. It surprised me that he'd never fucked her, but after meeting her, I understood immediately that she wasn't worth getting involved with.

"Yes."

"How do I fit into this? If I can't talk him out of it, I'm not forcing him. I won't risk upsetting the balance between our territories or the agreements we have in place. Not for your daughter's ineptitude."

"If she's already spoken for, he can't force her to marry him."

The hackles on my neck went up. "I know you're not asking

me to marry your daughter." The thought was sickening and insulting.

"No, of course not. I would never...but Tyson—"

This time, my laughter filled the car.

"I'm serious, Mason. It doesn't have to be real, just long enough for this to blow over."

"You must be joking. You want me to convince Tyson to have a sham marriage with your daughter until Tirenti's son turns his attention to someone else?"

"Exactly."

"Fuck, Donelli. That's the most ridiculous thing I've heard in ages. He won't go for that, I can assure you of that."

"He will because you'll convince him. I'll tell Tirenti she has an offer I can't refuse, and he'll back off when he finds out it's Tyson."

"And cause friction between my family and his."

"I can always tell him how you and Tyson aren't exactly a team right now. I'm sure that knowledge would be beneficial to a boss whose loyalty to you isn't as secure as mine, especially one who would love to take control of the assets you provide him and spread his power to a territory like Treemont."

They were bold words, a threat that would have had my gun to his head if I'd been with him. I sat back, resting my head on the seat. He had me cornered, and I didn't like being in that position. But it was a temporary one. Once I worked things out with Tyson and had Casey with me, there would be no threat, no loose strings.

"I'll talk to Tyson about it. I can't guarantee he'll agree, even if it is a façade to appease Tirenti."

"Good, because I've already told him his son won't be touching my Angela."

"You what? Dammit Donelli, you play a dangerous game."

"And you're weak right now, Mason. My game could be more

dangerous if I wasn't loyal to you. Right now, I have Casey protected and safe. But she doesn't have to be."

I sat up, gripping the phone. "Are you threatening me?"

"No, of course not. I'm merely reminding you of what you stand to lose if my loyalty ever shifted."

"I'll talk to Tyson. But if you ever pull this shit on me again, ever threaten me or any of my family, I'll burn you down so fast, Tirenti will be the least of your problems."

I hung up, slamming my fist against the seat in front of me. I needed to fix things with Tyson quickly before I lost not only my hold on Casey but my hold on the empire I'd built as well.

CASEY

Angie was babbling about some hunk she'd hooked up with the night before, not leaving any details out as I stared at my coffee. We'd gone for coffee at the tiny shop in town after she insisted we go shopping. It was the last thing I wanted to do, but her father had encouraged it, saying I needed to stop staring at numbers and have some fun.

This wasn't fun. This was torment. My mind wandered to Mason. I hadn't talked to him since he left, too afraid to call him or even text him. But I missed him dreadfully, and I was worried about him. I was concerned about my brother as well. Tyson had called me several times, screaming at me for letting Mason touch me, not listening as I tried to explain that he hadn't used me, that it had been mutual, that I loved him. The words had spilled from my lips easily, confirming what my heart had been trying to tell me. They were words I hadn't spoken aloud before, that I hadn't told Mason, but their truth weighed heavy on my soul.

Tyson had ignored me, and finally I stopped answering his calls, putting him on ignore because I couldn't take his accusations or the vileness of his words. He was being an ass, deaf to everything I was saying to him, and to what I imagined Mason had said to him. He only saw the betrayal and lies, seeing me as a victim in this when I had been the instigator. I had been the one to push Mason, to finally break him. I'd done this, and I didn't regret it because I loved Mason with a certainty I didn't question.

"Are you paying any attention to me, Casey?" Angie's voice jerked me from my thoughts.

"Sorry, my mind wandered." I would have told her what I was thinking about, but she wouldn't have cared. She only cared about herself. Her conversations were always one sided. "What were you saying?"

"I said that guy behind the counter is flirting with me. He's cute."

I rolled my eyes. "Is that all you think about?"

"Yes...well, that and getting drunk and shopping. I like sex, Casey. And I'm going to get as much of it in while these tits are perky and my ass is tight. I'll settle down when I'm older. For now, this body is getting used like it should and as often as possible." She gave the guy behind the counter a sexy grin.

We'd been to this café often. It was a place we always stopped when we were out shopping, fueling up on caffeine before she dragged me to watch her spend her father's money. I'd never seen this guy. The owner's son usually fixed the coffee, but neither the owner nor his son was there today.

"Is he new?" I asked, trying not to stare at him. There was something that seemed off about him. Tattoos covered his arms, reminding me of Mason. There was an unusual tattoo that was mostly covered by his T-shirt, but the top portion stuck out on the side of his neck. It looked like the beginning of a word, maybe a name. But inside of the second letter was the start of a distinct shape. Something about it bothered me and I gnawed my lip, trying to place it.

"He was here the last time I came in. I chatted with him. The owner took his family on a vacation and he's covering until they get back."

I glanced at her. She was staring at him, her eyes flirty. Grabbing her wrist, I leaned in closer to her. "Doesn't that seem odd?" I whispered.

"What are you talking about, Casey? There's nothing odd about it," she answered loudly. She was so oblivious, and I wanted to reach over and smack her.

I peeked over at Runt, who was standing guard close by with Billy and two other henchmen, ready to attack if anything happened. Maybe I was just being paranoid. All this talk of Bad Omens.... Bad Omens. My eyes flew back to his tattoo, recognition slapping me upside the head. Tyson had shown me the tattoo, the sign to look for, the one he and Mason had missed when Randall had taken Riley. The shape in the lettering was the start of a skull. That's why it had bothered me.

"Fuck," I muttered. "Runt." I tried to quietly call his attention to us. "Runt," I hissed, wondering how they had missed it.

He looked my way, but a loud pop split the air and blood seeped down his forehead before I could warn him. He collapsed and pandemonium broke out, gunfire filling the air along with Angie's screams. I grabbed her, pulling her under the table. The sudden movement knocked my chair over and sent my bag, which was hooked on the back, flying. It slid across the floor, out of reach.

"Dammit," I muttered as Angie whimpered next to me. My gun was in the bag and now I had no way of defending us. My phone, however, was on the table. I scooted to my right, squeezing my hand between the wall and the table, my fingers feeling around for it. Splinters splattered when a bullet hit the table and scraped past my pinky. The urge to panic surged, but I tempered it, ignoring the sting on the side of my hand where the skin had broken. My index finger hit something solid and I grabbed at the phone, securing it and drawing it down. A sigh of relief would have accompanied the sight of the phone in my hand but for Runt's lifeless eyes, which stared back at me when I shifted my body toward Angie. I stifled my sob and hit Tyson's number, praying he would pick up.

Angie muttered incoherently next to me as the gunfight continued. I took the scene in through the thin white tablecloth while the phone continued to ring. There were three men behind the counter, including the cute guy Angie had been flirting with.

"Fuck, Ty," I mumbled when his voicemail picked up. Another of Donelli's men fell, knocking into the table and flipping it over. I snatched Angie's wrist and crawled to the next table.

Angie was crying hysterically next to me. "Shut up, Angie. We need to find a way out."

Two more of Donell's men had entered, and the gunfire was continuous. My eyes darted around in a feeble attempt to find a way out, but there were no exits that offered a safe escape. The pounding of my heart was almost as loud as the gunfire as I dialed Mason, knowing he never let his phone go to voicemail like Tyson had. Another man fell, blood covering his body from all the bullets he'd taken to protect us. Every ring of the phone was a slow-motion rival to the thumping of my heart. When Mason picked up, I spoke frantically, a false sense of safety overcoming me just knowing he was on the other line. Feet stopped in front of me and ripped me from under the table, and I knew it was too late. The phone flew from my hand, and I thought I heard Mason's voice screaming in the distance just before something solid hit my head and the world went dark.

MASON

The tension in my neck was thick after my call with Donelli, and I expected it to remain that way when I walked into the gym. Rubbing my neck, I spotted Tyson sulking in the corner, watching two fighters in a training match. Nerves tumbled through me, and each step I took toward him was like walking across a muddy bog, my legs heavier the closer I came. Rolling my shoulders, I shook the nerves away. This was going down now, and nerves were something I couldn't afford. Tyson would read them and take advantage of the weakness, as if I were any other prey he was hunting.

Hardening myself to what faced me, I nodded to Petey and strutted over to Tyson.

"Office, now," I barked, walking by him.

He didn't bother looking my way when he replied, "I don't take orders from you, fucker."

There was nothing in that statement reflecting any recognition of our friendship. Instead, venom poisoned each word.

My jaw ticked, and I tried to keep my temper in check. It was already unsteady after my call with Donelli. Grabbing him by the collar, I yanked him from the seat. "You will today. Now stop pouting and get in the fucking office."

I released him and walked into the office, crossing my arms and waiting for him. He took his time, but he finally came in, slamming the door and leaning against it. He stared me down, the anger in his eyes palpable. Tension seeped from him like a trail of thick fog that coated the room.

"There's nothing to talk about, asshole. You betrayed my trust and used my sister. Nothing you say can take that back," he sneered. And when Tyson sneered, it was like looking a rabid animal in the face. I'd seen that expression turned on our enemies, seen it when he broke bones and took fingers, but never had I seen it turned toward me.

"Would you settle the fuck down and listen for once?" I said, my fists bunched. I just needed him to hear me out, to put his anger aside for two minutes and actually listen to me. Maybe then I stood a chance of repairing the damage.

He moved fast, slamming me against the wall. "No amount of bullshit you give me will make this better. We're through."

I shoved him from me, saying, "You pigheaded asshole. If you'd calm down—"

He punched me and I snapped, plowing into him and ramming him into the opposite wall, which shook from the force.

"Stop this, Tyson. Think about what you're doing."

"I am thinking about it," he said, shoving me back and punching me again.

I rubbed my jaw, ready to punch back, but he brought the barrel of his gun to my temple before I could stop his quick movement. My heart dropped, and something in me broke because his action told me there was no resolving this. Rage blinded him, and in his eyes, nothing could ever fix what I'd done.

"You hate me that much?" I stared at him, looking for any sign that the brother bond we'd shared since elementary school remained. Not even a glimmer shone for me to see, and my hope crumbled. My best friend held a gun to my head. There was no reconciling this in his eyes.

"You fucked my sister," he snarled. "My little sister, like she was nothing but some common whore." His voice cracked and his expression shifted.

I'd never seen him so filled with hatred and hurt. Hurt I'd caused because I'd crossed a line neither of us had ever questioned. But for him to think I would ever treat Casey like that was like a bullet piercing my chest.

"You really think I would do that to you? To her? After all the years we've been friends, do you think I would hurt her?" I pushed his gun down, dropping my head in defeat. An ache sat in my chest that matched the one I'd carried since I left Casey. "I give up," I said, meeting his eyes and seeing the pain behind them that matched mine.

His phone rang, and he ignored it, our eyes staying locked as it continued until it went silent.

"I made a mistake in not telling you, in fearing you'd act just like you are and think I'd betrayed you, betrayed our friendship. But as much as I regret that mistake, I will never regret what I have with her."

My phone rang too soon after his, and my instincts flared. Something screamed for me to answer. The crease of his brows reflected the same worry that was striking me. He dropped his gun to his side and nodded for me to answer. I pulled my phone out, my heart thudding upon seeing Casey's number flash on the screen. Tyson had insisted she have both our numbers years ago, but this was the first time she'd ever called me. We'd avoided talking while I dealt with Tyson.

I glanced up at him and his anger dissipated when he saw the look of fear in my eyes. I answered, bringing the phone to my ear. A barrage of noise and the sounds of gunfire came through immediately. "Case?"

"Mason, help. They're here. They have me and Angie—"

There was more shooting, then the muffled words of a male's voice and a definitive sound of a thud, and Angie's scream in the background.

Fear wound its tentacles into me, and I screamed, "Casey!"

The phone went dead and with it, my heart screeched to a halt.

Tyson went stiff, his anger at me put aside with his fear for his sister.

"They have her," I said.

Neither of us had to ask who had her. We both knew. The Bad Omens. And I'd led them right to her. I didn't hesitate to consider that Tyson had been ready to shoot me only moments before as I called to have the plane readied and burst from the office. Tyson followed, his gun tucked away, his focus, like mine, only on Casey.

"Airport. Now!" I bellowed to Breck as we ran to the car.

I went to jump into the front seat, but Tyson shoved me toward the backseat. He stared me down, his chest puffed out, but I refused to let him intimidate me. I was tired of his shit. Stepping into his space, I challenged him with my glare.

"Get in the fucking back seat where it's safer. Your head isn't on straight, asshole. You didn't even bring two men with you," he said, pushing me away. "Open your own damn door. Breck, get in the car."

Breck looked between us, stopping on me and waiting for my direction. Knowing Tyson was right, I gave Breck a nod. I hadn't been thinking clearly since Casey left and it had only gotten worse since this thing with Tyson.

Road sped by as I stared out the window trying to calm my racing heart. I tried calling Donelli, but he didn't answer, and he knew better than to avoid my call. Something major was going down in Armina and I was hours away. Too far to stop whatever was happening, too far to save the woman I loved.

My mind raced through all the possibilities, none of which

were good. I hadn't felt this out of control, this terrified since the situation with Riley.

"Pull yourself together," Tyson said, and I flicked my sight to him. He hadn't turned around to address me, which told me this was a temporary truce. "You're no good when you're not controlled."

He was right. Control was what I did, and I did it well. Rolling the sleeves to my button-down up, I flexed my hands, clearing the worry from my mind and thinking of only one thing: bringing my wrath down on the Bad Omen.

Tyson didn't say another word to me, but what he'd said had been enough. No one hurt the members of my family. And no one touched my girl.

Chapter Eighteen

CASEY

There was an aggressive throbbing in my head as I blinked my eyes open, squinting them until my vision cleared.

"I told you; we keep her here until we lure Brinks," a man's voice said.

I tried moving in order to see him, but my hands were bound, my mouth gagged. I glanced down to see thick rope surrounding my ankles.

"What about that brat?" he motioned behind me, and I strained my neck to see Angie glaring at him. Her words came out muffled as she mouthed off to him, her gag ensuring he didn't understand what she said. They had tied us both up, two metal poles keeping us in place, our hands tied behind them. I scanned the room we were in, noting the signs that told me we were in a building that was still under construction. The lighting was dim, and I thought we might have been in the basement. Cement blocks lined the far wall, plastic sheets hung behind them. A wheelbarrow with bags of cement sat next to them, and I swallowed down my fear that it was there to hide our bodies once they killed us. Even after all the time I'd lived in this world and known what could happen to Tyson or me, the threat had never seemed so real.

"We keep her. Donelli's boy will come to find her, and we'll take him out. The old man is no threat. It's only his connection to Mason Brinks that keeps him safe and once we kill Brinks, the old man will fall to the nearest family."

"Is that what the boss wants?" asked the guy who had been behind the counter at the coffee shop.

I could see more of the skull in his tattoo now that he was closer, and it matched the tattoo on the bicep of the guy he was talking to. This new man's tattoo was of a classic car with flames down the side, but hidden within the wheel was the skull and dagger. The second guy was massive. He reminded me of Runt and the thought saddened me. The image of his dead eyes staring blankly ahead was something I would never erase from my mind. I didn't know what had happened to my other guard, Billy, but seeing that Angie and I were here, that left little hope that he was still alive. I stifled the wave of sadness that climbed within me, knowing the situation was too dangerous for tears.

Closing my eyes quickly so they wouldn't know I'd woken, I listened to the two as they talked. It seemed strange that they would talk openly in front of us, but maybe they assumed we'd both be dead before Tony or my brother and Mason found us.

"Yeah, we take Brinks down, but only enough to immobilize him. The boss wants to torture him some before we off him. These two come with us." That blew my theory of burying us in cement. It should have left me relieved, but instead it filled me with dread. If they were keeping us alive, they had plans for us I didn't want to imagine.

Their lack of secrecy puzzled me, especially since they weren't planning to kill us. Even if they thought I was still unconscious, Angie was hearing it all. Angie wasn't a threat. She didn't care about her father's business, and they most likely assumed she had no idea what they were talking about. But even then, talking plans in front of prisoners was foolish and assumptive, and Tyson had taught me that both things could be your death.

Footsteps fell before a blunt kick to my hip forced me to open my eyes. That was going to leave an ugly bruise, and a few muffled expletives came from me. The bigger guy kneeled in front of me, his beady eyes hooded, and yanked my gag down. "Think you're smart, pretending to be unconscious, bitch?"

I spit at him and he hit my face so hard it left my ears buzzing. "You wait until my brother finds you. You're gonna regret ever laying a hand on me."

A laugh that scraped its way down my spine came from him. "I'm going to fuck your brother up so bad, you won't recognize him. But he'll get a fast death compared to Brinks. Brinks is the one you're going to torture."

"Me?" I stared at him, watching as my spit continued to slowly drip down his face.

"You, honey. Since Brinks was kind enough to show us just how important you are to him, he gets to watch as we sell you to the highest bidder."

"Damn, that's gonna be fun to watch," the ass behind him said.

I was trying to keep my expression hard, but that was difficult with the way my stomach had curdled at the thought.

"Not as fun as the way he'll die." He lifted his finger and wiped the line of spit, bringing it to his mouth and sucking it from his finger. The contents of my stomach threatened to spill. "The Boss wants your buyer to break you in while Brinks watches and then he'll kill him. What do you think that will do to him before the boss kills him?" He put the muzzle of his gun in my cleavage and pulled my shirt down further. "Pretty little thing like you would be fun to ruin."

A gut-wrenching wail clawed at me for release, but I refused to show him my fear. His eyes glimmered with excitement, a nasty smile spreading on his face as the other man laughed. The thought of another man touching me, of them forcing Mason to watch, was sickening, and I swallowed back the bile and the wail. I wouldn't let these men know they had any effect on me. That's what they wanted. To break me down.

I knew this business was dangerous, that every day Tyson's life was at risk but I never questioned my safety, no matter how many men guarded me, no matter that men with guns were everywhere I turned, no matter that the man I loved was one of the most feared killers of all the territories along with my brother. I'd never been worried. Tyson always kept me protected.

He jerked my gag back in place as I glared at him.

The guy from the coffee shop didn't know when to shut his mouth and asked, "What about the other one?" He nodded toward Angie, who had gone quiet.

The spit eater rose, his eyes slow to leave my cleavage before he walked over to Angie, taking her face roughly in his hand as she violently screamed at him through her gag. "This one gets sold to the second highest bidder."

Coffee shop guy let out a booming laugh. "He doesn't fuck around, does he?"

"Nope. These two will fetch a pretty price. Then we turn to Tides."

"Tides?" There was a distinct shake in his voice. Almost as strong as the one going through my body. I expected them to stop talking, but the idiots kept going. The more they said, the more I wondered how they could be Bad Omen.

"What's wrong, fucker?" asked his partner. "You afraid of Greyson Tides? Fuck Tides. He doesn't scare me."

Coffee shop guy didn't appear to agree, his skin looked a little paler. Maybe he was new to the Omens, or maybe he was a mark. But that made no sense considering the spit eater gave me the vibe of someone who fit the description of an Omen, other than his loose mouth. "He's a heavy hitter. You sure we're going after him next?"

"This will force his hand. You remember who his girl is? If Randall hadn't fucked it up, we would have had him already and the bitch would be on her knees obeying some big roller's kinks. But Randall deviated from the plan."

"Well, he fucked it up the first time by not following the plan and bringing her home."

They just wouldn't stop, and my doubts about the Omens increased. These guys were off their game and spilling too much information. Information that I took and stored. I'd be happy to report every word of this back to Ty and Mason while they slowly dismembered these guys, starting with their loose tongues. And as much as I avoided the violence of the families, I would get my bucket of popcorn and watch with delight.

"Yeah, he wasn't the smartest. He had a second chance. Fuck, both Tides and Brinks would have chased her to our turf and both would be dead by now. But he wanted to play around first. Was supposed to bring her back so we could sell her, then bring Tides and Brinks to their knees."

"Good thing Tides killed him, or the boss would have skinned him alive."

"If he was lucky," the other one muttered.

Angie had gone silent, and I peered over at her. She looked exhausted, and I wondered how long she'd been yelling at them. She was a bitch and a brat who never stopped to consider her words or the insults she threw around, but she was a spit-fire and no matter how docile she looked, I pitied anyone who got on her bad side.

The spit eater's phone rang, taking my attention from Angie.

"Yeah."

"Good." He hung up, saying to his buddy, "Let's go. No need to worry about Donelli's son. They took him down, and the old man has himself locked up in his safe-house. It won't be long before he falls." Angie's strength broke, and she let out a muffled cry. "Brinks is on his way. Let's give him a warm welcome when he steps off his plane."

Shit, how many men did they have, and why hadn't Donelli flushed them out? If they were here, they could be anywhere. Bad Omen were the ghosts of the families, hiding in the shadows, waiting to take down a family. They'd been dormant for years, but ever since the attack on Mason, they were ramping up their efforts. But after everything I'd just witnessed, these guys didn't strike me as that calculating, otherwise their mouths would have stayed shut in our presence. They were sloppy, and that was something Bad Omen weren't.

"What about these two?" coffee shop guy asked.

Spit eater looked at us and laughed. "They're harmless women. That's the problem with these families today. They keep their women submissive. Weak, controlled women who couldn't fight back if they wanted to because they'd break a nail."

"Some of us like them like that," the other guy said, licking his lips at Angie.

"Don't let your woman hear that. She'd smack you upside your head and feed you to the dogs."

The two laughed as they left the room, taking a flight of stairs across from them and never looking back. Let them think I was submissive. Sometimes I was, especially when Mason pulled that dominating shit on me that made me soaked. But I was anything but submissive, and Tyson had taught me well.

I searched the room, looking for something I could reach with my feet. Angie was yelling something at me, but I ignored her. She probably had to pee, or maybe she did really break a nail.

There was nothing close by and no matter how I worked my wrists, the binds didn't loosen. I pushed my feet out, giving myself leverage and cursing myself for wearing such a short skirt as my skin shredded under the abrasion of the cement floor. Once I had solid footing, I scooted my back up the pole one inch at a time until my footing was secure enough to move faster. I was halfway up when something sharp tore into my back. I yelped into my gag, swearing at the pain that flared through me. Dropping back to my butt, I looked up, seeing the sharp piece of metal jutting from the pole. It blended in so that no one would see it unless they were looking from that angle. My back was throbbing and there was a streak of blood down the pole.

Angie was quiet, and I glanced over at her. Her eyes were wide as she looked back down from the sharp piece. There was hope in them and it gave me the urge to move again. I manipulated my body, scooting around the pole until I had the metal aligned with my wrists, then I began my ascent again. It was painstakingly slow, and I worried I might not make it in time. Not that I had a plan beyond freeing myself. All I knew was that Mason's plane was landing soon. Since I didn't know how long I'd been unconscious, I had no idea how close his plane was to landing. He would bring his men, and I knew no matter what had gone down, Tyson would be with him. And if these men got to the hangar first, I stood to lose them both.

My arm hit the metal, sending a searing ache through it. I cursed again and shifted until it hit the rope. I was at an odd angle, my legs not completely standing, my weight on my back, increasing the pain from my wound, but I gritted my teeth around my gag and worked the rope against the metal. The more my thighs burned from the mini squats I was doing, the more I vowed to hit the gym more when this was over. The pain was so intense, my thighs were quivering uncontrollably. Sweat beaded down my face and I wondered if my work was getting me anywhere or if I just looked like a fool until I felt the give in the rope. My heart thudded with excitement and with a few more lifts, my wrists freed, the rope snapping. The motion sent me sliding around the pole, and my ass landed hard on the cement floor.

Angie was yelling with an enthusiasm I'd never witnessed from her usual prissy demeanor. Untying my legs and then my gag, I stood, my legs still trembling from my workout. I was bruised and bleeding, but I was free. I considered leaving Angie for a fleeting moment as punishment for all the nasty things she'd ever said in her nonchalant way, but decided now wasn't the time to reprimand her. Instead, I freed her, waiting for her thanks but getting none as she complained about the men who'd manhandled her and vowing to kill them all if they'd really hurt her brother.

I highly doubted she could physically kill anyone, but she could annoy them to death.

She marched to the stairs, but I stopped her, yanking her back. "Are you mad? We don't know who's out there or even where we are," I scolded.

"And what do you propose we do?" She snatched her arms away before crossing them and staring me down.

Ignoring how badly I wanted to smack her, I grabbed a brick that was lying next to the pile of cement blocks and a hammer I found after rummaging through the wheelbarrow.

"Here," I said, handing her the brick instead of hitting her with it.

"What am I supposed to do with this?"

"File your nails with it. What do you think you should do with it?" I snapped, wishing I'd left her tied up.

Taking the stairs one by one, hammer at the ready, I held my breath and prayed they'd been foolish enough to leave us alone. But they were Omens, so that wasn't likely. When I reached the last step, I saw one flipping through his phone. His gun was on the table, far enough away to divert his attention from it. And again, I wondered at the way these men were handling things. Even men assigned to guard me never relaxed on the job. They always remained vigilant.

Turning, I put my finger to my mouth and grabbed the brick from Angie.

"Do what you do best, and get that guard's attention," I whispered.

"What I do best? What does that mean?"

"It means be the slut you are and show him your tits. Fuck him for all I care. Just keep him occupied."

"He'll kill me!" she hissed.

But I didn't think he would, not from everything I'd seen so far. "Just do it."

She frowned but pulled her shirt down, letting her breasts spill over even further. With a wiggle, she pushed her shorts down so that her hips were visible, along with almost half her ass. Sashaying over to him, I watched her in action. He stood no chance as he fumbled for his gun, dropping his phone at the same time Angie sat on his lap. The gun slid out of reach, dropping onto the ground with a thud.

"What the fuck?" he asked, grabbing her arms.

"Fuck? I'm not against that," she purred. "Those two weren't my type but you..." her fingers dug at his pants, "you seem like you'd fuck me like a real man."

He was speechless, clearly regarding her as no threat, because he let her arms go and grabbed her waist, pulling her onto the bulge in his pants.

"You want to be fucked, honey?"

"So hard it breaks me."

He grunted, his hands cupping her breasts and pulling her shirt down. Her tits would have impressed me if mine weren't bigger and she hadn't forced me in the changing room with her countless times over the years I'd known her, bragging about how perfect hers were compared to my chubby ones. Chubby, my ass. My tits were perkier and fuller, but I'd bitten my lip each time, knowing it wasn't worth the battle.

I dropped to the floor and crawled to the gun.

Just as he squeezed her breast, I squeezed the trigger, my aim precise after years of target practice with Tyson and Donelli's men. The bullet tore through his neck, blood splattering everywhere. Angie screamed, jumping from his body as he fell against her.

"Shut up, Angie!" I hissed, taking her arm and pulling her with me.

"There's blood...in my mouth," she cried, wiping her fingers over her face.

"Better than that guy's dick between your legs or the dick of some sex slave buyer."

"His dick was big; it might not have been as bad as this."

Glaring at her, I yanked her shirt back up and dragged her behind me, surprised there were no other guards. They'd seriously underestimated me, grouping me in the same defenseless category as Angie, who was still complaining about how I'd ruined her designer outfit. My urge to leave her behind was growing. Something felt off again, and I readied my gun as a precaution.

"Do you know where we are?" I asked, surveying the empty construction site from a corner.

"Daddy's new shopping mall," she said.

"The one in east Bayport?"

"Yeah, see, you can see the city to the west of us."

We weren't far from the airport. There was no one around, but I spotted a pickup parked a few feet from us. "Angie, how long was I out?"

"I don't know. A long time. They had us both stuffed in the trunk forever before they dragged us out and tied us up."

That didn't help me determine how much time we had before Mason landed. He wouldn't expect an ambush since I was the one who had called him. Unless the idiots had told him they had us. Which, given the three men who had underestimated us, gave me hope they had, and that Mason would be extra cautious.

Donelli had told me he'd kept our relationship quiet. But someone knew. Someone watching Donelli from the outside, or worse, from the inside.

"We need to get to that truck."

Angie looked over my shoulder. "It's so far away!"

"There's no one here." Just as I said it, a man rounded the corner. This one was alert and armed. He was alone, but that didn't mean there weren't others. I didn't see any other cars, which told me they had parked in the back. Deciding to take the chance, I aimed. All the years of Tyson's training came back to me as I released the trigger. He turned too late, and the bullet tore through his head. I heard a muffled scream as his body collapsed. Angie's hand was over her mouth, muting her fright.

"Let's go!" I dragged her with me, fearing the shot would send more men coming.

There were no keys in the truck, but two more guns were under the seat. And there was a phone. It was an ancient flip phone, but I didn't care.

"Who uses those things anymore?" Angie said, throwing me a disgusted look from where she stood inside the passenger door.

Rolling my eyes, I flipped it open, only then realizing the battery was dead.

"Dammit!" I threw the phone, my eyes darting to the building and my fear compounded until I heard the jingle of keys.

Angie held a pair of keys out to me.

"How—"

"I know how my father's men work and the ones he hires for these jobs don't hide their spare keys well."

That statement left me with too many questions, so I kept my mouth shut and hopped into the truck. She tossed the keys to me, standing there, that disgusted look morphing her features again.

"You don't expect me to sit in this...this thing, do you?"

"Get in the fucking truck, Angie, or I swear I'll deliver your ass to the Bad Omens personally when this is over. As much as you like getting fucked, I don't think you'd like some dirty old man buying you and making you his sex slave for the rest of your life."

She pursed her lips. "If he's buying me, he'll be rich, right?"

"You're gross. Get in the truck." My patience was running thin, my time running out.

I bit back my rage as she gingerly climbed into the pickup, closing the door with her thumb and index finger as if shit layered it.

A gun shot fired, the windshield shattering as the bullet hit the seat between us. I ducked, starting the truck and tearing from the site while bullets rained on us. When the sound stopped, I peeked at Angie, seeing her huddled on the floor but with no injuries. We had a head start, and I made the most of it, flooring the accelerator as I weaved in and out of traffic, swerving off the highway at the next exit and hoping they would assume I'd stayed on the highway.

The airport was about thirty minutes out and I had a full tank of gas and the determination that those assholes weren't laying a finger on my man or my brother. The pressure of the gun sat against my leg where I'd tucked it and the other two in the seat, reminding me that I'd blow anyone's brains out if they even dared.

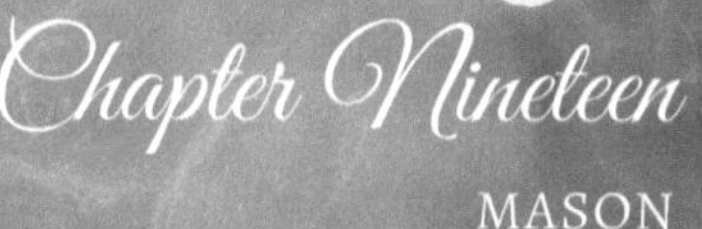

Chapter Nineteen

MASON

Tyson hadn't spoken to me, ignoring me, even as I watched the worry etch further into his face. I paced the cabin of the plane until I could take it no more.

"Are you ever going to talk to me again?" I asked him, throwing my hands in the air.

He remained silent, and I ran my hands through my hair in frustration.

"What do you want from me, Ty? I can't take it back, nor would I if I could."

Still, he stayed silent.

"Fuck you, then. If you can't trust me enough to know I won't hurt her, to believe me when I say I love her, then you're a bigger ass than I thought."

I sat, staring out the window, clenching my hands over and over to calm the nerves that were ricocheting through me.

"Why didn't you tell me?" he asked, his voice calm.

It was a question I'd asked myself repeatedly, questioning if it would have made a difference. The clouds swam by as my gaze fell upon them.

"I struggled with my feelings," I admitted. "I didn't want to fall for her, knew you'd see it as betrayal, that you'd hate me for it. But it happened. We said it would only be one night but..." I turned back to him, meeting his hazel eyes. "One night wasn't enough. I'm lost without her. It wasn't just one night, it was deeper, and she left a mark on me that I can't and won't erase."

He dropped his head in his hands. "She's my little sister, Mason."

"And I'm in love with her, Ty. Love like I've never felt. To lose her would destroy me."

He peered back up at me and I saw the question in his expression, the thing he needed to hear from me. The test of my loyalty to our friendship. The one that would leave Casey broken, and me riven. I swallowed back the pain that squeezed my heart like a vice so that each pound reverberated through me with a sharp ache.

Those eyes were penetrating as he waited for me to speak, and I wondered if he knew what my response would do to his sister. What it would do to me. I turned back to the window.

"When she's safe, I'll leave her alone." The words left my mouth like dead weights, each shredding through me with the impossibility of ever healing. "I won't touch her again nor see her again."

I heard him sit back in his seat, my mind so riddled with thoughts of never seeing Casey again that I barely heard him say, "Do you really love her?"

"Yes, she...she makes me feel complete. Like there was a void in my soul before she filled it, one I didn't know was there until she was in it."

"Fuck, Mace." He rose, and I glanced back at him just as he grabbed my collar and tore me from my seat. I didn't fight back this time. There was no fight left in me except the one that wanted to murder the men who had taken her. There was nothing left to give Tyson because as much as I didn't want to lose Casey, I didn't want to lose him, and I hated that he was forcing me to give her up.

"Tell me what you love about her," he demanded.

My brow creased as I questioned him.

"Just tell me."

I thought about her, my heart wrenching with each thought. "Everything. I love how she challenges me, how she talks back and tests my patience." My smile spread at the thought. "I love her confidence, how she can evaluate a situation like the one with Tides as if she's head of the family. She's intelligent and sharp and I love that about her. But I also love the amber in her eyes and how it deepens with her mood, the way her curls bounce when she's happy, and the way her smile lights every part of my dark heart. There isn't anything I don't love about her."

He jerked my body, bringing me closer to him, his eyes studying me. I was being vulnerable, and Tyson was the only one aside from Riley and now Casey who ever saw that side of me.

"Will you keep her safe?"

I scrunched my eyes, not sure where he was going with this. "I'd die to protect her."

His lips pursed, a lethal gleam overtaking his eyes. "You hurt her, Mason, and I won't care that we're like brothers. I'll tear you to pieces."

He shoved me back and walked down the aisle, raking his hand through his auburn hair so that it formed messy spikes.

"And if you knock her up, you marry her."

"I'll marry her anyway," I said, surprising myself. He looked back at me, his eyes wide, as wide as my own were.

"Damn, you do have it bad. I don't want to hear any details. Keep that shit to yourself and if I hear you fucking her or catch you doing it, I'll beat the shit out of you."

I snorted, knowing it was a meaningless threat because he still wore the fading bruises from our last fight.

My phone rang. I expected it to be Donelli again, but Casey's number flashed, sending my adrenaline soaring.

"Casey," I answered, her name coming out in a rush as Tyson moved next to me.

"Mason Brinks," a male's voice came through the phone.

"Who is this?" I asked, all vulnerability gone. "And where the fuck is Casey?"

"You don't get to ask the questions, Brinks."

"Where the fuck is she, asshole?"

"You know, it was so easy to unlock her phone with her bloody finger. And perfect that your number was the one in her most recent calls."

"If you hurt her, so help me, I'll gut you until you're screaming for mercy, then leave your body out for the crows to pick at until you're dead."

"So full of that bravado, Brinks. My boss wants you dead... well once he sells your whore off to the highest bidder. Imagine how that will feel watching her get fucked right before he puts a bullet through your eyes."

"You're dead, fucker," I roared, my calm obliterated. "I'll cut a piece of you out for every insulting word you just muttered. And your boss can put the pieces back together while I carve him up until I'm satisfied that enough of his blood covers the ground."

"Bring it. We're waiting at Donelli's latest construction site. One he won't be completing because he won't make it. If his son's death doesn't kill him, knowing we sold his snotty daughter to another high bidder certainly will." Shit, they had Angie, too, and Tony was dead. The nightmare kept getting worse. "Get here soon. Your girl's got a nice set of tits, and I might need to break her in before the boss sells her off."

The line went dead. Tyson was pale, the anger creased into every part of his face, the same anger that was burning through me. I looked over to see my men with the same expressions. No one threatened one of us, especially either of our sisters. Especially not my girl. The ire that lit my bones mingled with the terror of her being hurt, of anyone touching her. I would burn the world down around the Bad Omens if they hurt her and Tyson would be at my side. If we died, we'd go down fighting and taking as many of them with us as we could.

"We'll get her back," I told Tyson, trying to bolster my confidence and his. I'd almost lost Riley this way, and now I might lose Casey. The Bad Omens had found my weakness, and it was the women in my life. Riley was safe now. Of course, I'd thought she was safe before. But now there was no way anyone was getting close to her with Tides on guard. After Randall broke through his ranks, I was certain he'd dealt with any faults in his defenses. And once we found Casey, she wasn't leaving my sight again. I didn't care if she complained that I was making her uproot her life. She would deal with it. There was no way I would let her outside my protection.

"Damn right we will. And then I can beat the shit out of you every time you touch her."

"You're gonna have bloody knuckles then, because I plan on touching her often, especially after this."

He gritted his teeth, but I noted the slight tug of a smile.

"Let's go murder some Bad Omen."

"Fifteen minutes until we land, boss," Breck called out, and I took my gun out, readying it, then grabbing another and tucking it in my waistband.

"Shame you didn't bring the sexy flight attendant," Tyson muttered, arming himself. "My tension could use some release."

"Are you shitting me?" I asked. "I thought you said she wasn't worth the fuck?"

He shrugged. "She wasn't, but having those pretty lips around my dick right now sure would feel good."

"There's something wrong with you, Ty. Get your head out of your pants and focus."

"I focus better after I come. You've had me off my game and I haven't had a good fuck in a week."

"You need help," I teased, shaking my head, my anxiety growing with every minute that passed until we landed.

As we pulled into the hangar, the tension rolled in waves through my body. Breck lowered the stairs, exiting the plane first, his gun at the ready. Three more of my men followed before Tyson and I exited.

My car was in the hangar, and I headed to it, not taking notice that my men hadn't finished sweeping the place. It was a rookie error, one I was too calculating to let happen, but my mind was on getting to Casey in time.

"Mace," Tyson said, stopping me at the bottom of the stairs. I peeked back at him just as he caught up with me, his eyes frantic. "Get your ass back on the plane and let them do their job."

Only then did I realize my mistake. Tyson snagged my shirt to yank me back to the plane as I cursed myself. "Fuck, I—" A gunshot split the air, cutting my thought short. The bullet ripped through my shoulder, sending me stumbling several steps back, but I managed to get a round off before all hell broke out. Tyson yelled something about them being hidden and pulled me down and toward the plane tire. I'd been sloppy, too rushed and worried about Casey to follow normal protocol. And that one reckless move might have cost us everything.

Chapter Twenty

CASEY

inutes crawled by like ice thawing as I sped down the road, taking random turns to throw anyone following off my trail. My gut told me they'd been too far behind to see me take the exit, but I wasn't taking a chance. I still couldn't shake the feeling that there was something off about these guys, and the fact that only two men had rounded the building to shoot at us as we left only further solidified that thought.

Angie sat next to me, her knee bouncing, her hands so tight on her seatbelt that I worried it would snap.

"What are we doing?" she asked, her words coming out between shivers.

"I don't know," I answered honestly. I really didn't know. There were a hundred possible scenarios ahead of us and only one held a positive outcome—me making it to the hangar before the bad guys. But that was irrational because they'd left ahead of us.

Scratching my arm, I continued to stare at the road, taking a sharp left turn and throwing Angie's body into the door.

"Dammit, Casey. I'm bruised enough."

I drummed my fingers on the steering wheel to stave off some of my nerves. "Sorry, but I'm running out of time."

She was quiet for about a mile until she said, "Do you think Tony is dead? And my father?"

I looked over at her, seeing her as I never had before: vulnerable and scared. Two things Angela Donelli would deny if ever questioned about.

"No, Tony's tough. If anybody can survive this, he can." But I wasn't sure because Tony didn't have any interest in learning the ropes of the business. I didn't even know if he knew how to shoot the guns he carried. "And your father won't go down without a fight. I'm sure that guy was just trying to get to you."

"Okay," she muttered, looking back out the window and gripping the seatbelt tighter.

Silence filled the remainder of the drive and as I rounded the corner to the small airport, I pulled to the side of the control tower. The airport was a local one, for private companies and the few people with enough money to afford a private jet and the hangar rental fees. I'd been here a few times to see Tyson off and, of course, the day I returned to Armina. Mason's hangar was the second to the last. It wasn't far, but just as we got out of the car, a plane descended. Mason's.

I thought through my options: driving out to the runway or running after the plane as it taxied. Driving out seemed to make more sense, and as the plane touched down, I yelled for Angie to get back into the truck.

She shook her head, and I was about to shoot her for being stubborn about sitting in the dirty truck when she pointed behind me. A quick turn of my head and I spotted movement at the end of the row of hangars. The Omens were here, and they were ready to attack. I chewed the inside of my cheek as the plane taxied past us, oblivious to the danger that lay in wait for its passengers. Grabbing the guns from the car, I tucked one in the back of my skirt and threw the other to Angie, who fumbled and dropped it.

Cursing her, I ran to her side of the truck and picked it up, regretting that the safety was on and a bullet hadn't taken her off my hands.

If only I had my phone. I could have called them and warned them, but I didn't and all I could do was pray they had their defenses up when they parked. The plane was too far down the runway now, turning toward the other side of the hangars.

Taking Angie by the shoulders, I forced her to look at me. She was shaking, her façade of the put together mafia daughter cracked.

"Here's what we're going to do. We're going to skirt the edge of the tower and make our way to the end of the hangar where Mason's plane is going. You will follow me and keep your mouth shut. Understand."

She nodded, her eyes darting nervously around.

"You're a bitch, Angie. Remember that and act like one."

Releasing her, I ran, knowing my time was short. The plane was likely at the hangar now. Dashing around the tower, I thanked Angie's fashion sense and her manipulating pestering to get me to follow it. She'd insisted that sneakers were this week's fashion trend, buying us each a pair and making me put them on before we'd left the store. The pink and purple pair with the glittering white rhinestones that I'd vowed to burn when I got home were currently protecting my feet with each step I ran. The bags with all our other purchases were likely blood splattered and still lying on the coffee shop floor along with the heels she'd insisted I change out of and replace with the sneaks.

There was no sign of the Omens as we ran across the open airstrip, my heart thumping, adrenaline overtaking the fear that was threatening to send me to my knees. I ducked and moved to the corner of the hangar, peeking my head around. An Omen was at the opposite corner, squatting down like we currently were, his attention toward where I imagined the plane had parked. But I couldn't tell how many more there were or where they were.

I really didn't know what I was going to do. If I shot him, it would draw the attention of the other Omen. I needed a distraction to bring him to us and away from the others, but I didn't think Angie's breasts would cut it this time.

"Get back and stay down," I told Angie.

With my gun drawn, I ran toward the guy, muttering, "This is reckless, Case."

As if on cue, my foot hit a loose rock, and my ankle turned, sending me sprawling, and my gun flying from my hands. I cursed myself, thinking I looked just like one of those weak damsels in distress I always made fun of in movies. Tyson would have ripped me a new one if he'd seen how clumsy and stupid I'd been.

I watched my gun slide to a stop at the feet of the man who had once had his back to me. Lifting my head, I met the steely eyes of the guy from the construction site—the spit eater.

"What the fuck?" He closed the gap between us before I could move. "What the fuck are you doing here?" he asked, gun pointed at me.

"I missed you," I said as innocently as I could.

My heart thudded when he stepped over me, his feet on either side of my back. Stooping down, he yanked my head up by the hair and brought his gun to my temple. "Get the fuck off the ground, stupid cunt."

"I don't like that word," I complained, trying not to scream from the pain in my scalp.

He pressed his knee into my spine, and my scream almost escaped, but the sound of a thick thud stopped it. His grip on my hair released right before another thud accompanied the squishing sound of broken flesh and bone, and his gun dropped. I grabbed it and turned just in time for his body to collapse on top of mine. Blood splattered with each downward fall of the brick Angie held.

"Angie, he's dead." I hissed from under his torso, praying she'd stop before she hit me.

The brick paused its motion, and I rolled his body over, trying not to look at the collapsed mess of brain and skull his head now was.

"That's impressive," I said, taking the brick from her. "And terrifying."

Splattered blood covered her, and she looked to be in a state of shock. But I couldn't worry about her mental state, not with my men in danger.

"Stay here," I said, running over to the gun she'd dropped in exchange for the brick. A random pile of bricks sat next to it, and I didn't bother questioning why they were there. I was just happy they had been, and that Angie had the nerve to use one.

I jogged back over to her. My knees had taken the brunt of my fall and were aching from the impact. I was certain bruises would form soon.

Handing the gun to Angie, I noted how it shook in her hand. "Remember who you are, Angie. You're the daughter of Vince Donelli, and you just pulverized a man."

"Yeah," she murmured, the glaze on her eyes fading. "That's what he gets for being mean to me."

I would have laughed, but the sound of gunshots erupted. Turning, I ran, leaving her there and knowing my time was up. Rounding the corner, I shot a guy heading toward the hangar door in the head. He collapsed as I spotted two others who had been running toward the hangar but had stopped short with my involvement. My shot tore through the neck of the first guy and, as the other aimed at me, I rolled to the ground, getting two rounds off. The second one hit him in his chest and knocked him over.

"That was a bad move, you stupid cunt." I looked up to find a gun pointed down at me. I'd been reckless once again. This time not checking my surroundings and assuming all the men were heading into the hangar to join the fight. This one looked like the type to play with his prey, a fact he validated by grabbing me by the neck and hoisting me up.

"I really don't like that word," I muttered, wondering if these guys had any other words in their vocabulary.

"Drop the fucking gun or I'll kill you now."

"And if I drop it?"

"I'll have some fun with you first and then kill you."

"Don't you need to join your buddies in there?" I asked, stalling and hoping he would slip and remove the gun from my head.

"They've got it covered. Besides, I prefer to be a lone wolf, and you look like a delicious meal."

Lone wolf? That didn't make me feel any better. Bad Omen were dangerous, but one who turned his back on his family had to be homicidal because they had a reputation for what they did to traitors that stemmed all the way back to the turf wars.

I dropped the gun, my mind whirring through my options as he turned and dragged me by the neck away from the hangar. Guns were still going, but the volume of shots had decreased, and I prayed that meant my guys were winning.

My fingers were struggling to free my neck from the strangling grip he had on it when a shot cracked through my frantic thoughts and he stumbled, his hand slipping. I broke free as he swiveled around, trying to raise his gun. Blood seeped from the hole in his back where a bullet had pierced it. And tucked in his waistband was another gun. Sloppy but fortuitous. I grabbed it and shot before he could react. His body jerked, but he looked like he wanted to turn around and so I put another two rounds into him. He slumped to the ground, his gun hitting it before his body did.

Gun in her shaking hand, Angie stood across from me, no longer looking as fragile or as psychotic. She dropped the gun, looking down at her hands just as the gunfire ceased. My chest clenched so tight with fear that I didn't know if I could function well enough to make it to the hangar door.

Nodding at Angie, I forced myself to run, coming up short at the open door and closing my eyes to steady myself before I allowed myself to look in, the vision of seeing my brother or Mason dead so vivid in my mind that it threatened to swallow me whole.

Chapter Twenty-One

MASON

Adrenaline thrummed through me. Bodies layered the hangar, mostly Bad Omen, but they had downed two of my men and injured another. The ache in my shoulder reminded me of its presence now that the fight was over. I signaled to Breck and two others to check for danger outside the hanger and was rolling the tension from my neck when a flash of auburn curls captured my attention. I lowered my gun and heard Tyson's sigh of relief as Casey's hazel eyes wiped the remainder of my stress away.

She dropped her gun and ran to me, cussing Tyson out as she fussed over my wound. She was like a firecracker, her mouth laced with so many profanities even my ears were burning. I pulled her to me, silencing her with a kiss and ignoring Tyson's complaints.

"You bastard," she muttered between kisses. "I thought you were dead." Her voice cracked, and I pushed her back, wincing with my arm's movement.

"I'm fine, princess."

"Princess?" Tyson grumbled, taking her from me and holding her in a bear hug that looked like it left her breathless. I wanted to make a joke about me being the only one who could leave her like that, but the situation had me too distracted. My pilot handed me a towel for my gunshot wound, talking about a hospital when Breck and the other two men returned from outside the hangar, dragging Angie with them.

"All the Omens are dead, boss. And we found this one hiding around the corner."

"Get your dirty hands off me."

"Good job. How many did you take out?" I asked, ignoring Angie's complaints. The bitch was the last thing any of us needed to deal with right now.

"We didn't," he replied, scratching his head. "They were already dead. Four of them."

I looked at Angie, confused at how the spoiled woman in front of us could have pulled that off without any of us noticing.

"Don't look at me, although those sexy eyes of yours can undress me anytime." She pushed her hair back, trying to look sexy. I didn't want to break it to her that she had blood splattered all over her, some of which was still plastered on her face.

"Always the little slut," Tyson muttered.

Angie's eyes narrowed, but before she could reply, Cassie said, "You flirt with my man again, Angie, and I'll lay you out, too."

I swiveled to Casey, my brows creased in confusion. She walked over to her gun, locked it and put it in the waist of her skirt. "What?" she asked. "My brother is partners with the sexiest, most deadly boss in the territories. You don't think he taught me how to shoot?"

I threw a glance at Tyson, who shrugged. "I taught her to fend for herself. She hits her mark every time."

Casey put her hands on her hips, a proud smile on her face.

"Fuck, princess, I thought you were sexy before, but that takes you to an entirely different level of sexy."

Tyson's punch to my good arm threw me off balance.

"That's still my sister, prick."

"Better get used to it, Ty. And once they patch this arm up, my hands are gonna be all over her."

She gave me a glorious smile, healing my heart and erasing the pain in my shoulder. The stress of the last few days and hours slipped away like the emptiness in my soul, the one she had replenished.

MY EYES COULD NOT HAVE BEEN any wider as Casey explained how she'd freed herself and Angie, then drove to the airport to stop her captors. The way she nonchalantly talked about killing them had me so hard it was a wonder I hadn't come in my pants. The only reason I hadn't was that Leo's hands were on me, bandaging my wound after he sewed me up.

"You killed men from the most violent crime family like you were playing a game?"

"Eh, Angie killed one and shot another. Bashed the one guy in the head with that brick so many times there wasn't much left of his skull."

"Damn, you are something."

"They weren't hard to kill, though."

My brows furrowed, and I tried not to wince at Leo's rough touch. "You think they were marks?" I asked, knowing she knew enough of the business to know the difference.

Giving me a shrug, she said, "Not sure, but there was something off about them. For as deadly as the Omen are, they seemed..." she hesitated "...almost novice."

"Case, they took out Donelli's men, kidnapped you, and led an attack on Donelli. They weren't novice."

"Maybe I'm wrong."

If she wasn't so sharp, I would have considered that. "I'll talk to Ty about it when this settles down."

I had other plans first and with Tyson and our men heading to check on Donelli with Angie in tow, I had time to indulge myself.

Leo handed me a sling. "I'd put this on you and warn you about keeping that arm still, but I know you won't listen."

"Not right now, I won't. Thanks Leo, once again your med school skills came to the rescue."

"Good thing I dropped out to run in your pack, boss."

"Good thing. Close the plane door on your way out," I said, pulling Casey onto my lap. "And no one disturbs me."

"Yes, sir," he replied with a smirk.

My phone rang, and I answered, using my damaged arm to hold Casey in place.

"They only left two men on Donelli," Tyson said. "I took care of them. They must have assumed he wasn't a threat once they had him cornered and Tony down. Most of Donelli's men are dead or injured. You were the bigger threat, so they sent all their men to greet us."

"I'm surprised. Bad Omen don't take chances." I glanced at Casey, thinking of what she'd said that echoed my earlier thoughts. "Did you case the entire grounds?"

"Yeah, nothing."

Something didn't seem right about that either, but I couldn't pinpoint what. "And Donelli?"

Casey ran her hands up my chest and I gave her a grin, yanking her hips into me. I pushed her skirt up, hitting the edge of her lace panties, and narrowed my eyes.

"Donelli's fine. His men had him secured in a safe room. Tony's not dead. He's close to it, but he held on. They just rushed him to the hospital. He's full of holes, but the fucker's tougher than he looks."

I pushed the panties aside, my fingers slipping between her legs.

"He'll be down for a while if he's that injured," I said, sinking my fingers into her and watching her bite her lip. "That and the fact that they attacked his family head-on will make them look weak. Call Tirenti and Stirk. Ensure them we handled the situation. Spin it so Donelli doesn't look like he's vulnerable. I need stability in this province."

"And the Omens?"

They were like a fungus that was spreading. "Let me handle the Omens. I have a plan to keep them in their place, at least for the time being."

"Fine. I'm gonna stay here a little longer and help Donelli get situated. He's shaken up, and that's the last thing we need. Keep your hands off my sister while I'm gone."

"Not gonna happen, Ty. In fact, they're on her now."

"You're an asshole, Mace."

"I know," I said, sliding my finger over her clit. My shirt was still unbuttoned, and she was kissing her way up my chest. She froze, pushing down on my hand and moaning. "And she's gonna make me a very satisfied asshole as soon as I remind her there are consequences for wearing these skimpy panties."

She jerked back, her eyes wide, as Tyson started swearing at me. Hanging up, I tossed the phone to the other seat and gripped her hip.

"What did I tell you about wearing these sexy panties?"

"I'm with you, aren't I?" she said with a coy smile.

"That's a technicality, sweetheart. You were wearing these when I was hours away." I pinched her clit, and she jumped. "And then you went and wore this tiny skirt, showing everyone those sexy thighs and calves."

"But you like it," she said, leaning toward me.

"Damn right I like it, but these," I snapped her panties on her hip. "Are for my eyes only."

"I will not wear ugly panties, Mason."

"No, you won't. You're going to wear these tiny things or nothing at all from now on."

Her eyebrow arched beautifully. "I am?"

"You are. I told you once your brother and I worked it out, you were coming home with me."

"And what about my life here?"

I squeezed her waist, shoving her body against mine. "Your life is with me now."

Her inhale was enough to send me over the edge and stop my game.

"With you?" The hazel in her eyes was a rich amber.

"Yes. You're mine, Casey. I claimed you that night in Treemont, and I'm not giving you up again."

"What are you saying, Mason?"

Her eyes searched mine, looking for something to convince her to give everything up for me.

"I'm saying that I love you, Casey. I won't live without you anymore and I'll be damned if I can't touch you every day of my life and have you in my bed every night of it."

Her eyes sparkled, her smile lighting the space around us. She took my face in her hands and kissed me, stealing the air from my lungs with the emotion in it. "I love you, too, Mason, and I don't want to be away from you. It hurts to breathe when you're not next to me and there's an ache in my chest that won't disappear." I knew that ache. It had hounded me since she left.

Threading my fingers through her hair, I brought her lips to mine, kissing her again and knowing the ache in my chest would never return because Casey belonged to me now and I was never letting her go.

Chapter Twenty-Two

CASEY

Mason's words resounded through me like an acknowledgement that encased my heart and bound it to his forever. He loved me. They were words he didn't speak often, just like my brother didn't, the two not attaching themselves to anyone, the armor they wore too thick to penetrate. But he loved me, and I loved him.

Our lips parted, and I pushed back, my hands on his firm chest. "So, you ruin me for any other man and now you want me to give up my life so that I can do what? Prance around in my lingerie while you work?"

"Fuck yeah. You can interrupt my business calls anytime you want, sweetheart. In fact, if you want to drop to your knees and use that gorgeous mouth on me while I'm talking, I'll be happy to punish you once you've swallowed."

"Punish?" I asked, layering my voice with as much seduction as I could. "I thought you didn't dole out punishments on anyone but your enemies."

His hand rose under my shirt, taunting my nipple through the fabric of my bra. "I don't, but I think I'll make an exception from now on because the idea of smacking that ass again until you come is making me hard. And you're definitely getting punished for wearing this outfit and those panties."

My heart raced in anticipation.

"Turn around princess." Damn, he'd called me princess again, and it soaked me every time he did.

I stood, letting my eye drop to his hard-on. "Don't worry about that. You'll take care of it in due time."

He grabbed my waist and turned me. I wanted to scold him for continuing to use the arm with the injury, knowing it had to hurt, but he'd stood and had me bent over before I could say anything. He weaved his hand through my hair and tugged as his other hand caressed my ass. His arm put pressure on the cut on my back, the one that had remained hidden under my hair, and I hissed. He stopped, pulling me up and lifting my hair.

"What the fuck, Casey? You're injured?" There was so much worry in his voice I felt bad that I hadn't mentioned it. He shoved my shirt up, slowing down as he reached the gash. I gritted my teeth against the pain. The material stuck to the wound now that the blood had dried. "Shit, Case. Did they do this?"

"No," I whimpered as he pulled it up the rest of the way. He forced my shirt up further and moved my hair around my neck.

"That's gonna leave a scar." I felt his fingers gingerly touching the surrounding skin before they lifted. He moved from me and rummaged through the medical case Leo had left on the seat across from us. "Take that shirt off the rest of the way, Case."

I followed his order, noting how his eyes dropped to my chest when he turned. "Damn, those tits are by far the sexiest I've ever seen."

Arching my brow, I said, "And should I ask how many you've seen to compare them to?"

"Enough," he answered with a chuckle, tossing the bottle of water Breck had used into his stronger hand. "But I won't be seeing any but yours from now on, sweetheart."

My heart jumped at his words. "That's going to sting," I said, biting my lip.

He moved behind me again, yanking my hips back. I heard his grunt and knew from the sound it wasn't because of my position. His shoulder was hurting, but he wouldn't admit that to me.

"It won't sting as bad as my hand will when it's smacking that ass later."

A shiver shuddered through me. His hand smoothed along my ass, causing a moan to softly fall from my mouth.

"None of that, sweetheart." The warmth of his hand disappeared and within seconds, the sharp sting of the water on my wound scalded through me. I yelped, biting the inside of my cheek to silence it. "That's a sexy sound," he teased.

"Fuck you," I bit back through my teeth.

"Be patient, princess."

That word he'd stolen from Tony had become my favorite word. Where it had made my blood curl when Tony said it, it sent a rampage of butterflies through me when Mason said it. He could bring me to climax with the way it fell from his mouth.

"Wanna tell me how this happened?" he said, while he cleaned my back. "It's bad enough the assholes bruised your face, but this..."

"This wasn't them. Remember how I said I got out of the rope they had tied around my wrists?"

"Yeah." He blotted the wound gently, but it still burned, and I clenched my teeth against the pain before continuing.

"Well, I may have left out a minor detail. They had us tied to poles and when I scooted up the pole, I sliced my back on a jagged piece of metal."

"Fuck," he muttered, bandaging the injury.

"It was worth it. I used the metal to slice through the ropes once I lined myself up with it. It took a few tries and a few more cuts." I lifted my wrist to show him the other wound that had long ago dried up.

He grabbed it and examined it.

"It's fine, Mason."

"No, it's not. I don't like you hurt, Case."

I glanced over my shoulder at him, seeing the worry lines that had formed around his eyes.

"It's part of the business, right?" I whispered.

He shook his head, his eyes holding the weight of sadness they'd carried the first night I'd seen him.

"It shouldn't be," he mumbled.

"But it is, and I accept that. The men in my life don't have normal jobs, but they're stronger than any men I know. And my man is sexier than any man I know. So, if my life comes with a few bumps and bruises, so be it."

The melancholy lifted, that sexy smirk I loved forming. "Your man?"

"Yeah, my man. And my man better finish patching me up because he left me so wet, it's uncomfortable."

The smirk grew, his eyes sparkling. He pushed my head back down and finished applying the bandage to my back. Tossing the bottle and some trash to the other seat, he brushed his fingers over my back.

"That'll do. It's not pretty, but the rest of this body makes up for it." He yanked my ass toward him. The sound of my panties ripping sent a flood between my legs. "Let's not let that wet pussy wait any longer. I owe you punishment for looking this hot without me near you."

He shoved my skirt up and before I could say anything, his hand met my ass. Warmth flushed through my body.

"Fuck," I complained with little fight because I couldn't deny the way it turned me on.

He smoothed the heat away before he smacked me again and wrapped his fingers in my hair. With the tug of my hair, he jerked me against his chest, the sensation dimming the brief flare of pain from my back. My body ignited, becoming an inferno that was one touch away from erupting, but he didn't bring me the release I was craving. His hand followed the path of my body, cupping my breast as his thumb teased my nipple. I squirmed as he edged me closer to my climax.

"Not yet, sweetheart," he murmured against my neck. He rolled my nipple between his fingers, tearing a moan from me before he dropped his hand back between my legs. With a tug to my hair that soaked me further, he sank his fingers into me. I bucked as flames blazed a path through my body.

"Mason," I murmured, the word a cluster of broken syllables.

He pulled them back out and circled my clit, causing my entire body to shake.

"Do you want to come, Case?" he asked, his breath warm against my neck, his voice hoarse.

"Yes," I cried as he pulled my hair harder.

"Who are these sexy panties for, sweetheart?"

"You." He rubbed my clit, then slid his fingers through my wetness. "Only you."

"That's a good girl," he said. His fingers sank between my legs, and I lost it, coming so hard my body shook in his hold. Waves of pleasure soared through me, and I clenched my thighs around his hand.

"Damn, you're beautiful when you come for me, princess." My climax tripled in force, a cry escaping as his fingers went deeper.

His hand was now holding me by the neck, and I could feel the shake in it, his wound weakening his arm. As the last convulsions of my orgasm pulsed through me, his fingers slipped from me, taunting my clit before he removed them.

"That's enough punishment for today, princess." I glanced at him to see the naughty grin he wore, and my insides quivered. That grin became more devious when he pulled my purple scarf from his pocket and pushed my head down in the seat. "It's time for some fun," he said, grasping my hands and loosely tying them with the scarf. The move had me so wet, my stomach flipped in anticipation, worsening when I heard his zipper, followed by the drop of his pants.

"If that was punishment, I think I'll continue being naughty," I said, lifting my head, which he immediately shoved back down, thrusting into me. His groan was his only response.

His hand stayed on my neck, his other holding my waist as he drove into me. "Fuck, Case, you look so sexy and feel so amazing," he growled, his words drenching me along with the feel of him filling me with each thrust. Being bound only increased my arousal until I was right on the edge.

I didn't care how he took me, as long as he was touching me. I needed to have his touch, his words, his body moving against and with mine. Releasing my neck, he tugged me back up against his chest, pushing my bra strap down and encasing my breast. My back flared, but the pleasure masked the pain. His fingers caressed my breast and taunted my nipple until I was so close to breaking that my body shook.

"Am I the only man who gets to see this body, Case?"

"Yes," I moaned.

He drew his hand up around my neck, his other reaching down to where he was still embedded in me to stroke my clit. "And am I the only one who will ever break you again?"

"You're the only one who has ever broken me," I cried.

"Dammit, Case," he growled, biting my shoulder.

"Am I breaking you, Mason?"

"Shit, are you ever." He slid from me, freeing my hands before turning me around and slamming me into the wall of the plane. I was grateful the shades were all down because he took me hard, his intensity numbing the sting of my back. Smashing his mouth against mine, he lifted my leg and penetrated me. His mouth captured my cry, his kisses greedy and forceful. My kisses were just as desperate, a need tearing through me to be as close to him as possible, to have his touch bring me to ecstasy again. He tried lifting me, but his arm gave out, his irritated grunt loud. Knowing what he wanted, I worked my foot onto the armrest and lifted myself so that as my other foot maneuvered onto the other seat, he went so deep his growl was feral. His fingers dug into my ass, the hand with his wounded arm threading through my hair. He broke our kiss, giving me a confused look before I wrapped one leg tight around his back.

"Guess you forgot about those years my mother forced me to go to gymnastics, thinking it would turn me into one of those thin, athletic girls?" It hadn't worked, but I'd continued going and still practiced a few times a week to maintain my strength and flexibility.

I dug my heel into him, pushing him even further into me while I wrapped my other leg around him, the grip of my legs and the wall the only thing keeping him buried in me until his hand encased my ass, giving me extra support.

"Fuck, I'm glad she wasn't successful because this is the only way I want you, princess. Every fucking sexy inch of this curvy body is perfection," he said, lighting my soul with happiness. I pulled his mouth to mine. "But I won't complain about that flexibility. I think you need to show me more of your tricks, Case."

Nibbling his bottom lip, I said, "I plan to," as I moved my leg up higher.

His thrusts increased, each one driving so deep my climax was climbing again. The airplane was shaking with our moves, the silence filled with our moans as he brought me over the edge once more and joined me. Our kisses didn't stop until our bodies did. Residual quakes coursed through me, and I clung to him until he drew back to look at me. I dropped my legs from him, hating how he slid from me, and as if he knew, he pushed me further into the wall, forcing his body against mine so that we were one again. In a moment that I knew defined his place in my soul forever, he brought his hands to my face, cradling it, his fingers slipping into my curls.

"I love you, Casey. I don't think I ever knew what love truly was before you and I will never love anyone the way I love you. I don't want to. I only want you...forever."

My lips parted as his finger brushed the corner of my eye. "You have the most beautiful eyes. Ones I won't ever stop gazing into. I will love you and worship you until my last breath and long after death has taken me." He kissed my forehead, dropping his head to mine, his green eyes so intense I thought they could see right into my soul and witness the way it stretched and twisted at his words, becoming his completely.

"I'm yours forever, Mason. Yours to have, to hold—"

"Til death?" he said so softly it was almost like a feather falling through my heart.

"Til death and beyond."

I held onto his arms as he brought his lips to mine, his kiss claiming every cell in my body that his words hadn't reached.

"Marry me, Case," he muttered between kisses.

"I thought we just established that I would," I returned with a chuckle.

His laugh was light, and I held onto it as he drew back to look at me again.

"As romantic as this is, I think we should leave out the part about us being naked and how you asked me after taking me against the wall of your plane," I joked.

"You're not naked. Your skirt and bra are still on," he said with a wink.

I threw my head back and laughed, and he dragged his lips down my neck.

"We may want to leave that part out for our kids," I said, not thinking before the words came out.

He lifted his head, giving me a naughty smile. "Damn, princess. Seeing you with a massive baby bump would do nothing but keep me hard non-stop."

That hadn't been the response I'd expected, but everything

about Mason's reaction to me gave me butterflies, and this was no exception. "Let's leave babies on the back burner for a while. I want to continue testing you with my naughtiness so you can continue to spank me before I'm ready for that."

He tipped my chin, bringing my mouth to his and kissing me again. "I like that idea."

I watched as he dressed, taking a moment to stop him from buttoning his shirt so I could trace each of his tattoos, memorizing each one before I buttoned it for him. His eyes never left mine, the green in them on the cusp of sage by the time he helped me put my shirt on. His fingers lingered on the swell of my breasts before he pulled it all the way down. I lifted my ripped panties, shaking my head. Snatching them, he bent and picked up the scarf, tucking the panties into his pocket.

"That's dirty," I joked. He wound the scarf around my neck and used the two ends to pull me to him.

"I'm gonna keep them with me so I can think of that pussy anytime I have to be away from you."

"Stop getting me wet, Mason. I already need to go clean up," I complained.

"Why? I want your cum dripping down your legs so that every man out there knows you're mine."

"Ha! We just shook this plane so hard it almost overturned. I think they know."

He gave me a smirk that lit my insides on fire. Releasing the scarf, he shoved me playfully toward the bathroom and smacked my ass. "Go clean up. But I'm keeping the panties. You can go without them for the trip home. I think I'll have you sit on my lap so I can finger you while the others sleep."

I rolled my eyes as I made my way to the bathroom. "Tyson will never agree to that and good luck even getting a seat next to me when he gets back."

"Maybe I'll leave him here. I don't need him chaperoning us."

He adjusted himself, walking to the front of the plane as he neatly folded my scarf. "Shit, Case, you got me hard again. They're gonna think I couldn't finish the job."

"No one will think that," I replied with a laugh.

I went into the bathroom, shutting the door and leaning against it. My legs were still shaking. The adrenaline of the day and of what we'd just done on top of what Mason had said had left me weakened to the core. He loved me. He'd said the words. We both had. And then, he'd asked me to marry him and there was no question his words had been sincere and that he'd meant it. I couldn't imagine living without him again. I knew he would give me no choice but to go back to Treemont. Tyson would be the same now that the Bad Omens had compromised Donelli, and I'd been a victim. Neither of them would let me out of their protection again. Where in the past that might have bothered me, now I welcomed it. I could give up my life here, the identity I'd built for myself if it meant Mason would be in my life. If it meant I could touch him and see him every day. And I knew I never wanted him to be farther than my reach ever again.

I cleaned myself up and splashed water on my face, looking into the mirror. My hair was a mess, my curls mussy from Mason's hands and the events of earlier. The day had gone from a nightmare to a frightening adrenaline filled rampage to save my brother and the man I loved to the most erotic and romantic moments of my life. This was the life I had accepted when I'd said yes. Had I said yes? I hadn't actually said the word, but my heart had screamed it.

I smoothed my hands over my shirt and pulled my skirt down, hoping no one would notice my lack of underwear. Leaving the bathroom, I rushed out of the plane, searching for Mason and needing to say the word, to solidify my answer so he knew it without a doubt. I spotted him talking to Tyson and my heart lifted again at seeing them talking to each other. They'd always been inseparable, and it had hurt knowing my attraction to Mason had caused that rift.

I ran over to them and jumped into Mason's arms, not caring that Tyson grumbled about it.

"What was that for?" Mason asked, holding onto me with his good arm. I had my legs wrapped so tight around him that his words came out raspy. Or maybe my move had turned him on again.

"Yes," I said. "I forgot to say yes."

He smiled, pulling me closer and kissing me.

"What the fuck, you two? I'm still getting used to this. Don't think you're going at it like this every time you're together. And yes what?" Tyson rambled.

"Yes, I'll marry him."

"Marry?" Tyson flipped, causing Mason to chuckle. "Are you shitting me?"

"No, deal with it, Ty. Your sister is going to be my wife, whether or not you like it."

"Dammit. First Riley, now this? What the fuck?" His complaints continued, but Mason just smiled, his smile lighting his eyes. Tyson lifted the hem of my skirt. "Are you not wearing any underwear? I'm gonna beat the shit out of you, Mace."

Mason's laughter filled the hangar, his kiss muffling it. Tyson's complaints fell away, the world with them and all that was left was Mason and his love for me.

The soft curls of Casey's hair fell gracefully through my fingers as I pretended to watch the movie. My mind was more on her and the feeling of having her so close. Her head was in my lap, her face turned to the fantasy movie she'd chosen. I would have taken advantage of the position if she hadn't gone down on me when we'd first escaped to the basement, her mouth leaving me so weak I didn't argue when she chose the movie. She was something, and she was mine.

My hand continued to play with her hair, my eyes trained on each strand as they floated down. I loved her curls, the way they gently framed her face, bouncing with her steps or swaying in the breeze when we went for walks on the grounds.

"Are you trying to distract me from the movie?" she asked, her voice lazily drifting over my ears.

It had been three weeks since the Bad Omens had struck, three weeks since the thought of losing her had wrenched my heart, nearly gutting me, three weeks since I'd moved her in with me. Three amazing weeks where I'd explored every inch of her fantastic body and she'd done the same to mine, taking me to new heights every time I indulged in her, which was frequent. But there were times like these when simply being in her presence made me the happiest, leaving me contented like I'd never been before.

Tyson still grumbled about us, but it had become playful, his complaints waning with the passing of time. He'd moved back in but now used the apartment more frequently to give us space.

I still planned to marry Casey, but with the newness of our relationship, she wanted us to take our time, to wait until after Riley's wedding to make plans. Whatever made her happy made me happy, so I didn't argue, content to know she loved me.

"I might be," I replied to her question as she peeked up at me. "But you left me pretty tired with that stunt you pulled earlier." I gave her a crooked grin, which she returned with a radiant smile. I'd found I never tired of her smiles or the way they warmed my soul.

My phone rang, ruining the moment, and I reached for it, seeing Greyson Tides' number.

"Duty calls, princess." Watching the sexy shiver run through her every time I called her princess had made it my favorite nickname.

"Tides," I greeted him. "Calling to tell me how much you liked my gift."

"Don't pull that shit again, Brinks. Your sister threw up when she opened it."

"You let my sister open packages sent to you?" I tried to remain calm, but it was hard. Tides grated on my nerves and anything that had to do with Riley sent that irritation skyrocketing.

Casey sat up, her eyes questioning me.

"You wanted her to be part of this world, Brinks. She needs to deal with dead bodies if she is. Personally, I prefer my women soft, not like you who let your woman take down your enemy for you. How is that shoulder doing, by the way?"

My grip on the phone tightened. I heard Riley complain in the background that she wasn't soft.

"You're not soft, baby girl."

"Don't call my sister that," I groused, the nickname turning my stomach.

"And stop pouting like that or I'll put those lips to use," he said to her.

"Why you fucker," I yelled, but I heard Riley retort back that if he didn't stop, her lips wouldn't be of any use the rest of the day. I wasn't sure that made my thoughts on the subject any better, but it shut him up.

"I sent your message to the Omens," he said, changing the subject.

When we'd rounded up the bodies, including the ones Casey had taken out, I kept a souvenir. The head stayed on ice until I sent it to Tides as an engagement gift. He may have enjoyed taunting me about his relationship with Riley, but I hit him where I could, when I could. The head was a purposeful show of my power. One I knew he'd use to send a warning to the Bad Omen. He was the only boss I knew who had a way of contacting them, although he'd never divulged how.

"And?" I asked.

"They didn't respond, but I doubt they'll come after you for a while. They may turn their attention away again, like they did with Donelli. The families you have alliances with will be safe for the time being. You struck them hard. Or maybe I should say your girl struck them hard."

"Fuck off, Tides." I didn't bother arguing that my men and I had taken most of them out. If he wanted to believe Casey had done all the work, then let him underestimate me. I had a feeling he knew exactly how it had gone down, but he enjoyed goading me as much as I enjoyed goading him.

"I plan to when I get done with this conversation." I could

hear the smirk in his voice and my urge to reach through the phone and strangle him grew.

"They're using marks, Tides."

He stayed quiet for a few seconds. "I know, and it means they could be anywhere. I don't know when they'll strike again, but they'll come after you and now that it's out that Riley connects us, they'll come after me." Riley muttered something in the background, but I couldn't make it out. "We're moving the wedding up," he finally said.

"You promised her a Christmas wedding."

"I did, but I won't wait that long. There's too much at risk with the Omen stirring things up. The wedding needs to happen sooner. I'll give her something special at Christmas to make it up to her."

"Damn right you will." This time, I heard her loud and clear.

"What did I tell you about running that mouth, baby girl? Now be a good girl and take those clothes off. I'm almost done with this call."

"Dammit Tides, you say that shit to stir me up and I swear the next time I see you, my fist will be in your face."

"Idle threats, Brinks. The wedding is being moved to next month. She gets a spring wedding. Until then, make sure your men stay on guard. Lock down every business, every loose end you have, every mouth the Omen can leverage to get to you. And make sure those families in the west are still loyal. I've heard rumblings about Tirenti."

"I'll take care of those rumblings. You worry about keeping my sister safe."

"Keeping her happy is the hard part. This wedding shit is killing me."

"Hey!" Riley yelled.

"Sounds like you've got a pissed off woman to deal with and I can tell you from experience, my sister is a handful when she pissed."

"I know she is, but she understands there are consequences if she acts up." The phone went dead, leaving that thought in my head. I hoped his punishments weren't anything like mine because that was disturbing. I shook the image from my mind, meeting Casey's bright eyes.

"They moved the wedding up?" she asked, almost bouncing in her seat.

"Yeah, sounds like it."

She leaned into me. "That means wedding planning, wedding dress shopping, bridal showers. I wonder if she'll make me her maid of honor." She bit her lip, a worry crease forming between her eyes.

"Of course she will. And I bet you'll look stunning all dressed up in one of those fancy dresses, a pair of sexy stilettos, your curls all done up." The thought made my dick twitch. There wasn't a speck of Casey's body that didn't turn me on. She had curves that were never ending, and I had touched, kissed, and licked every one.

"Why are you grinning like that?" she asked, a subtle blush filling her cheeks.

"Just thinking of you with no panties on under that bridesmaid dress and those luscious tits of yours spilling over the top of the dress." Even picturing her that way was making me hard. "Although maybe that's not such a good idea, I don't want other men staring at my girl."

She gave me a kiss, giggling against my lips and I pushed her back on the couch, pulling her legs out from under her so that she was laying down as I hovered over her.

"I think I need a taste of you, sweetheart," I muttered between kisses.

My phone rang again, and I groaned, pulling away. She jerked me back to her, saying, "Ignore it."

"No can do. You know the rules." She came first, but I always took business calls.

She whined, but I took my phone back out, seeing Donelli's number. Sitting back, I answered, running my hand down the length of her body.

"Brinks," Tony said.

"Why are you calling from your father's phone?"

"Pops is handing the business over to me. Now that I'm recuperating, he says it's time to bring me all the way in. That means I'm the voice and the face of the family now."

"That's not terrifying," I muttered.

"I'm ready this time, Mason. I wasn't before, but seeing death so close has changed me."

I wanted to say I'd see with time, but I kept my mouth shut, letting him ramble about his near-death reawakening. The bullets had missed his major organs, and they'd sent him home from the hospital with a new lease on life and the scars to prove it.

"What do you want, Tony?"

"Pops is calling in the favor he asked of you. Remember how Tirenti's son was harassing my sister?"

My insides clenched because I'd hoped with all that had gone down, Donelli would forget about his proposal for us to help Angie.

"Yes," I said with some hesitation.

I looked over at Casey. She'd wiggled out of her jeans, her tiny thong the only thing blocking me from tasting her like I'd planned.

"That's a dirty move," I mouthed.

"Well, he's back at it," Tony continued as my eyes followed the path of Casey's leg where she bent it. "He and his father were here for a business meeting, and he made a move on Angie. The prick touched my sister. I about killed him, but there's tension between our families, so I held back." That tension was worrisome, especially after Tides' comment about them. I'd need to pay them a visit to remind them who had bailed them out when they were struggling to keep hold of their territory.

"I'm proud of you, Tony. That was a big thing to do. I would have cut his hands off and stuffed them up his ass."

By now, Casey had her shirt and bra off, her breasts staring temptingly at me. I wiped my hand over my face as Tony bragged again about how he was a changed man. Ignoring him, I cupped her breast, leaning forward and flicking my tongue over her nipple. She bit her bottom lip, letting her head fall back.

"Are we done, Tony?" I said, hearing how hoarse my voice had become. I wanted Casey so badly I was aching for her.

"No, we're not. I need you to take Angie. You told pops that the fake marriage with Tyson would be okay."

I stopped, dropping my head against Casey's stomach. Her hands played through my hair, and I rested my cheek on her skin. "I never agreed to it. I told him I'd talk to Tyson about it."

"About what?" Casey asked. I put my finger to her mouth to silence her, and she pouted her lips.

"Don't pout," I mouthed before I ran my hand down her body and pushed her panties off.

"Well, your time is up. My father announced it to Tirenti before things went down and reaffirmed it when Tirenti was here. I expect Tyson here by the end of the week to take his new bride home."

Fuck, that was a disaster and a move that was sure to push Tirenti another step further to questioning his allegiance to me. This entire situation had gone from bad to worse. The only thing keeping me sane at the moment was the gorgeous brunette whose naked body had my cock in a frenzy.

"Are you giving me orders, Tony?" I rubbed my fingers through Casey's wetness, forcing my groan to stay silent. Her legs spread, and I teased her clit before slipping two fingers deep inside of her. "Because we're done here, and if you're threatening me, we're done completely."

"Shit," he mumbled. My fingers moved in and out of Casey, her moans growing louder. I really needed this call to end. "No,

I'm not threatening you. Please take her. She needs protection, and I'm not in the position to give it to her without starting a turf war. If we go to war, your alliance breaks up and your business will hurt as much as ours will."

Damn, he had a point. Although I wasn't certain Tyson taking Angie would make it any better. I freed my fingers, sliding over Casey's clit again, causing her legs to tremble enticingly.

"Fine, I'll have Tyson on a plane by Friday. Make sure Angie's ready. And Tony, if she's as mouthy as she usually is, I can't guarantee Tyson won't kill her within the first day of this sham."

I hung up on him, throwing my phone aside and shoving my fingers back into Casey, grabbing her breast with my other hand.

"What sham?" she moaned.

"I'll tell you later, princess. Right now, I'm ravenous, and I need to taste you." I didn't wait for her reply, burying my head between her legs and sinking my tongue into her sweetness. I wrapped my arms around her legs, jerking her further into my face, feeling her oncoming climax and waiting to experience her euphoria. Every lick got me harder. Every moan that shivered through her body sent my desire for her rising until she came undone, her body shaking so hard that I couldn't resist freeing myself. I gave her a long lick, flicking my tongue against her clit as her body calmed, then sat back and freed my cock, stroking it while I watched the quivers that were still running through her stomach.

"Damn, you are the most beautiful thing when you're coming, sweetheart."

"Only when I'm coming?" she teased, her voice unsteady.

"You're always beautiful, princess." She grabbed my shirt and pulled me over her, pushing her heels into my back as I penetrated her, both of us grunting in unison.

I knew I needed to talk to Tyson, but I needed Casey more and the desperation that always hit me when she was close had me in its grip. I took her, luxuriating in every touch, every cry that escaped her sexy lips until I broke. My climax crushed me with its force, knocking the wind from me until I could gain control of my body again.

Lifting myself, I gazed into her hazel eyes. They were a deep amber right on the cusp of brown.

"Still love me?" she asked, her smile reaching in and tugging the heart she owned.

"Always, Case."

And it was the truth. There would never be room for anyone else in my heart because she filled it so that it was overflowing with the love I had for her. There would never be a day when I wouldn't love her, wouldn't desire her, wouldn't be owned by her. Because Casey was my everything now, awakening my hardened heart and capturing it so there was no escape.

"Mind telling me what sham?" she asked, pushing my shirt up and running her hands over my muscles.

"I'd prefer not to and to have you continue touching me like that," I mumbled, leaning down and kissing her neck.

"Mason."

I lifted myself, narrowing my eyes. "Are you scolding me, sweetheart?"

"Will it get me punished if I say yes?" Her eyes sparkled with the devious smile she wore.

"I can guarantee it."

She groaned and bunched my shirt in her hand. "Tell me what you and Tony were talking about."

My fingers grazed her ass before squeezing it, and she purred. The sound was like her hand stroking my dick and I started moving in her again, feeling it come back to life.

"Can it wait, sweetheart? I'm feeling hungry again."

"When are you not hungry?" she played.

"Never with you around."

"Mason, what's going on? And what does it have to do with Ty?"

I sighed, stopping my motion and knowing I needed to deal with the situation. Tyson was bound to find out soon enough, and he needed to hear it from me. Ignoring the throb in my lower body, I pulled from Casey and rose. She whined, but I stopped her with a shake of my head as I fixed my pants.

Casey sat up, her eyes questioning me. She grabbed for her clothes, but I stopped her. "Uh, uh," I said. "Keep them off. That ass needs a few handprints on it, and I plan to take it hard once I've marked it."

The sigh that fell from her lips was glorious. Leaning over her, I kissed her, indulging myself once more before I dealt with what was likely going to be a blowup.

"Is that a promise?" Damn, she was something. My girl liked a good spanking, and I enjoyed doling them out and watching her break.

"Sure is. Now why don't you get that ass in the air for me, so it's ready when I return."

She giggled, a sound that rippled through my heart, owning it further. "Then you'll tell me what's going on?"

"Only when my cum is leaking out of your ass, princess."

Her moan set my soul on fire, and I forced her hands from around my neck, kissing them before I dropped them. Walking away, I realized just how much of me she owned now. It was like there had never been a part of me that wasn't hers, like I'd been waiting for her to return and claim it all these years. I peeked back at her, watching her snuggle under the blanket that had been on the back of the couch. I should have scolded her for covering her body up, but she looked too adorable, her curls spilling around her bare shoulder, her knees drawn up as she turned her attention back to the movie. Stealing one last look at her, I fortified my heart to being away from her, something I was finding more difficult by the day.

Tyson was in the home gym, pounding his wrapped fists into the punching bag, when I found him.

"Little late to be working out, isn't it?" I asked, my hands in my pockets as I walked in.

"I'm keeping my mind from images of you taking advantage of my sister in the basement."

"I wasn't taking advantage of her; I was fucking her."

He stopped, his glare lethal. "Asshole."

"Better me than another guy, Ty."

He shrugged, then returned to pulverizing the bag.

"What do you want, Mace? Must be something important to tear you away from Casey."

I prepared myself, knowing I was about to ruin his night and an unforeseen number of weeks. There was no telling how long the façade would need to be in place. With the Bad Omens in the picture and the trouble brewing with Tirenti, there was a chance it would be at least through Riley's wedding. Donelli knew the ruse of a marriage between Angie and Tyson would secure his family's protection. No one would touch them if they were now merged with my family, especially not the Tirenti's. But Angie was a handful, and Casey was the only one who could tolerate her for long periods of time.

Tyson stopped punching and looked at me, waiting for the words I was dreading to tell him. That I was cutting off his playboy ways and sinking him in a fake marriage with a woman he despised. There was no way this was going over well.

"It's time you settled down, buddy. No more one-night stands or playing with the girls at the club." His eyes creased, lines forming around his tightened jaw. He knew my tone wasn't play-ful, that this wasn't a warning to keep his hands off the employees, that there was more to it. I braced myself. "You've got a wife now and trust me, she's not one for having the attention on anyone but her."

THANK YOU FOR READING FORBIDDEN CRAVINGS. IF YOU ENJOYED MASON AND CASEY'S STORY, PLEASE CONSIDER LEAVING A REVIEW. REVIEWS GO A LONG WAY IN SUPPORTING AUTHORS.

THE CRAVINGS WORLD CONTINUES WITH TYSON AND ANGIE'S FAKE MARRIAGE IN **HOSTILE CRAVINGS**.

SIGN UP FOR MY NEWSLETTER FOR NEW RELEASE UPDATES AND NEWS. OR JOIN MY READER GROUP, WICKED LITTLE FLOWERS, FOR EARLY NEWS AND REVEALS.

About the Author

J. L. Jackola is a writer of love stories with fantasy, darkness, feisty women, and morally gray men. She's an admitted sugar addict with a penchant for anything with salted caramel. When she's not weaving tales, snacking on sweets, or downing her morning cup of tea, you can find her logging miles in her running shoes, watching movies with her family, or curled up with a book.

She resides in Delaware with her husband and three children.

To learn more, visit her website at
www.jljackola.com